Gwen Bristow

TOMORROW
IS
FOREVER

Published by

CONSOLIDATED BOOK PUBLISHERS

CHICAGO

1944

*Again, for
Bruce*

1.

ELIZABETH HERLONG looked across the coffee-cups at her husband. "Feel better, Spratt?"

He began to laugh. "Yes, I do. Talking to you is such a relief. You're good to drop everything and drive all the way here just to listen to me."

"You know it's no bother," said Elizabeth. "I rather enjoy being a wastebasket for you to toss your troubles into."

"Call it that if you like," said Spratt. "Anyway, you're always there when I want you."

They smiled intimately at each other. They had been through this a hundred times in the past twenty years, since long before Spratt Herlong became a major producer of pictures at Vertex Studio. It was always the same, with minor variations—a picture that simply would not get itself made, actors who quarreled with the cameraman, writers who couldn't write, directors who antagonized everybody on the set, unexpected costs straining the budget, release dates creeping maddeningly closer, and Spratt desperately grabbing the telephone. "Elizabeth, if I don't get out of this place and see a reasonable human being I'm going wild. Meet me for lunch, can't you, and let me talk?"

She always responded. Since gasoline rationing began she had taken care to keep a few coupons in reserve, riding her bicycle on errands to the village, so she could always drive out to meet Spratt at the studio gates when he called her. She could rarely offer any concrete advice, for he knew his business a good deal better than she did, but she had a sympathetic ear and a sense of humor, and she knew how to keep silent about what he told her. She had, in fact, exactly what he needed. Spratt remarked,

"Now that I've got it off my chest to you, I'm beginning to see daylight. This new German writer ought to be a help. He's starting out like a pretty smart fellow."

"Can he write English dialogue?"

"Oh yes, funny expressions sometimes, but any competent collaborator can fix those. He's been in this country two or three years, in the New York office awhile and then on pictures here. I gave him this script to read and he's coming in this afternoon to tell me what he can do with it. Tough story. Also some scenes about motherhood that can be good if they're right and awful if they're wrong."

Elizabeth's eyes twinkled across at him as she sipped her coffee. "Don't expect any suggestions from me, darling. If you want somebody to get romantic about motherhood, ask a man who's never changed a diaper."

"I don't want him to get romantic," Spratt retorted, "and as for you—"

"—as for me, I'm no help whatever." Her attention caught by a sudden clatter of china, Elizabeth began to chuckle. "Spratt, on the way here I noticed a shop with the sign 'Henry K. Dishington.'"

"What's that got to do with anything?" Spratt inquired.

"Nothing, except that I amused myself all the rest of the way by thinking what fun it would be to find a partnership, especially a restaurant, called Washington and Dishington."

Spratt laughed again. "You've never learned anything about pictures, but you do take my mind off them."

"Let's hope the German writer is more sympathetic. Oh, how do you do, Mrs. Farnsworth," Elizabeth broke off brightly, as Spratt sent her a Good-Lord-what-have-I-done-to-deserve-this look and the cushiony wife of one of the Vertex directors billowed down upon them. Spratt got up, trying to hide his annoyance, while Mrs. Farnsworth began telling them they simply must come to a party she was having at her house for the benefit of the Greek War Relief.

"And *don't* keep standing up, Mr. Herlong, I'll just sit down a minute and tell you about it," she exclaimed, spreading herself over an extra chair the waitress had left at their table. Spratt sat down again, politely assuring the lady that he expected to be working the night of her party.

"Oh, but don't you, either of you, want to do *anything* for the war?" she persisted plaintively, ignoring that they both wore silver buttons indicative of their having given three pints of blood apiece.

"I'm sorry, Mrs. Farnsworth," answered Spratt. "Of course I understand the Greek War Relief is a deserving cause, in fact, I've already made a contribution to it. It isn't necessary for me to attend a party to appreciate the need."

"But that's not quite the idea," urged the worthy creature. "It's what your *presence* will do for the cause, don't you understand? We want prominent *personages* to be there. And it will be a very good party—first-class bartenders, and professional entertainers—" She paused expectantly.

"Why don't you just give the war relief all it will cost for the liquor and entertainment?" Elizabeth inquired. She knew it was a useless question. But she was not always as good as Spratt about being polite to bores.

Aggrieved, Mrs. Farnsworth exclaimed, "But you don't understand!"—which Elizabeth reflected was quite true. She did not understand people who got drunk for the sake of the starving Greeks. Before she could say anything else, Spratt interrupted suavely.

"I'll tell you what I'll do, Mrs. Farnsworth. I can't come to your party, since I'm close to a shooting date and have to spend a great many evenings at the studio. But I'll be glad to give you—" he took out his wallet—"twenty dollars to be added to the funds raised by your entertainment."

"Why thank you, Mr. Herlong, how good of you!" she

cried beaming, accepting the bill he handed her. "I knew you'd understand the need when I explained it to you. And if it happens you don't have to work, I do hope you will come, you and Mrs. Herlong too. And couldn't you bring that dear boy of yours? We'll need some young men for the dancing, and it's so hard to be sure of service men these days, and anyway, you don't know *who* you might be getting," she added in a lower voice. "You know, it's all right at the USO, but when you invite them to your *home*, it's different. Couldn't you bring your boy?"

"I'm afraid Dick is rather young for late parties," Elizabeth demurred. "He's only seventeen, you know, and he has to be up early to go to school."

"Only seventeen? Really? He looks older than that, because he's tall, I suppose. I'd wondered why he wasn't in the army. Does he still go to school? Seems almost useless, don't you think, when he'll be in the service so soon anyway. Where does he go?"

Elizabeth told her Dick had matriculated this fall at the University of California at Los Angeles.

"Oh, I see," said the fat lady dubiously. "Does he *like* it there?"

"Why yes, he likes it very much. Why shouldn't he?"

"Oh yes, it's a *good* school, I've no doubt of that," their tormentor conceded. "But the student body—oh, I know a good many *nice* boys and girls go there, but so many others—do you really think it's wise for him to mix up with all those people?"

"Why, what people?" asked Elizabeth. "They get good and bad in any big university, I suppose."

"Oh yes, but at UCLA—you know, all those *Negroes*, and—" again she lowered her voice—"I'm told the place is simply brimming with Jews. And when it comes to the colored students, they tell me that at UCLA they simply *require* the white students to treat them—well, you know, as equals—they insist it's democratic, and all that—"

She left her sentence hanging in the air, ominously.

She had touched Spratt at a point where he no longer felt it necessary to be suave. "Frankly, Mrs. Farnsworth," he said tersely, "I should not like to think my son was ashamed to be courteous to anybody God Almighty was not ashamed to create. I'm afraid we must leave you now—it's late, and I have to get back to work." He stood up.

"Oh, if you must. It's been such a pleasure to see you, and do come to the party if you can. Goodby now, Mrs. Herlong. Now that our husbands are in the same studio you and I will be seeing a *lot* of each other."

Elizabeth nearly answered, "Not if I can help it," but she lied brightly and said she hoped so, and added no, she couldn't possibly drive back to town with Mrs. Farnsworth, because she had called for Spratt at the studio and had to drive him back there. Spratt put a bill on the table to pay the check, and without waiting for change he and Elizabeth got out to their car.

"Oh Lord!" he groaned as he sank into it. "Haven't I got enough to put up with without having to run into fools like that?"

Elizabeth got in under the wheel. "I was wondering," she remarked, "when you said Dick shouldn't be ashamed to be courteous to anybody, if we shouldn't be ashamed to be courteous to her. This town really has more than its share of overfed imbeciles. What sort of man is her husband?"

"A very good director, thanks to her," Spratt returned. "He works himself to death to keep from having to go home. That's why she'll believe any yarn about night work."

"Why on earth is he married to her?" Elizabeth wondered.

"God knows. Maybe she was cute and cuddly when she was eighteen, and now she's so excessively virtuous he can't get rid of her. And she cost me twenty dollars."

"It's not quite lost if any of it gets to the Greeks."

"It won't," said Spratt. "It will go to buy Scotch for her party. Don't you know how those things are run? They pay for the liquor out of the contributions, and if anything is left over it goes to the cause."

Elizabeth began to laugh. "Forget it, Spratt. Twenty dollars is a small price to get away from her. My Aunt Grace was like that. Right now she's probably having a lovely time in heaven, organizing a campaign to get brighter haloes for the lesser angels. Do you still feel better about the picture?"

"Yes, in spite of that nitwit." He grinned at her as she guided the car along the boulevard. "Maybe I need a brush with some dame like that once in awhile to appreciate my own good fortune."

"That's a left-handed compliment, but thank you. I'll keep my fingers crossed for your refugee to have an inspiration."

"I rather think he will. He's a good fellow. You should meet him sometime."

"Bring him to dinner."

"I will, one of these days. I imagine poor Kessler could use a little amusement. He's a cripple—can hardly walk, and only one hand."

"What a shame. Did the Nazis do that to him?"

"I don't know. I suspect they did. He doesn't say so, but he turns a sort of furious greenish white whenever anybody mentions them. Anyway, he does have ideas. I hope he has one today." Spratt turned toward her and repeated, "And thanks for coming out."

"You know you're welcome."

She took her eyes from the traffic for an instant to give him a comradely smile. Spratt smiled back.

"We do have a pretty good time, don't we?" she said, looking down the road again.

"Yes we do. In spite of war, meat shortage and bores. Elizabeth."

"Yes?"

"You aren't worried about Dick, are you?"

"I try not to be," she returned briefly.

"Don't be. He's got to go next year when he's eighteen, you know."

"I'm trying not to think about it until then."

"That's all right. Just remember this. He's had a good life, he's a mighty decent kid, we never did expect to keep him at home forever. Besides, this war *is* about something."

"Yes, it is," she answered in a low voice. "But I'm not going to pretend it doesn't hurt. I wish Cherry had been the oldest, so both the boys would be under age. That's cowardly, isn't it? I've had a good life too, and one reason I've had it is that I happened to be born in the United States. I ought to be willing to give something back to my country. But—well, I think I can promise that when it happens I won't be a weeping little mother, but you know how it is."

"Sure I know. I feel like that myself. But we might as well figure it this way. Nothing we can give up to win this war can be compared to what we'll give up if we lose it. Don't forget that."

"I won't. I really don't think about it very much, Spratt. I don't want to. It isn't necessary yet. I'll face it when I have to."

"Okay," Spratt said understandingly. "One day at a time. That's enough."

They were passing the high wall that surrounded the studio lot. Elizabeth turned the car in at the gate, stepped on the brake and changed gears while she paused a moment for the officer on guard to recognize them. He glanced into the car. "Oh, I see, Mr. Herlong. How are you?"

"Fine, Kennedy," said Spratt. "How's the baby?"

"All right again. Just a cold. Nothing to worry about. You all right, Mrs. Herlong?"

"Never better," answered Elizabeth, and started the car again. She drove into the lot, turned to the left and went along a street of bungalows, each occupied by a suite of offices, until she came to the one with "R. Spratt Herlong" printed on the door. Spratt got out, and standing on the gravel drive he turned back to look at her as she sat behind the wheel. She saw his eyes going over her, appreciatively. Spratt had gray eyes, cold as fog until they looked at something that stirred a luminous warmth within them, when they had the gentle grayness of olive leaves. Spratt looked over the glistening car and over Elizabeth, trim and alert behind the wheel in her dark green autumn dress and mink jacket. He looked at her well-brushed hair, her face, lean and clean-cut with its healthy skin, her still excellent figure, her hands in brown leather gloves resting competently on the wheel. Spratt smiled, taking her in with the same comprehensive grasp of detail that enabled him to spot one incongruous cigarette box in a studio set containing a hundred items. He nodded with satisfied appraisal.

"Not bad," he observed, "for a little girl from Tulsa, Oklahoma."

Elizabeth laughed at him. "Are you coming home for dinner?"

"I certainly am. Why the query?"

"It may be pretty noisy. Dick and Cherry are having a couple of youngsters in."

"What on earth are you feeding them with?"

"I was very lucky. I got some short-ribs of beef. And shrimps to start with."

"Better than anything I could get at the commissary. I'll be there. If Kessler turns up with an idea worth talking about, I may be a bit late."

"All right. But I'll have to feed the children. We'll start at seven-thirty whether you're there or not. How's that?"

"Okay. I'll have to go in now."

He waved her goodby. Elizabeth watched him until he went into his bungalow, then turning the car around she went

back through the gate and started toward the canyon pass that
would lead her home to Beverly Hills.

It was a gay, bright October day and as the cars rushed past
her the sun scurried over their fenders in a string of little white
fires. Elizabeth liked their brightness and their hurry, and the
whole general atmosphere of everybody's being importantly
busy. Her few minutes alone with Spratt had smoothed her
irritation at Mrs. Farnsworth. There were always people like
that in the world, and they really shouldn't matter; you could
usually avoid them, and when you did run into them, as Spratt
said, they served the good purpose of reminding you of how
lucky you were in having somebody interesting to live with.
Spratt was such a dear; success never went to his head and hard
work never gave him the wretched disposition that made life
so difficult for the wives of some executives. "Twenty years,"
Elizabeth said to herself with a pleasant warm feeling, "and I
like him better than ever. That's really something, with all the
strain Hollywood is supposed to put on marriage."

Elizabeth had a high opinion of marriage, because it was an
institution in which she had found a great deal of happiness.
She had been married twice, the first marriage joyous but
brief, for it had been ended in 1918 by a shell at Château-
Thierry. Strange to remember now that she had thought her
life was over, for she was only twenty when it happened, and
nobody could have told her she was going to meet Spratt. She
had had no children by her first husband and there was nothing
concrete in her present life to remind her of him. But it was
her memory of Château-Thierry that made her more frightened than Spratt when they spoke of their son's approaching
military age. Spratt loved Dick as much as she did, but he had
not had a personal experience of the price of war. Though
Spratt was an eminently practical man, his mind simply did not
accept the possibility that Dick could be killed. Her mind did
accept it, because she had been through it once and knew it

could happen. But she tried sincerely not to think about it, and for the most part she succeeded. Dick would inevitably be eighteen; what took place after that was up to him and his country. Horrible as it was, this war was nevertheless a battle against evil that must be stopped or it would make the world unfit for Dick to live in. There was no use letting herself get useless and shaky with dread. "I won't have to face it for nearly a year," Elizabeth said to herself for the thousandth time. "Anything can happen before then." So she let it go. Dick was still seventeen, and she had everything she had ever wanted—a congenial marriage, three children, and days full of worthwhile occupation. "It's a good life," she thought as she turned into the canyon road and the fragrance of sage blew up to her from the glens. "A very good life. I like it."

On either side of her the mountains stood brown against the bright sky, thirsty for the winter rains. Here and there along the slopes were what looked like dead sticks five or six feet high. Next spring grass like green velvet would cover those gaunt hills, lupin and wild poppies would be blowing in sheets of purple and gold and the dead sticks would be tall white plumes of yucca blossoms. Along the roadside were houses half hidden in the folds of the hills, each with its garden a tangle of bloom. The wind blowing over the gardens brought rich damp odors to mix with the odors of gasoline and scorching tires from the cars hurrying along the pass.

The road wound magnificently through the canyon, one of those triumphs of engineering that Elizabeth could never regard as commonplace though nobody could live here without seeing them every day. It always lifted her spirits to be reminded of the energy that had conquered this countryside. She wished sometimes that she had been alive to come here in the early days, when the pioneers were confronting California like the knights of legend who drew their swords before a dragon guarding a pile of treasure. For had there ever been, she wondered as she drove among the mountains, another country where such wealth had been guarded by such barriers?—as though nature itself had stood up to say, "This, at least, you shall not take."

It must have seemed impossible, if they had been people to whom anything seemed impossible, to live in a country of such tremendous mountains and such killing thirst. But they had conquered, not with swords but with machines and mathematics, and though Elizabeth's knowledge of both was too sketchy for her to have described how it had been done, she was thrilled to comprehend the victory. When she reached the peak of the canyon road and looked across miles and miles of her country, and smelt the wild odors of dust and sage and gasoline and eucalyptus, and heard the swish of a hundred tires together with the swish of the wind in the glens, she felt, as she always felt at the top of the pass, that this was what it meant to be an American. It was no accident of birth, it was a way of thinking that made you part of the future instead of something leaning back on the past, an attitude that made you more excited by the Los Angeles Aqueduct than by any castle or cathedral left over from the Middle Ages.

Some people did not like it. That was all right for them; if they didn't like it they could go rest on the mossy stones of some civilization that was old and tired, where they couldn't possibly put in a new drainage system because there was a precious ruin standing in the way. Well, it didn't get them much, this reliance on the old way of doing things. War and terror and hate, because the world did change, and if you resisted change it exploded on you. The future insisted on pushing the past out of the way, that was all there was to it—even Hitler, trying to enforce his ancient barbarism, admitted this when he called it the New Order, though as somebody had remarked, it wasn't order and it certainly wasn't new. Why couldn't the Germans and Japanese understand that the whole trend of human thought was away from their brutalities? Why couldn't they yield to the new world of science that made human beings healthy and their lives more worth living? Why couldn't fools like Mrs. Farnsworth understand that their non-sense was as outmoded as it was ugly? No matter how much you liked the Middle Ages you couldn't go back to them. The new world was here, it was real, it was California where they built highways over awful mountains and stored water until the desert was alive with ranches that could feed half of tor-tured Europe if only their submarines would let the food get in. It was so stupid, so maddeningly senseless.

Ahead of her a transport plane buzzed like a fly across the face of a cliff. Elizabeth wondered if it would be very difficult to learn to pilot a plane. "I'd probably break my neck," she thought as she started downhill and put her foot on the brake. "Suppose I did? I'd rather break my neck having fun than let it get stiff with being bored. I'm certainly not bored," she re-flected as she guided the car along the downward curves. "Run-ning a household for a movie producer and three youngsters is hardly what you'd call a life of effortless ease."

The road flattened, and ahead of her lay the flowering plain of Beverly Hills. Elizabeth drove home. How pretty her house looked, glittering in the sun. It was not elaborate, but it was big and comfortable, and though everything about it was well kept it had a pleasant air of being in use. The gardener, who was busy among the chrysanthemums, had turned on the sprin-klers to get the grass watered while he was working. On the lawn were three rows of six sprinklers each. Above them the mist spun like a dancer's veils, throwing rainbows back and forth across the grass. From the back Elizabeth could hear shouts of young voices and the splashing of water in the pool. The children were at home, and evidently their dinner-guests were already with them.

In the driveway she paused to give some directions to the gardener. Her youngest, Brian, aged eleven, appeared with his bicycle. She called to him.

"Where are you going, Brian?"

"Scout meeting." He looked up and down the street. "Peter's supposed to come by and go with me. I said I'd wait in front for him. He ought to be here now."

"All right." She nearly added, "Be careful of the traffic," but stopped herself. Brian was as expert with a bicycle as she with a car. He had never got himself hurt riding, and there was no sense in being overly fussy with him. From scanning the street he turned to look up at her.

"Mother, can I stay for dinner with Peter?"

"Has he asked you?"

"Not yet, but I'm going home with him after Scout meeting to see his lepidoptera—" Brian got out the word importantly —"and he might. I mean if he does, can I stay?"

"Not unless his mother asks you," she answered gravely. "You mustn't ever go to dinner with any of the boys unless their mothers ask you, Brian. If Mrs. Stern invites you to stay, tell her you aren't sure, and ask her to call me up."

"If Mrs. Stern calls you up, can I stay?"

"You won't say anything about wanting to stay unless she suggests it first?"

"No, I won't. Honest. I promise."

"All right then, if she calls me."

"Okay," said Brian, with confident satisfaction. "Oh, there he is. Hi, Peter!" He swung to his bicycle and was off.

"How busy they are," Elizabeth thought as she looked after the two little boys whisking down the street. "Everything they do is so important. I wish life was always like that. Oh, fiddle-sticks and fury, I don't either. Getting wistful about childhood is a temptation, but how dreadful if childhood lasted sixty years. Living always on the top of things, with no idea what goes on underneath."

Laughing at herself, she started the car again and drove toward the garage at the back. The children did not notice her at once, so Elizabeth pressed the brake and paused a moment to watch them. Her two older children, Dick and Cherry, were there by the pool with their two friends. One of the latter was a leggy freckled girl named Julia Rayford, whom Dick for some obscure reason considered beautiful. Elizabeth could not see that the child had any beauty except what went with health and high spirits, but she was glad Dick admired her, for Julia was a nice girl and as she was Cherry's best friend they all got along amiably together. Cherry, now, was a really adorable creature, all curves and a cascade of dark hair, and her two-piece bathing suit, clinging wetly to her luscious person, did more to emphasize her hips and her round young breasts than to conceal them. Elizabeth suddenly thought, "Good heavens, how fast I'd have been arrested if I'd gone swimming as nearly naked as that when I was her age! But she's really lovely."

Since Cherry was his sister, Dick rarely paid much attention to how she looked, but it was quite evident that the fourth member of their party was aware of her charms; he was a classmate of Dick's, who, since his name was Herbert Clarendon Whittier, was known to his intimates as Pudge. At the moment Pudge was shaking the lemon tree while Cherry scrambled around gathering the lemons as they fell. Dick stood poised on the diving-board, evidently about to perform some marvelous feat for the admiration of his girl friend, who sat with her legs dangling into the water at the shallow end, watching him. What a healthy-looking creature he was, Elizabeth thought, and how he was growing up. He really looked more like a man than a boy now, and she suddenly thought of Dick as he had been when he was so tiny she could carry him on one arm, and he was soft and warm and smelt like talcum powder. "That's how it goes," she thought. "Strange, and of course it isn't strange at all, it's been happening like this for ten thousand years, but it still seems strange when it happens to yourself. Now before many years more he'll marry some immature little girl like that Julia Rayford, and she'll have a baby, and he'll come in and bend over it with that same Good-

Lord-it's-alive expression that Spratt had the first time he saw Dick. If it's a boy they'll name him Richard Spratt Herlong III and if it's a girl they'll argue about every name from Amaryllis to Zillah and compromise on some prosaic family name like mine, and I'll get a smug matriarchal air about me, and we'll all have a grand time and be just as excited about it as if it hadn't happened to anybody else. Of course, before that we'll have to get through the war. Oh, why should any group of power-mad scoundrels have the power to send the world into a holocaust? Boys like Dick—I will *not* think about it now. He doesn't think about it. Or I wonder if he does?"

She recalled Dick at the radio the day of Pearl Harbor. She came into the living room, as stunned as everyone else was that day, to find him listening, his lips drawn back from his teeth in an expression of horror almost grotesque on so young a face. As she entered he looked up at her and said deliberately, "The yellow-bellied bastards." She gave an exclamation, shocked to discover he had such an expression in his vocabulary, but all he did was grin mirthlessly and reply, "I know some worse words than that and if you don't want to hear them you'd better go out and listen to the portable in the garden with the boss, because I feel like saying them." Elizabeth was astonished, not only at his words but at his vehemence. It was the first time Dick had ever seemed to her like anything but a fun-loving little boy. The news from Pearl Harbor had shocked him into a strange and sudden maturity. She went out to the garden and told Spratt what he had said. Spratt answered tersely, "I know just how he feels." "So do I," said Elizabeth, "I couldn't have scolded him with any conviction." They listened awhile to the enraging radio voices, and suddenly she exclaimed, "Spratt! We're in the war. That means that before long—it means Dick." Spratt said, "Yes. I wish it meant me." Elizabeth got chilly all over, but she told herself that day for the first time, "I don't have to face it yet!"

She wondered how Dick felt about it now. She was not sure.

Dick spoke of the war sometimes, with the matter-of-fact assumption that when he came of age he would get into it, but right now it seemed less important to him than campus affairs, probably because by the reckoning of seventeen anything a year ahead was too remote to be of pressing concern. "Good heavens above!" she broke off her thoughts, for Dick rose up from the board, turned over twice in the air and cut like a knife into the water, reappearing just in time to hear Julia exclaim, "Dick, that's wonderful! Do you think I could learn to do it?"

Pudge saw Elizabeth first. He called, "How do you do, Mrs. Herlong?" and the others turned to wave at her. Elizabeth waved back as she drove the car into the garage. When she had put it up she walked across the grass toward the pool.

"Hello, all of you. Cherry, what on earth are you going to do with all those lemons?"

"Make lemonade," said Cherry, and Pudge added, "You don't mind, do you?"

"Of course not, but you've shaken down enough to make about four gallons. Pick up the rest of them in a towel or something, Cherry, and bring them in; we can use them."

"I'll get the ice," Dick offered, scrambling out of the pool. "Julia, you and Pudge wait for us here, you don't know where things are." He took up a towel from the grass and began scrubbing his lean brown legs. "The trunks are drippy, but I won't go anywhere but in the kitchen," he promised before Elizabeth could give him any orders.

"All right," she agreed, and started for the house. Crossing a balcony that ran along the back, she entered the den which the children were allowed to use as their own, and paused to glance with curiosity at some disreputably dusty old magazines stacked up against the wall. They looked like the accumulation of years from an attic; what the children meant to do with them she could not imagine, unless one of the schools was having a drive for the Salvation Army.

The door leading to the kitchen burst open and Dick put his head in.

"Mother, do you want a glass of lemonade?"

"Why yes, I'd love one."

"You'll have to come get it, unless I'm allowed on the rug."

"I'll come get it," she said hastily, and went into the kitchen before he could bring his dripping trunks into the den. Dick and Cherry were making a great racket with ice cubes and glasses, their suits leaving puddles on the linoleum and bringing unhappy glances from the cook. "What are all those old papers doing in the den?" Elizabeth asked as she accepted a glass from Dick.

"They're ours," Cherry answered, "Julia's and mine, I mean. We've got to write an essay for costume design about the evolution of twentieth-century clothes. Julia found those old magazines up in the attic at her house and we're going to get some ideas from them."

"I see. Don't bring them into the living room unless you dust them off."

"Okay," said Cherry. She disappeared with the pitcher of lemonade, and Dick held up a box of cookies he had found on a cupboard shelf.

"Can we have these, mother?"

"Such appetites! Very well, take them."

"Thanks." He followed Cherry out to the pool. When she had conferred with the cook about dinner, Elizabeth went upstairs.

She glanced into Spratt's room. Everything there was in order—cigarettes in the boxes, matches and ashtrays beside them, *Time* and *Newsweek* on the table, along with a couple of novels from an agency and a notebook in which Spratt could scribble ideas about their picture possibilities. She made sure his pencils were sharpened, drew a curtain across one window through which the sun was pouring in to fade the rug, and went through the communicating doorway into her own room.

This was her favorite spot in the whole house. Much as she loved her family there were times when she was glad to be alone, and this was the only place that was entirely hers. Here everything was arranged to please herself—the bed with its monogrammed blue cover, the dressing-table with long lights down either side and convenient shelves for her creams and perfumes. In one corner stood her radio, so she could listen to the programs she liked without interruption, and in another corner the desk and wastebasket that Spratt called her office, since it was there that she wrote letters, paid bills, jotted household memoranda and took care of the various other tasks that had to be performed with pen and paper. By a window was her chaise-longue, and on the table beside it lay the book she was reading, her cigarettes, a desk calendar, her private telephone and notebook of unlisted numbers. Though the windows were usually open her room always had a faint fragrance of its own, compounded of toilet soap and the lotions she used to protect her skin from the dryness of the air. Whenever she came inside and the familiar scent greeted her, Elizabeth felt delightfully welcome.

She took a long lazy bath, brushed her hair and got dressed for dinner in a white satin hostess gown Spratt had given her on her birthday, a fragile, impractical garment of the sort one would hardly ever buy for one's self but which one loved to receive. As she stood before her glass drawing up the zipper, Elizabeth considered her reflection and decided that she looked extremely well. She took care of her skin and hair, for one thing, and what was more important, she had kept her figure under control, so that her waist and hips were as firm as ever. Her husband's favorite gifts to her were beautiful clothes—a candid tribute, for a picture producer had to know a good deal about women's apparel and Spratt would not have brought her clinging gowns if he had not been sure she could wear them.

For a moment she stood turning the radio knob. The radio

mourned that there were no flowers in its garden of love, offered her a remedy for acid indigestion and inquired persuasively if she was troubled by nagging pains in the small of her back. With a wrinkling of her nose, Elizabeth switched off the voices and decided to read until it was time to get out the makings of the dinner cocktails. If she started now she could probably finish her novel. Stretching out on the chaise-longue, she took up the book and found the place where she had left off last night. It was not an intellectual treat, but it was interesting—after reading *All This and Heaven Too* she had learned that the English author who wrote under the pseudonym of Joseph Shearing had published, several years before, another fictionized version of the Praslin murder, and Elizabeth was well enough acquainted with the sinister Shearing heroines to be sure that the governess as portrayed here would not be a fit companion for anybody's children. She had not been disappointed. Having begun an evil career on page one, the damsel was now behaving most wickedly, demure in her bonnet and shawl while she dreamed up yet more sins. Absorbed in the lady's beruffled iniquity, she was annoyed when she heard the buzz of her telephone. This phone was not connected with the others in the house and its number was known only to her best friends, so the call could be for nobody but herself. She pulled her attention out of the book, put her cigarette into the ashtray and reached reluctantly for the phone. Spratt's voice greeted her.

"Elizabeth, are we having anybody to dinner tomorrow night?"

"No, do you want to bring in somebody?"

"Kessler. I've just been talking to him. He's got an idea for clearing up this story. So don't have anybody else around. I want to go into it with him after dinner."

"All right, tell him tomorrow at seven-thirty. Has he got Hollywood ulcers, or can he eat anything?"

"He can eat anything, so far as I know, but remember what

I told you—only one hand. Have something that won't be too awkward."

"Oh yes, I'm glad you reminded me. Soup to start with, and what about chicken patties? Then he won't have to use a knife and fork at once."

"Sounds fine to me."

"And one thing more—has he got a wife or anything that I should call up and invite with him?"

"No wife—come to think of it, though, I did hear him mention a daughter, but I don't know how old she is. I'll find out if she's grown and let you know. You'd better tell Dick to stay around and take her out of the way after dinner so Kessler and I can talk."

"Oh dear," exclaimed Elizabeth, "oh dear. Does the girl speak English?"

"I've no idea." Spratt laughed penitently. "Tell him my heart bleeds for him, but this is the way I make a living for my family and there's no way out."

"You'd better start your heart bleeding for me. I'm the one who'll have to break the news to him. All right, I'll do my best, dinner, Dick and everything."

"I know you will. I've got to go now, three people waiting for me. Thanks," said Spratt, and hung up.

Elizabeth screwed up her face as she reached for her desk calendar to make a note of tomorrow's dinner. She did not mind it, for she was used to entertaining Spratt's colleagues, but she felt sorry for Dick. He could take the girl to a show, if she understood the language well enough. She ought to, Spratt had said something at lunch about Kessler's having been two or three years in this country. Elizabeth hoped Miss Kessler would at least be pretty. Flipping the leaves of the calendar, she tried to remember what the date was. Sunday, Monday, Tuesday—today was Monday, so here was the page for tomorrow, blank but for a note reminding herself of an appointment with the hairdresser. She was scribbling "Kessler to dinner 7:30," when the date at the bottom of the page leaped up at her, and struck her and glared at her and made her start backward to put the calendar down quickly, but she could still see the date and she put her arm over her eyes as though by doing that she could shut it out of sight of her mind. October 6, 1942. Her imagination was making such a fierce effort to adjust itself that even with her eyes covered she could still see it, October 6, 1942. For though the figures did not resemble each other, there had been a fraction of a second when by some trick of the light or of her own mind it had looked like October 6, 1918.

And now all her power of will and reason was insufficient to hold her back from the shadow into which she was slipping, into which she still went down once every two or three years in spite of her full life and happy marriage, impelled each time by some trivial incident that had no connection with the pain it brought. October 6, 1942. October 6, 1918. Twenty-four years. She tried to stop it, but nothing she had learned in her lifetime could stop this darkness once it began to close around her.

2.

SHE was remembering that day, and nothing she could do or think of could make her stop remembering. It was just about this time in the afternoon, and the autumn sun coming in by the front door glittered through the hall and fell on the yellow telegram she held in her hand, with its letters blue-black against the shining sheet of paper. ". . . regrets to inform you . . . Sergeant Arthur Kittredge . . . killed . . ."

There was no reason for this, Elizabeth was telling herself angrily. She had fought and conquered it years ago, she had rebuilt her life in the knowledge that she had conquered it, she was a perfectly rational woman and a very happy one, there was no reason why every now and then some incident of no importance should strike her down and leave her as she was now, quivering under an assault of pain. Lying on the chaise-longue, her arms crossed over her eyes and her hands pressing against her temples, she fought it with all the strength she had. But it did no good and she had known it would not. She might as well have tried to argue with an earthquake as with these rare but terrible re-livings of the days when she had been put to the torture. Every time she thought it would be the last. But a year later, or two or three years later, some occurrence too small to be otherwise noticed would stir up the fire that she had been so sure was finally out. There was no escaping it; that day came back as though it had been that day and not this that she was living in.

It was such a cool, shining day, the trees reddening, and it seemed that nearly every house in Tulsa had a flag rippling from its front porch. After spending the day rolling bandages

22

at the Red Cross headquarters, Elizabeth came home with her knitting-bag on her arm. There was very little she could do to win the war, but if knitting sweaters and rolling miles of bandage was of any value she was glad to do it. Anything that might shorten the war by five minutes would bring Arthur back that much sooner, and for five minutes more of his presence she would give up all the years she had to spend without him. She ran up the steps, singing. It was a silly song, but everybody was singing it about that time, "I'd like to see the Kaiser with a lily in his hand." Their little house welcomed her brightly as she ran in. She and Arthur had lived here for the year before he went to the army, and she now shared it with a girl friend who was releasing a man for war by working for the telephone company.

As she opened the door the sun fell in a long rectangle on the floor of the hall. Dropping her knitting-bag on a chair Elizabeth turned by eager habit to look at the table where the colored maid always put the mail. Arthur wrote her often, but the ships from France were not regular; sometimes she would go weeks without a letter and then get a pile of them at once. Wonderful letters he wrote, mirthful even in the blood and dirt of the trenches, telling her very little about the awfulness of the war but describing every amusing incident he had observed and only now and then changing to wistfulness when he told her how much he missed her. Only once, when she wrote to him saying the war could not be only what he told her, he answered: "Please, Elizabeth, don't ask me to write about what I've seen. When I write to you I can forget for awhile that I've seen it. Let me keep it like that. I love you so. Haven't you got any new pictures of yourself?" She sent the pictures, and never suggested again that he write her anything but what he wanted to.

There were no letters on the table today, nothing but the telegram. She picked it up and slit it open, wondering vaguely who could have anything to say to her important enough to be sent by wire, and then she saw that it came from the War Department. The message was mercifully brief. It merely told her that Arthur was dead. She did not know then that he had died of wounds received at Château-Thierry. They told her that later, in a letter from the Red Cross.

She did not understand even the little they had told her. She stood still, staring at the sheet of paper in her hand, all her instincts of self-protection rising up to prevent her understanding what it said.

(Wasn't it enough to have lived through this once, twice, ten times? Elizabeth tried to think of something else, tried so hard that the palms of her hands were damp with the effort. But she lived through it again, helplessly.)

She folded up the telegram and put it into her purse. She picked up a vase of flowers on the table and straightened the cloth under it, looked at the picture on the cover of a magazine lying near by, brushed a speck of dust from a chair, picked up her knitting-bag and went upstairs to the bedroom she had shared with Arthur before he joined the army. The windows were open to the afternoon sun. Arthur had said, "Let's find a house that has the bedroom on the west side. There's no sense in inviting the sun to come in and wake us up at four or five o'clock all summer long. Any time we have to get up at dawn we can use an alarm clock, so why not let ourselves sleep late when we have a chance?" Elizabeth had never thought about it, but once he called her attention to it she wondered why everybody didn't make allowance for such an obvious fact. It was odd, she had thought at first, that Arthur should be so much interested in dwellings, for he knew nothing about architecture; he was a research chemist employed by one of the oil companies. But Arthur was interested in everything. He had never been bored in his life, and never understood how anybody could be, with a perpetually fascinating world to be enjoyed and the longest lifetime too short to enjoy all of it.

Even in this ordinary little house he had arranged their room perfectly—the bookshelves within reach of the bed, the light excellently placed for reading, her dressing-table between the windows, the long mirror so she could see herself from hat to shoes when she got dressed. "You have such fine ankles," he said to her, "imagine your having to dress in a room where you haven't a chance to see whether or not your stockings are on straight." He had planned everything for her. She had let him do it, without realizing that since they could not afford everything, he would get what she needed and take what was left. So she had not noticed until later that his shaving-glass did not turn properly and he had to stretch his neck to get at those hairs around the angle of his chin. She was saving part of her army allowance now to buy him a new mirror when he came back, and a better light for his writing table, though she was going to let him pick out the latter for himself. Arthur was not, thank heaven, a sentimental goose. He might have worn a hideous necktie if she had given him one, but if she should give him an inadequate gadget for his work he would not use it any longer than it took to buy a better one. So she was going to give him the money she had saved for the lamp and let him select it, as soon as he came back and got to work again.

A hundred hammers started to beat on her head. She dropped her knitting-bag in the middle of the floor and grabbed at the catch of her purse to get out that thing inside, which she seemed to remember had said what it could not possibly say. But it did say just what she recalled. It told her Arthur was dead.

Then all of a sudden she knew what had happened. The purse dropped out of her hand and fell softly on the half-made army sweater that was tumbling out of her bag. The telegram dropped with it, and a little wind from outside picked it up and began blowing it merrily around the room. Her legs went down like strips of macaroni. She caught at the nearest solid object, which happened to be the bed, and then at the nearest object on that, which happened to be a pillow, and she clamped the corner of the pillow between her teeth and heard herself making fierce choking noises down in her throat, like an animal strangling.

At first she was not thinking of anything. The world was simply full of a wild pain that had clamped on her and crushed out of her everything but consciousness of the pain itself. Then after awhile she began to recall everything she had read or heard about what those explosions did to men in battle. She wondered if it had hurt him very much. It did not seem possible that anything could have hurt him. He was never sick. He never complained of anything. Arthur was strong as an athlete. She could remember his arms around her and herself saying, "Arthur, you're hurting me!" and when he said, "I'm sorry, dearest," and relaxed his grip she was sorry she had spoken. None of this was possible to understand. That any man so alive could be blown out like a match, could be annihilated, could be not coming back to her—it didn't make sense, it wasn't true. But all the time she knew it was true, Arthur was simply not there and nothing was left but herself, muffling screams in the covers of the bed where they had slept together.

It was quite dark when her friend, Frances, knocked on the door. When Frances came in from work and the maid said she had not seen Elizabeth, Frances came up to her room. Elizabeth did not hear the knock, so Frances opened the door, saying, "Elizabeth, are you here?" and then, "Why, what's the trouble?" She switched on the light and ran to the bed.

Elizabeth managed to say, "Please leave me alone." Looking around in astonishment, Frances caught sight of the telegram where it had blown into a corner. She picked it up. "Oh my dear," she gasped. "Oh my dear." After a minute in which she could not say anything else, she asked, "Do you want me to call your aunt?"

"No!" cried Elizabeth. "Please go out. Please just let me alone."

Frances hesitated, but being a sensible girl she only said, "You're going to catch flu in this cold room," and brought a blanket from the closet to throw over Elizabeth's tense body, and went out.

Elizabeth did not call up anybody that night, not even her Aunt Grace, an omission which Aunt Grace never forgave her. For weeks afterward Aunt Grace could not think of this without exclaiming, "But I was just like a *mother* to the poor girl! She needed me. And just when she needed me most, she didn't call me." Aunt Grace loved to hover over people in distress. She could well believe that her dear niece had been grieved when she was told of her husband's death, but she was always sure this grief would have been lessened if she herself had only been around to offer sympathy and a nice cup of tea.

She told all her friends how inconsiderately she had been treated. And after all she had done, too! Why, now it was all right to say that a previous telegram had come for Elizabeth saying Arthur was missing, and she had read it and torn it up, and hadn't told a soul except a few of her most intimate friends, no use distressing the poor dear girl when everything might turn out to have been all right. She had found it by the merest chance, or perhaps it would be more reverent to say Providence had guided her to it, one day when she dropped in and Elizabeth was still at the Red Cross. While she was there a messenger had delivered the telegram, and since it might be bad news she just opened it herself, wanting to break it gently, but when she found it said Arthur was missing she went home and didn't tell Elizabeth at all—now what could be kinder than that? If she had only been there to receive this second message! She would have told the dear child gradually, preparing her for the shock, and then she would have stayed with her all night, comforting her. But in spite of such affection, Elizabeth hadn't even let her know. It was hard. Not that she meant to complain, but it was hard.

Elizabeth had no use for her aunt's ministrations. She did not think of wanting anybody. Later, she was able to appreciate her friend's kindness in leaving her alone. But that night she was not capable of appreciating anything but the fact that she was alone and would remain so. For the first few hours the pain stayed with her, blotting out everything except an occasional confused recollection of some minute of her life with Arthur and then closing around her again like a red-hot shell. Then, slowly, she began remembering everything about him, not merely his strength and humor and gentleness, but the tiniest details of his appearance, little unimportant words he had spoken to her, the way his eyes would catch hers across a crowded room and make her feel warm with his love. She remembered his splendid mind, the energy with which he went to work—why should the world want to destroy a man who had no purpose but to contribute to its happiness?—and more than that, his goodness, his large tolerance—"Oh Elizabeth, why get so bothered about it? Who are we to think anybody different from ourselves is wrong?"—and for herself, more even than all of these, their exquisite sense of unity. "Elizabeth, I couldn't say this to anybody but you, but you'll understand. . . ."

She had had so much with him. And yet she had had so little of it. Two years ago she had not known Arthur existed, and now she had lost him.

Her thoughts went back to the beginning. If she had only known him longer! She might have, if she had stayed in Tulsa, for Arthur had lived there several years before she met him. But her aunt and uncle had deprived her of those years by sending her away to school, though of course they had not known they were depriving her of anything and she had not known it either. She liked going to school much better than staying at home with them, for even in her early childhood she had comprehended that though they had a strong sense of duty they really did not know what to do with her. After fifteen years of childless marriage they had hardly been prepared to welcome an orphaned baby left on their hands. Luckily her father's life insurance prevented her being a financial burden. So they provided her with a competent nurse until she was old enough to go to boarding-school, and in the summers there were always camps and other supervised vacations. It had all seemed a matter of course to her until the summer after her first year at college. She was spending a few weeks with her uncle and aunt before the date of an educational trip to Canada with a group of college girls, and one day she went to swim at the country club and met Arthur.

She went swimming alone, expecting that she would meet some acquaintance at the club, which was always full of people on Saturday afternoons. She was practicing a swan dive; she had already gone through it several times, but she liked to repeat it—standing poised in the sun high above the green stretch of water, the spring, the swift plunge down through the rush of air with her arms out like wings, and then at the right split-second bringing her arms together to cut the water and feeling it close around her, cold on her hot skin, and then up again into the warmth and brightness, so vigorous that she felt like crying out, "I'm alive, alive, and I love it!"

She went down into the water again and came up, pausing an instant to shake the drops out of her eyes before she struck out for the edge of the pool. Her face half submerged, she swam quickly. As her fingertips touched the edge she lifted her head and laughed from sheer joy of being healthy. She was not looking at anything when she put out her hand to raise herself out of the water, and was astonished and for an instant embarrassed to feel her fingertips closing on somebody's leg.

Elizabeth started back, about to make an apology. But before she could speak the young man had grasped her arms and lifted her to the edge of the pool by him, and he was begging her, "There now, do it again!"

"What?" she exclaimed, moving back a step, but he insisted, "I've been watching you. Honestly, that's the most beautiful swan dive I ever saw—please do it again!"

She looked up at him, and in that first moment she liked him because he looked just the way she felt—young, joyous, alive with an extraordinary vitality. He was instantly so vivid to her that Elizabeth exclaimed, "Do you often come here? Why haven't I met you before?"

"I don't know. I was wondering the same thing myself. I come here a lot Saturdays and Sundays, when I'm not working. My name is Arthur Kittredge. Will you let me see you do that dive just once more?"

"Of course," she said, and ran back to the ladder leading up to the high diving board. At the top she looked down at Arthur. He lay stretched out, his eyes on her. As she saw him he smiled, raising his hand in a little gesture of praise, and it was as though everybody else in the pool had become invisible. Elizabeth ran forward and arched her body into the air, and as her hands touched the water she knew it had been the most graceful dive she had ever made. "That's what it does for you," she thought under the water, "to have somebody like that to dive *for*."

Arthur sprang into the pool to meet her. Though he was a big young man who gave an impression of great physical strength, he moved with the grace of one long accustomed to rhythmic exercise. They swam up and down together, trying to ride a rubber swan and falling off with shouts of laughter, till Elizabeth lost her cap and Arthur had to dive to find it for her, though by that time her hair was down her back, as soaked as though she had never worn any cap at all. "Now I look simply awful," she said, treading water while she wrung out her hair, but he retorted, "You do not, you look like a mermaid, tawny skin and sea-green eyes and your hair floating." They came out to sit in the sun, and while she shook out her hair to dry they talked without any sense of strangeness.

Arthur told her he was a research chemist. He was employed by an oil company to conduct laboratory investigations leading to additional practical uses for petroleum, and he had published several pamphlets describing his work. To Elizabeth the profession sounded erudite and cloistered, not at all the sort to engross a beautiful young athlete. But chemistry, he told her, was the most exciting subject on earth, though physics ran it a close second, or maybe he should give that place to biology —though it didn't matter, they were all divisions of the same subject, which was the fascinating way the various bodies of creation were made. "Even a smattering of it," he said, "makes you see things you never saw before, you feel as if you've been walking around blind." Pulling a leaf off the nearest plant, he called her attention to how glossy it was on top and how velvety beneath, and told her the tiny tufts on the velvet side were clusters of little nostrils through which the leaf breathed the air.

She was interested, so he went on, telling her how the leaf used air and water and the energy from the sun to make food for the plant. "Then animals eat the plants," he said, "and we eat the animals and the plants both, so we stay alive. But we don't know how to use the sun; nobody understands how that's accomplished, only the green leaves can do it. It's the fundamental life-process of the world. Our bodies can't do it. Only the green leaves know how, and if they should forget we'd die, all the life on earth would end, because we've never learned their secret."

Elizabeth was delighted. "But that's wonderful!" she cried. "Why didn't anybody ever tell me that before? Now whenever I walk across the grass or look at a tree, I'll remember it. What a lot you know."

"Oh no I don't," he assured her laughing. "I don't know anything, but I like finding out."

As they talked she discovered that his outstanding characteristic was a profound curiosity about how the universe and its inhabitants were put together. Everything from babies to planets interested him. He wanted to take them all apart and see what made them behave as they did. He told Elizabeth that before choosing his specialty he had hesitated before the attractions of becoming a chemist, a surgeon, a biologist, an astronomer—not because he did not know what he liked, but because he liked so many fields of study that he could not decide which one would be most interesting to enter. It was lucky he had his living to make, he remarked, as otherwise he might have turned into one of those scholarly recluses, a suggestion that provoked her mirth, at the notion that anybody who loved life as much as he evidently did should imagine it possible for himself to withdraw from it. "No, I guess not," he admitted, laughing too. "I love people. I can't imagine anybody's actually *liking* to live alone, can you?"

"I don't imagine you've ever been alone very much, have you?" she asked.

"Why no, I haven't. I always meet somebody."

"Have you been in Tulsa long?" asked Elizabeth.

"About three years."

"Where did you live before that?"

"Chicago."

Elizabeth began to laugh again and said, "That's where you were born, isn't it?"

"Yes, how did you know?"

"Because people born in Chicago always call it *Chicawgo*, and everybody from other places call it *Chicahgo*. Why is that?"

"Chicawgo," he said thoughtfully, and laughed at himself. "Why, I do. What do you call it?"

"Chicahgo," said Elizabeth.

"Chicawgo," repeated Arthur. "I can't seem to say it any other way. It's like a birth certificate, isn't it?"

She nodded.

"Did you ever hear anybody from England say it?" Arthur asked.

"No, what do they say?"

"Tchicago," said Arthur. "The Ch like in church. You can

tell them a thousand times that it's like the Ch in machine, but they can't seem to change."

"Any more than you can."

"Chicawgo," Arthur repeated. "Chicawgo," as though trying to change, and shook his head in amusement. "No, I can't. Shall we go swimming again?"

"Yes, let's." She rolled up her damp hair and tucked it under her cap. They caught hands and dived in together.

Elizabeth thought she had never had such a good time. Arthur was a magnificent swimmer. He moved with such beautiful control that when they came out of the water again she exclaimed, "I bet you're a wonderful dancer."

"Want to find out?" he asked instantly. "This evening?"

"Good heavens!" she protested. "I wasn't hinting for a date."

"Well, I am," Arthur retorted. "Only I'm not hinting."

Elizabeth had a date for that evening, but the young man was not nearly as attractive as Arthur so she reflected she could get out of it somehow. "All right," she said.

"I'll come for you," said Arthur, "if you'll give me the address. And by the way—"

"Yes?"

"What's your name?"

"Good Lord! Didn't I tell you?"

"No. It doesn't matter, except that they might think it a bit odd if I just rang the bell and said, 'I'm calling for the green-eyed sunburnt young woman who lives here, please.'"

"You'll say nothing of the sort. My name is Elizabeth Mc-Pherson. And something else—my aunt, the one I live with, thinks a great deal of being proper, so you'd better tell me just where you work and all that and we'll see if we don't know some of the same people, so she won't guess I picked up a perfect stranger."

He agreed and they sat down on the grass again. Like herself he had no immediate family, he told her. His parents had died long ago, and he had worked his way through the University of what he could still call nothing else but Chicawgo. After a few moments' conversation they found that Elizabeth's uncle, who was also in the oil business, knew several members of the company where Arthur was employed, so they justified their acquaintance by that. They went dancing that night, and as the next day was Sunday they went swimming again. A week later Elizabeth was refusing to undertake the projected trip to Canada. A month later she was refusing to go back to college. In September they were married.

There was no use in anybody's saying eighteen was too young to be married, she hadn't known him long enough, she would never have another chance to go to college, Arthur couldn't support her in the style to which she was accustomed, or giving any of the other sensible advice older people like to give young girls in love. She and Arthur wanted each other and nobody could keep them apart. Elizabeth found there was still some of her father's property left, so with what had been intended for the rest of her expensive schooling they furnished their home. That it was a very modest little place troubled them not at all. It was a place of peace and ecstasy. Elizabeth was tremulous with joy at finding out what it was like to be loved. She had always had plenty of friends, her masculine acquaintances had let her know she was desirable, and her aunt and uncle had done their dutiful best to be affectionate, but nobody had ever loved her. Arthur loved her.

She was not very good at expressing it. But in the evenings while he read, or worked on the pamphlets he wrote describing his researches for the benefit of other oil chemists, she would sit with the mending and look up to watch the line of light down his profile, and every now and then Arthur would glance up and smile at her and she would be unutterably happy. Sometimes when they went out together and did something quite ordinary like seeing a movie or playing tennis, she would say, "I never knew any two people could have as much fun together as we do," and he would grin at her and answer, "It's great finding out, isn't it?" That was all they really needed to say to each other about it. But Arthur had more talent for words than she had, and now and then he would make it articulate.

One night when she was nearly asleep he turned over and said, "Elizabeth, if you're still awake, I was just thinking about us, and how I get such a thrill every time I see you, and I remembered an old myth I read in the university library one day."

"Tell me," said Elizabeth. She moved closer to him and he slipped his arm around her as he went on.

"I don't know who thought it up, the Persians or Greeks or somebody. They said that in the beginning everybody in the world was happy. Then they sinned, and to punish them the gods decreed that every soul should be split in half. Since then each of us is born incomplete, and has to wander over the earth looking for the other half of himself, and nobody can be happy unless he finds it. But if you're very lucky you find it, and unite with the one who's really the other half of you, and then you're right with the universe because you're complete."

She drew a long joyful breath. "Arthur, how beautiful! And how right—I think I felt like that the first time I saw you."

"So did I. You came down off the diving board and I pulled you out of the water, and you were there, it was right. Funny to think back now—there was so much I wanted to do, so much I wanted to learn, about oil and plants and people and stars—I still want to do everything like that as much as ever, but it's so different now. You've no idea how different it is."

"Yes I have. Everything is different now that we're together. I do love you so!" she said.

Arthur kissed her shoulder in the dark.

They both wanted to have children. Elizabeth loved babies.

Ever since she was a little girl playing with her dolls she had looked forward to the time when she could have a real baby of her own. They talked about it eagerly. But Arthur, who had a deep sense of protection, thought they should wait a year or two. Elizabeth was so young. Besides, they had been married in the fall of 1916, and by spring it was evident that the United States was about to enter the war. "Suppose I should be called into the army," he said, "and have to leave you here alone."

Elizabeth shivered. Now that she had found Arthur, the idea of living without him was more than she could bear to contemplate. "The war won't last much longer," she said. "I'm sure it won't. We don't have to have children right now—we've got years and years before us, but you do want them, don't you?"

Arthur grinned at her with tender eagerness. "You're mighty right I do."

Then the United States was in the war, and there was no keeping Arthur back from it. Arthur loved people. The people of France and Belgium and Great Britain, cloudy masses to Elizabeth because she had never seen them except on one or two schoolgirl tours of Europe, were as real to Arthur as the people of Tulsa, though he had never been to Europe at all. While she had been seeing the war in terms of newspaper accounts he was seeing it as human beings starving and bleeding before a force of evil that decent men must stop. Arthur had registered for the draft, though he had been deferred because he was married; but he wanted to go. Terrified, Elizabeth pled with him.

"Arthur, have mercy on me! Suppose I wanted to go out to France or Flanders—don't you understand?"

He doubled up his fists. "Yes, I understand."

"Have you thought about it? I mean *thought* about it?"

"A lot of times. While you were asleep. I'd look at you in the dark. You looked so trusting."

"Arthur, you're not going. It's different with some men. I suppose I mean it's different with some women. They've got somebody besides their husbands. Please understand. My father was a bank and my mother was a bell. The bank sent the checks and the bell rang to tell me what to do. I'm not trying to say I was unhappy—I wasn't, because I didn't know any better. But then, all of a sudden, you."

Arthur said, "Do you have to make it so damnably hard to do?"

"You don't want to go, do you, Arthur?"

"No, I don't. But my darling, we've got to win this war or lose it. If we lose it, God help us. Don't you see it? We're fighting so other people will have the same chance at life that we've had—not only the foreigners, but Americans, the Americans who aren't born yet. We've been thinking, here in our favored corner of the world, that we were safe. Now we've found that we're not. Not even this country is safe unless we're willing to fight the brutes of the world so we can keep it so."

Her mind yielded, for he was incontestably right. But she could not help protesting still.

"What about those children I was going to have?"

"If we win this war," said Arthur, "you'll have your children. If we don't," he added grimly, "you won't want them."

3.

SO, AFTER not quite a year of marriage, Arthur joined the army. From the day they were married until the day he left, he and Elizabeth had not been separated for as long as twenty-four hours. The first night she slept alone the bed seemed twice its usual size and the room seemed enormous.

Crumpled up on that same bed, Elizabeth was telling herself the room would always be empty. She had nothing. No husband, no children, no desire for anything else without them. She was alive, and that was strange, she thought dully as the hours of that dreadful night dragged by, strange that when two persons had interlaced their lives into such a unit as theirs, half of that unit could be torn away and leave the other half still breathing, alive for no purpose but to feel the anguish of the separation.

She felt nothing else. The morning came at length, and other mornings followed it, but for a long time Elizabeth was not conscious of anything but the immensity of her pain. She went through the usual movements of existence, because the routine was so automatic that she followed it without paying attention to what she was doing. Every day blended into the next without anything to mark the transitions, so that she would have found it hard to say how long it had been since they told her Arthur was dead, or whether some occurrence had taken place yesterday or a week ago. It seemed to her that she was alone all the time, though this was not true, for a great many friends came to see her. She was grateful, but they could not penetrate her loneliness. The shock had been too great. Sometimes she wished they would stop coming in, talking and making her

38

answer, but it did not matter very much. She simply drifted from day into night and back into day again, without expectation. Whatever happened around her, she was not really aware of anything except that Arthur was dead, she had to get through the time without him, and she hoped she could do so without being too much of a nuisance to anybody.

Several weeks after the end of the war she received a tactfully worded letter from the Red Cross, telling her that Arthur had died in a German field hospital. There were some gentle phrases about how the stretcher-bearers paid no attention to international differences in their errands of mercy. Before she had read halfway down the page Elizabeth recognized it as a form letter composed by some expert writer to soften the regret that would be felt by recipients on learning that their loved ones had had to spend their last hours among foreigners. It was very kind of them, no doubt, to have gone to the trouble of getting up such a pretty letter, but neither this nor any other literature could help her. She tore the sheet of paper into small pieces and let them dribble out of her hand into the wastebasket.

By this time it was as if her single great pain had changed into a thousand small ones striking her with swift short anguish, each in a different place from the one before. Earlier, there had been no details. Now whatever she saw, every object she touched, stabbed her with its own small blade of memory. She could not pick up a table-napkin without remembering what fun she and Arthur had had choosing the linens for their home. Every time she opened the china-closet she could hear their secret laughter as they garnished the top shelf with the atrocities some of their relatives had thrust on them as wedding presents. If she looked out of a front window she could almost see Arthur coming down the street from his office and raising his head to see if he could catch sight of her anywhere and wave at her before he came into the house. Arthur was everywhere, so vividly that there were even moments when she forgot he would not be there any more. She would wake up in the night and begin to turn over softly so as not to disturb him; sometimes if the library door was closed she would find herself tiptoeing past it, lest the sound of her approach interrupt the work he had brought home to do. When this happened she would bring herself up with a start that reminded her, "But he isn't there, he'll never be there again." The pain would slash into her, deep and quick, until she thought, "This is worse than it was at first. And there'll never be anything else. Arthur is *dead*."

She did not make any display of her grief. This was partly because she had an inborn dread of public weeping, but mainly because it did not occur to her to do so. What she and Arthur had shared had been too profound for them ever to talk about it except to each other. Now it would have seemed sacrilegious and obscene to try to tell anybody else what he had meant to her. Arthur had been *her* husband; no matter how much his friends valued him, he did not stand in that relationship to anyone but herself, and only she could feel the severing of that tie. So she bore what she had to bear alone and in silence.

It was a matter of embarrassing astonishment to her Aunt Grace. Aunt Grace was very fond of Uncle Clarence, and would have been deeply distressed to lose him, so when Elizabeth said nothing whatever about Arthur, Aunt Grace was reluctantly forced to the conclusion that Elizabeth had no soul. To Aunt Grace one's soul meant the sum of one's emotions, and to her an emotion was synonymous with its expression. When she was happy she laughed, when she was unhappy she cried, if she liked you she kissed you and if she was angry with you she lost her temper. Regarding these manifestations as identical with the states of mind that inspired them, when she observed that Elizabeth expressed nothing she concluded that Elizabeth felt nothing, and therefore had no soul.

Elizabeth took no interest in her aunt's reactions, nor, for that matter, in anything else. Her friends were being very kind to her. They urged her to go out with them, saying it would do her good. She tried going out, but it did her no good whatever. For they did the same things in the same places as when Arthur had been among them; whether they played in the snow or had dinner at a favorite restaurant or sat around someone's fire and talked, every gathering reminded her of him. She would come home and sit down wearily, sorry she had gone. It was easier staying at home, where at least she did not have to put up any ghastly pretense of being cheerful.

And then one morning, in the spring after the Armistice, she discovered that she did not have much money left to live on.

It gave her a start, not because she had thought she was rich but because in the past few months she had not thought about it at all. She had been spending very little, mechanically writing checks for such necessities as food and rent since it was part of the inescapable routine. When a phone call from Uncle Clarence—who had again constituted himself her guardian, as he saw she was in no state to attend to her affairs herself— advised her that she should meet him at the bank the next morning, she obeyed his summons, mildly wondering what it was about. Uncle Clarence and the bank vice-president told her it was to make arrangements for her pension as a soldier's widow.

The words revolted her. Without trying to understand her reaction, she exclaimed in protest. Arthur had given his life for his country and that was all there was to it. Nothing his country could give her could restore him and she had no desire for anything else. But when she tried to tell them this, Uncle Clarence and the banker, two kindly men with gray mustaches and sympathetic if astonished eyes, explained to her as gently as they could that it would be very foolish of her to insist that she had no need of a pension, since she unquestionably had. Most of what her father left had been spent on her education. And then—didn't she remember?—when she married she had spent a good deal on furnishing her home. Arthur's insurance, though as much as he could have afforded, was small—and in short, the American lawmakers had taken all these matters into account when they provided pensions for the widows of men who died for their country. Uncle Clarence knew this was a painful subject; he would have liked to spare her these details, in fact, he had already attended to everything, but there were a few forms to be filled out, and then her signature here, and here, and here—the banker dipped the pen into the ink and held it out, the handle pointing to her.

Elizabeth took the pen and looked at it an instant, then as though it were a horrid object she threw it down on the blotter and stood up. "No!" she exclaimed, and she meant it, though she could not just then have told what prompted her. "No. I don't want the government to pay me for Arthur. I can earn my own living. I'd rather."

Before they could reply she ran out of the bank, leaving Uncle Clarence to apologize for her strange behavior, and the banker to answer Uncle Clarence that it was quite all right, he understood, the poor girl was young and had no idea of money, and she had undoubtedly received a great blow, just come back when she's more reasonable, glad to see you both any time.

Elizabeth was walking quickly along the street. She felt somehow strong and free, stronger and freer than she had felt since the day she had received that terrible telegram. All her senses were abruptly alert. She noticed that there was a tingle of spring in the air. People were walking fast, as if they had somewhere of importance to go. All of a sudden she stopped in front of a store window and said "Ah!"—not an audible exclamation, just the swift little catch of her breath that she would have given this time last year at the sight of a smart black hat with a red feather.

Her thrill was gone in an instant. She had time only to think, "Why, this is the first time I've noticed anything," before the tiredness was back on her and she was saying to herself, "What difference does it make what I wear now?" Looking up at the store front, she remembered that she had bought many hats here in the past. One afternoon she had called Arthur and told him to pick her up here on his way home. He had come in while she was still hesitating, and had made the choice for her—"Here's the one for you, Elizabeth, black with a red feather." She caught her breath again, but this time it was to stifle a sob, and she hurried home as fast as she could.

Once at home she sat down tensely, asking herself with a sense of desperation, "Can't I ever get away from this?" Then, suddenly, she became aware that in asking the question she had unconsciously, by the words she was using, provided the answer. She had to get away.

But though the answer had come, it was not clear. For a few moments this morning she had been exhilarated, until the hat with the feather had brought him back. What was it, she asked herself now, that had given her that brief bright sense of being alive again?

It was something that had happened at the bank. She had said she did not want to be paid for losing Arthur. No wonder they had heard her with such surprise, for on the face of it that was a foolish thing to say. Nobody could believe a war widow lost her self-respect by receiving a government pension. But her words had given her the impression of shaking off a burden. As she thought of it she remembered what else she had said. "I can earn my own living. I'd rather."

Naturally they had been startled. She knew no more about earning her own living than a child. The idea of such a possibility had never occurred to her before. She had spoken without thinking, and yet she had somehow been thinking of something much more vital than the source of her income. She sought to recall it, more than once drawing back, for the operation was too painful to be continued without pause, but at last she found what she was looking for. "I was thinking of something, not about a pension or about my going to work. Just for a minute I got a flash of it and it was like being waked up with a dash of cold water—I know—I was realizing that I didn't have to keep on being dependent on Arthur."

That hurt. She stood up and walked around, her whole spirit protesting against the hurt of it. "I want to be dependent on him! I was so happy when all day I was thinking of him. 'I'll tell Arthur about this, he'll laugh and laugh.' 'I must ask how she makes that sponge-cake, Arthur would love it.' 'Do you really like my bracelet? Arthur gave it to me.' Arthur, Arthur, all the time, never anything but Arthur. Stop it, Elizabeth! I don't care how it hurts, *stop* it! Arthur is dead. Yes, say it and get used to it. He's dead, and you're burning yourself up like those Oriental women who lie down on their husbands' funeral pyres. Arthur wouldn't want this. He loved living and he wasn't afraid of dying, but he'd hate this imitation death you've been slipping into. If you're ever going to be anything better than a sick vegetable, you've got to learn to count on yourself. The only minute you've felt alive since you lost Arthur was the minute you said you didn't have to depend on him any more."

But as she walked around the house, or looked out at the sidewalk and its familiar trees, she knew more and more certainly that as long as she stayed within sight of these things she would continue to lean on her memory of him. She would be, not an individual, but Arthur's widow, a poor object standing around like something a traveler had forgotten to take with him on his journey. But if she turned down that pension and went to live in a strange environment it would mean she would have to take care of herself, no matter how much her resolution might waver. Her fists doubled up and her whole body tense with the effort, Elizabeth faced the necessity. She had to go. She was going.

She chose California because neither she nor Arthur had ever been there. Neither of them knew anybody who lived west of the Rockies, and there was nothing in California that would

remind her of him. Once her decision was made she set about
vigorously getting ready to leave Tulsa, doing everything
briskly lest she be overwhelmed with the pain of parting. Her
first act was to buy a ticket for Los Angeles. Having it there
bolstered her determination on the occasions when she thought
she could not go through with it. The ticket safely in her desk,
she began deliberately to strip herself of the physical objects
that linked her with Arthur. She had to do this, because if she
had taken them with her she would simply have built up another home like this one, where she could not pick up any
article of use without remembering that Arthur had touched
it. She sold most of her household possessions, and what she
could not sell she gave away. It was hard to do, but not as hard
as it would have been to live among these reminders of her lost
happiness. Her acquaintances were puzzled by her vehemence,
and Aunt Grace was volubly shocked. They could not understand what she was doing, and believing like most other people
that if they could not understand a matter it had no explanation,
they said, "Who would have thought Elizabeth was so heartless?" Aunt Grace agreed sadly, and told them Elizabeth had
not only sold the desk where Arthur had worked, but had even
given his clothes to the Salvation Army. Oh well, said Uncle
Clarence, Elizabeth was young, and the young were noted for
their springing adaptability. But Aunt Grace shook her head.
"She has no soul," said Aunt Grace. "And after all we've tried
to do for her." Contemplation of Elizabeth's lack of soul sometimes moved Aunt Grace to tears.

Since it was useless to explain to Aunt Grace, Elizabeth kept
quiet and went on doing what she had to do. If she was going
to leave, the break had to be entire. There was no other way.
She parted with everything except a few keepsakes too precious
to be given into alien hands, but even these she packed in a
covered box which she put underneath the clothes in her trunk
when she took the train for Los Angeles.

As she crossed the continent she looked out with amazement

at the immensity of her native land. No book of geography
had given her any conception of such space. This, she told herself as she looked out at the cities, the ranches, the desert, this
was what Arthur had died for. Every acre of it was a safe
place where Americans could live in security. Watching the
states go by, Elizabeth felt as if she was drawing strength from
the strength of her country.

In Los Angeles she learned to typewrite, and took the first
job that offered itself through the employment office of the
business school. It happened to be a minor clerkship in a law
office, where a large part of the business was concerned with
the contracts of Hollywood actors. This was before the days
of the great agencies, and actors were supposed to handle their
own contracts with the advice of privately retained lawyers.
Elizabeth's work was mostly routine, answering the telephone
and copying legal documents, but the moving picture business
was young and even her own small contact with its bounding
growth was interesting enough to demand all her attention.

When she woke up in the morning she no longer faced the
blankness of an empty day, and at night she was tired enough
to go to sleep. She had an apartment consisting of one room
with a bath and kitchenette, but she was not uncomfortable.
With the other girls in the office she talked about the immediate
affairs of the day. She never talked about Arthur. They had
not known him and could not be interested in him, and this
was the reason why she had come to California.

As for the men in the office, they might have been sexless
for all the thought she gave them. The first time one of them
asked her to have dinner with him she felt startled, with a
curious under-feeling of resentment; but it was the most ordinary sort of invitation from a friendly young fellow who
disliked eating alone, and she accepted, though still with a
sense of strangeness. But they had a pleasant evening, talking
about nothing more personal than the bad temper of their boss
and the unreasonableness of all actors, and when she came back

to her apartment she looked at herself in the glass thinking, "I do believe I'm getting normal again."

She was getting normal again; she could feel it, like the return of equilibrium after dizziness. Her fellow-workers liked her and she was beginning to enjoy their companionship. When she got a promotion and a raise she felt a justification of herself that was real delight. As her job in the office brought her into contact with a great many employees of the moving picture industry, her acquaintance increased and with it her invitations. She lost her sense of strangeness at going about with men who were not Arthur. There were plenty of them to go out with, and there was nothing unpleasant in discovering again that she was an attractive woman. She did not try to pretend to herself that she was happy, but she was not unhappy either. There were still hours when she ached for Arthur, but she was grateful for what she had.

She had been in California two years when she met Spratt Herlong.

Spratt worked in a studio publicity department. It was sometimes necessary for him to visit the office where Elizabeth was employed, to get information about screen players under contract to his company. The girls in the office liked him, because while he was always friendly he never stared meaningfully at their legs while he talked to them, or sat on their desks killing time that they would have to make up by staying an extra hour to finish the day's assignment. Though she had not been long in Hollywood, Elizabeth had already had sufficient experience of both these habits to appreciate the lack of them. She observed also that Spratt worked hard and got results in the form of a great deal of magazine and newspaper space for the actresses he was paid to publicize, and her own brief career in the business world had taught her to admire anybody who concentrated his attention on doing his job well. As Spratt was invariably good-humored and reasonable in his requests—in contrast to some of his colleagues, who were too impressed with ideas of their own importance to take the trouble of being either pleasant or reasonable with office clerks —she responded by giving him all the assistance she could, even when it meant extra effort on her part. Spratt was grateful, and proved it not only by telling her so but by sending her tickets to premières, coming by to drive her home in the evening, or calling up for lunch or dinner. Elizabeth liked him increasingly. Before long she found herself hoping, when she started for work in the morning, that there would be a call from him to enliven her day.

Spratt was very unlike Arthur. Later, Elizabeth thought that one reason for her immediate pleasure in his company had been that he roused her interest without at the same time rousing her memories. Spratt was terse, practical and coolly ambitious. He liked the moving picture business and intended to be successful in it. His expectation had no elements of uncertainty— he was as matter-of-fact about it as a man who walks toward a chosen destination with the purpose of reaching it. Elizabeth had no doubt of his getting what he wanted. Spratt knew his trade. Though he had never done anything in a studio more important than direct publicity build-ups for actors, he had learned so much about how pictures were put together that he astonished her with his technical expertness. He rarely talked about himself, but he enjoyed talking about his business, and he regarded it, with characteristic clearness, as a business and not an art. "Look around you," he said practically. "Hollywood is a factory town, where several big industrial plants manufacture a product that is packed in tin cans and shipped out to be sold to consumers. The honest manufacturers do their best to turn out a product that will be worth the money they get for it. That's all."

Elizabeth smiled appreciatively. "It's refreshing to meet a man as honest as you are."

"Thanks," returned Spratt, "though I didn't know there was any special virtue in speaking one's mind."

"There is in knowing one's mind," said Elizabeth.

Spratt laughed a little. They had finished dinner in a restaurant, and as Spratt happened not to have a show to cover that evening they had ordered more coffee and stayed to talk. She asked,

"What do you want to do in pictures ultimately, Spratt?"

"Produce them," he answered without hesitation. "I like the executive end. But I shouldn't want to be a producer until I've had some experience in writing, or at least supervising a story, and directing. It's a good thing to know what other people are doing before you try to tell them how to do it."

"And you'll do your best," she added, "to pack an honest product in your little tin cans?"

"Certainly," he said, laughing frankly. "A first-class product worth a first-class price."

She laughed back at him. "You're not an idealist, are you, Spratt?"

"Not the classic variety, at any rate." He paused a moment, and remarked, "Elizabeth, it's so much easier to dream about the ideals we can't reach than to do the best job we're capable of doing." He paused again, poured cream into his coffee, and in a rare expression of confidence he added, "I guess I saw too much of that when I was a youngster. I come from a long line of visionaries who were too sensitive to take the world as they found it and get anything done. I don't like it."

"Please go on," she urged.

He smiled wryly. "My father was professor of Egyptology and Semitic languages at Columbia University. We lived in one of those genteel apartments uptown where nice people spend generations putting new collars on their old clothes and keeping up appearances. In our family we never had enough of anything but soap. Know the type?"

She nodded, beginning to understand him.

"Half my father's salary was always going to support relatives so delicate-minded they couldn't do anything but write bits of verse for the magazines and lament the decline of culture. The other half went mostly for books, and soap. Books, soap, toothbrushes, neat patches and the appurtenances of gentility." He shivered.

"I think I'm really getting to know you," said Elizabeth. "May I venture a guess?"

"Go ahead."

"So now half your salary goes for postage on letters to the delicate-minded relatives, telling them they can either go to work or starve, it's all one to you."

"How right you are," said Spratt.

They began to laugh again, and Elizabeth started telling him about Aunt Grace and her cups of tea. "My aunt would really be sorry to see the millennium arrive, for if there were no affliction there'd be nobody for her to pester with good works. In consequence I sometimes think I'm hard-hearted. But I simply loathe patronizing the poor."

"Now we do understand each other," said Spratt. He gave her a companionable smile across the table. "I like you, Elizabeth."

"I like you too," she said.

By this time they were spending their evenings together several times a week. It was characteristic of Spratt's forthright habit of mind that several nights later, when they were having dinner again, he suddenly interrupted a pause in the conversation to say to her,

"Elizabeth, may I ask you a personal question?"

"You can ask it, of course," she returned, "though if it's very personal I don't promise to answer it. What do you want to know?"

"About your husband," he said.

Elizabeth looked down at the reflection of an overhead light on the surface of her coffee. "My husband was killed in the war," she answered briefly.

"Forgive me, won't you?" said Spratt.

She looked up. Spratt was regarding her with a friendly contrition.

"I'm sorry," he continued. "I can see it's not easy for you to recall it."

"No, it's not," said Elizabeth. After an instant's pause she went on, "Why did you want to know?"

He smiled. "Frankly, for self-protection. Shall I explain?"

"Why yes, I wish you would."

He leaned a trifle nearer her. "Well, this isn't an easy town to get around in, Elizabeth. You are Mrs., and you wear a wedding ring, but you live alone and I've never heard you mention your husband. We've been seeing a good deal of each other, and I'd like to keep on seeing you, but I wanted to make sure. I've had—well," he said with a shrug, "one or two embarrassing experiences with unexpected husbands turning up. I hope this doesn't make you angry," he added.

"Why no, of course it doesn't. I don't mind saying it surprises me. I suppose I take it for granted that everyone knows I'm a widow, or at least that if I weren't widowed or thoroughly divorced I shouldn't be going out with men as casually as I do. But maybe I've been a bit naive for Hollywood—and anyway, as you noticed, I'm still reluctant to talk about it."

"Then we shan't talk about it," he said gently. "Thank you for understanding why I brought it up."

There was a pause. "Were you in the army?" she asked.

"For a little while. I never got across."

"And when did you come here?"

"In the first winter of the world's hangover." He spoke readily, evidently glad to turn the course of her attention. "Before we went into the war I had worked for an advertising agency in New York. We handled a lot of moving picture advertising, so after the war they sent me out to organize a branch office in Los Angeles. Then I got a chance to do studio publicity."

From there the talk went back to moving pictures. As he

drove her home, Spratt said, "I'd like to see you over the week-end if you can manage it."

"I can, easily."

"Good. Would you rather go dancing at a night club Saturday night or spend Sunday at a swimming pool?"

"Sunday, swimming."

"Terrific, so would I. I've got to do a layout on one of my beauties, and I can do it either Saturday night or Sunday. So I'll get rid of it Saturday night, and pick you up Sunday morning. I belong to a rather good country club and we'll go there —swim, late lunch by the pool, get sunburnt in the afternoon. Right?"

"Splendid."

He stopped the car in front of her apartment house and went up with her. At her door Spratt said,

"Elizabeth, about what came up at dinner. Don't run away from it. Look at it hard, and take it."

"I do try to, Spratt," she said in a low voice. "I've been trying to for a long time now, but I can't always. Sometimes it —comes back. As if it had just happened yesterday."

"I think I understand. Though maybe I don't—nothing's easier than believing we understand experiences we've never had. But the longer you live the more you find out that life consists mostly of getting used to things we don't like. Keep trying."

"I will, Spratt."

He went on, "You know, most of us, when we say happiness, mean the absence of change. And that's just fighting the facts. Our lives are always changing in spite of anything we can do about it. Eventually, if we learn anything, we learn to take what happens and go on with it." He stopped abruptly, half abashed. "Queer, my talking like this. I don't often. But there it is—I wish I could offer you more consolation."

"Why, you have," said Elizabeth.

"Have I? How?"

"By being you. It's hard to explain."

"Thank you." He took both her hands in his and gave them a hard grip. "You're a swell girl, Elizabeth."

When she went into her room and turned on the light she felt a new elation. She had not seen this side of Spratt's nature before. Finding it made her feel that for the first time since she came to California she had acquired, not another companion to amuse her leisure, but a friend who would be there when she needed him.

The following Sunday, as they were driving home, after a brisk day of sun and water, she leaned back in the car, saying drowsily, "I'll probably be asleep by eight o'clock tonight. I'm so tired!"

"I am too," said Spratt, "fun-tired. Let's do this often."

"I'd like to. But I thought you worked most of your week-ends."

"So I do, but that's been because there was nobody interesting to play with. I work too hard."

"Are you just beginning to realize that?" she asked.

"Not exactly, but I'm just beginning to admit it. Work can be like liquor sometimes, an escape from too much of one's own company."

She glanced up, expecting him to go on, but Spratt remarked on the coloring of the desert hills in the sunset and said no more about himself. Remembering his remark later, however, she thought she should have expected it. She might have realized long ago that like so many other brilliant and ambitious men, Spratt was essentially lonely. Yet she had not realized it, and she was glad to do so now. She needed his friendship; it was good to know that in spite of his self-assurance Spratt also had need of her.

When he asked her to marry him she was not surprised. She did not answer him at once. Spratt had given her so much, more than she knew until now, when she had to consider the possibility of letting him go. But she wanted to be fair, and in fairness there were matters that had to be explained.

She explained them on an evening when they were in her apartment, Spratt listening with quiet attention while she spoke. She told him how she had loved Arthur, and how she had suffered at being told he was dead. "It can't be easy for you to hear this," she said.

"It's easier now than it'll ever be again," he answered. "Go on."

Elizabeth stood up. Moving around behind her chair she put her hands on the back of it and held it while she talked.

"Spratt, you told me to take this out and face it. I've tried to. I've tried to be practical, to tell myself everything I might tell somebody else. I've said to myself that maybe Arthur wasn't worth what I gave him, maybe nobody ever born could deserve so much. Maybe it was just a young girl's infatuation, taking all the romantic heroes of her dreams and embodying them in the form of a handsome lover. I can say all this, I can accept it with the cool reasoning part of my mind, but beyond that it doesn't go. My emotions, my spirit—what the poets would call my heart—simply won't accept it. Because I had what I had. The simple truth is that for the year we were married Arthur gave me an experience of ecstasy. If he had lived I might have been disillusioned. But what I'm trying to tell you is that I wasn't disillusioned, and now I never will be. Do you understand what I'm saying?"

"Yes. But you haven't said whether or not you want to marry me."

"I do want to. But I'm not sure you're going to want to marry me. If you don't want to, say so. You're too fine and honest to have anything less than the truth from me, or to let me have anything less than that from you. Spratt, when Arthur died something died in me. What I feel for you—it's strange to call it love, because it's so different. It's not adoration that sees no faults. It's thoughtful and realistic. I like you, I admire you, I have tremendous respect for you. I trust you completely. I'd tell you anything. I know you'll never fail me. But I can't give you what I gave Arthur, because I haven't got it to give. It's just not there any more."

She looked across the room at him, listening steadily in the half-glow of a reading lamp some distance away. She concluded,

"It would hurt me terribly to lose you. But it would be worse to know I had been less than completely honest with you. There may be another woman who can give you what I can't, and if that's what you want, please, please tell me so."

She heard a soft, smothered little sound from his direction, and saw to her amazement that Spratt was laughing. He stood up and came over to her.

"My darling girl, you told me I was honest. I am, and I'm going to prove it. If any woman offered me the sort of total worship you're talking about, she'd throw me into a panic."

He put his hands on her shoulders and squeezed them as he continued, in comradely fashion. "Forgive me for laughing. I wasn't laughing at you, but at the idea that anybody could possibly think I might want to be adored like that, which you'll have to admit is ridiculous. Elizabeth, if I may be brutally frank—if that's what you were like when you were a young girl I'm glad you got rid of it before I met you. I want you the way you are."

Quite suddenly, she began to laugh too. This way of talking about marriage was so different from the shining rapture with which she and Arthur had talked about it.

"Then you do want me, Spratt?"

"You bet I do."

"You're not going to be sorry for what's past?"

"I should say not. You see, Elizabeth, it's really quite simple. I love you as you are. What you are must be the result of what's happened to you before. If it had happened differently, you'd have been a different sort of woman now, and I shouldn't have loved you. It makes sense."

"You're the only man I know," said Elizabeth, "who always makes sense."

They were married soon after that. She had never had reason to be sorry. Spratt had been brilliantly successful in his work, they had their three children, their long unbroken affection, and the peace of mind that came from knowing themselves of supreme importance to each other. It was a good life.

4.

*I*T WAS a good life—then what was she doing here, curled up on the chaise-longue in a tight little knot of pain? Elizabeth sat up and looked around the room. A bar of sun had moved a little way across the rug. There on the table was her desk-calendar, open to the page for tomorrow, with "Kessler to dinner 7:30" scribbled across the bottom. No more than half an hour had passed since she wrote it, but half an hour of her old torture had been enough to make her feel now that she had waked from an intolerable nightmare.

But she had waked from it. Like its predecessors, this period of recollection had gone as abruptly as it had come. Elizabeth pushed a lock of hair off her forehead and reached for a cigarette. "What a fool I am," she said, her eyes on the picture of Spratt that was standing on her desk. She had a picture of Arthur packed away somewhere in the back of a closet, but it had been years since she had looked at it. She wanted Spratt there, Spratt whom she loved, her children's father. Spratt and her children were what she lived for. They filled up her thoughts—except for these rare minutes of agony, minutes that were more cruel because they had to be borne in silence. She could tell Spratt anything on earth but this. She could mention Arthur to him without self-consciousness, as she did sometimes— "There was a man like Mr. So-and-so in the company Arthur worked for in Tulsa, one of those pseudo-intellectuals who bought first editions for no reason but to show them off. I remember one day Arthur said he . . ." Just as simply as that. And they would chuckle over Arthur's wise-crack and go on talking. But no matter how seldom they occurred, she could not tell Spratt that there ever did occur such experiences of black anguish as the one she had just passed through.

And why in the world should she, Elizabeth asked herself now. It was over, gone completely until the next time, if there ever should be a next time. By tomorrow she would have forgotten it. Already the fact that she had been powerless to escape it was making her ashamed of herself, and glad to ignore such absurdity. The air was growing chilly. The children should have come in from the pool by now, and she hoped they had hung up their suits properly. It was about time she went downstairs and got out the cocktail tray to have it ready when Spratt came in.

The telephone rang again, and when she answered it she felt pleasure at the normal steadiness of her voice.

Her caller greeted her cheerfully. "This is Irene Stern, Elizabeth. How are you?"

"Fine, never better."

"And Spratt?"

"Working himself to death and flourishing on it."

"Any news on the picture, or do I dare ask?"

"Good news, I hope. Anyway, a new writer who seems to have ideas."

"Anybody I know?"

"I don't think so. He's just off the boat."

"Oh dear. Spikka da Inglis?"

"Fairly well, I believe. They're better at languages than we are."

"They should be, can't go a hundred miles over there without needing a new one. Elizabeth, I called to ask if it's all right for Brian to stay for dinner with Peter."

"Irene, you're an angel about that child, but are you sure it's no trouble? Brian takes half his meals with you as it is."

"It's no trouble and I wish you'd let him stay. He and Peter are upstairs getting starry-eyed over a new collection of bugs

—Elizabeth, is it really necessary for the Scouts to encourage such a fearful interest in natural history? Peter does nothing these days but mount insects."

"I know, Brian's room looks like all I've ever heard about delirium tremens. There's nothing we can do about it."

"It must be a recent craze," said Irene Stern. "I remember Jimmy—" she was referring to her older son—"Jimmy was an enthusiastic Scout, but he never had this passion for creeping things."

Elizabeth began to laugh. "You'd better send Brian home, Irene. He'll be a distressing influence on Peter."

"But when they're mounting bugs together they're so happy. I can't bear to separate them. So let him stay for dinner, Elizabeth. We'll bring him home by nine."

"All right then, and thank you for being so good to him. It's been ages since I've seen you—I'm going to ring you one day this week for lunch."

"Do. I'd love it."

They said goodby and Elizabeth put back the phone. She laughed to herself as she did so. Everything was back where it ought to be. Her friends, her children, the warm security of her life. Going over to the desk, she took up Spratt's picture and kissed him through the glass.

As she went downstairs she heard a babble of young voices and a sound of laughter. Dick and Cherry had evidently come indoors with their friends, and the four of them were making quite as much noise as might have been expected if they had been greeting one another after years of separation. "Doesn't their energy ever give out?" Elizabeth asked herself with fond wonder as she heard them. She glanced into the dining room to make sure the table had been set with two extra places, made ready the cocktail tray in the living room, and then went to the balcony that ran along the back of the house, to observe the state of affairs around the pool.

The children had hung their suits and towels on the line

provided, leaving the place quite tidy after their swim. They were really very good about that, except now and then when they had something important on their minds and forgot to clear up. What a good time they were having now! They had gone into the back den, the windows of which opened on the balcony where she was standing, and she could hear them as they discussed something that must be excruciatingly funny, for the conversation seemed to consist less of words than of laughter. Not wanting to interrupt whatever it was they were enjoying so much, Elizabeth sat down in a deck-chair on the balcony to wait for the appearance of Spratt's car in the driveway.

The shadows of the lemon trees were like dark lace shawls lying on the grass. A little wind rumpled the surface of the pool and moved gently past her, bringing odors of damp grass, lemon blossoms, torn geranium leaves. The air was full of the twittering of birds making farewell to the sun as joyfully as the children were laughing within.

Elizabeth leaned back, wrapped in a warm glow of pleasure. What a lucky woman she was, she reflected, and how much she had—a beautiful home, a husband who loved her, such charming, happy children. In the midst of all this, how foolish it was ever to remember anything else. It was good to have a few minutes alone, like this, to look at all of it and know she had a right to be proud because she had created it; good to take pleasure in her children's laughter and know they were so happy because of the love and security she had given them. No matter what might happen to them in the coming years they would have this to remember.

She found herself laughing too, in echo of the four mirthful youngsters in the den. They were reading something, for she could hear the rustle of pages—no doubt those dusty old magazines they had brought in from Julia's mother's attic—and their voices came through the window to her, breathless with merriment.

"Go on, Cherry—" it was Dick speaking—"what have you got now? Read it."

"This one's wonderful," exclaimed Cherry. "Listen." She read, grandiloquently. " 'In these days of bitter strife, when the earth shakes with the force of battle, a new future is being born. We make sacrifices gladly, for we know we shall be richly repaid with the glory of universal brotherhood. The world must be made safe for democracy! In this magnificent hour—' "

Another shout of laughter interrupted her. Cherry announced,

"*That's* an advertisement for raisins!"

"I don't believe it," said Pudge.

"It certainly is, here's a picture of a loaf of raisin bread to go with it."

"Did they have to eat raisin bread to get universal brotherhood?" Julia asked merrily.

"Oh, I get it," exclaimed Dick, as though looking over Cherry's shoulder. "It's easier to persuade the children to eat bread without butter if the bread has raisins in it. Butter is grease, grease makes explosives, and explosives make brotherhood. Very simple in that magnificent hour. Oh look," he continued, with a sound of turning pages, "here's a better one than that. They were having a campaign to sell Liberty Bonds—"

"What were Liberty Bonds?" asked Julia.

"Government bonds to pay for the war, like the War Bonds we buy now. Here's a question-and-answer department, and somebody writes in to ask if it's quite fair to sell long-term bonds to be paid for by future taxpayers. He asks, 'Isn't that making future generations pay for this generation's war?' and the editor answers—this'll kill you—he answers, 'Exactly so, and this is one of the *best* reasons for buying Liberty Bonds today. For the *fruits* of this war will be enjoyed by the generations yet unborn.' "

"Jumping Jupiter!" Pudge exclaimed as the four of them went off into another paroxysm of mirth.

"Generations yet unborn!" Cherry repeated. "That's us."

"And aren't we enjoying the fruits of that war!" said Julia. "Let me see that one, Dick. I wonder if this editor is still alive."

"If he is," said Cherry, "I bet his face is red. Oh do look, here's a beauty. A picture of a lot of babies, and the title is, 'The America of tomorrow, for whom the world is being made safe today.' "

"I bet every one of 'em's in the army now," said Dick. "Take a peek at this. A picture of a lot of soldiers ready to go abroad, and the line under it says, 'A payment on our debt to France.' "

"Any time France feels like making a payment on their debt to us," said Cherry, "I'm agreeable." There was another sound of rustling pages, and she burst out laughing again. "Listen, everybody. 'One of our greatest aims in this war is the reconstruction of Europe on such a basis that future holocausts like this one will be impossible. Out of the world's anguish must be born a new Germany, a nation in which democracy shall rule, where no tyrant and no group of bloodthirsty lunatics shall ever again have the power to plunge a whole continent—' " The rest of her words were lost in a confusion of laughter.

"For the love of Pete," murmured Pudge, incredulously.

"It's right here in print, only you didn't let me finish and the last sentence is the funniest of all. 'Germany will be defeated, but their defeat will bring the German people one tremendous gain: it will mean for them the complete and final overthrow of autocratic government.' How do you like that?"

"I get it," said Pudge. "We were just fighting the Germans for their own good, were we? Gee, when they look around they must be so grateful."

"I see by this paper," said Julia, "that the International Sunday School convention planned for 1916 has just been called off because the delegates are too busy shooting each other to attend this year."

"Where were they going to hold it?" asked Cherry.

"Don't look now, dear. In Japan."

They began to laugh again. Pudge exclaimed, "Be quiet and let me read you something funnier than that. These editorials about the first air raid on an open city. It seems the Germans had things called Zeppelins—that's a kind of blimp—and they sent some of these Zeppelins over Antwerp and dropped a few bombs, and here's what the American papers were saying about it. 'The attack upon Antwerp, made without warning to its innocent population, is completely contrary to all rules of civilized warfare—' "

"Rules?" Dick interrupted mirthfully. "You'd have thought it was a football game."

" 'Zeppelins have dropped bombs on an undefended city!' " Pudge continued reading with mock horror. " 'This is not only contrary to the laws of war, but can serve no legitimate military purpose—' "

"What is a legitimate military purpose," Dick inquired, "unless it is to kill everybody you can?"

"Shut up and let me read this. 'As those who were killed or injured by the bombs were women and male non-combatants, the airship attack was nothing but a plain act of savagery. This is not war, but murder!' "

"Did you *ever* hear anything so naive?" asked Cherry.

"Was that first attack a bad one?" asked Dick.

"I was saving that for the last," answered Pudge. "If you can believe it, that first air raid, that dastardly, bloodthirsty, savage raid that made everybody sit back and yell with horror —that raid killed *ten* people and wounded *eleven*."

"Holy smoke!" exclaimed Dick, and the others joined in his derision. A moment later Dick added, "Here's a swell side-angle on the air raids. It says the men in London were taking to wearing pajamas instead of nightshirts because when the blimps came over everybody ran out into the streets, and they wanted the neighbors to see them running around in something more becoming to British dignity than nightshirts."

They chuckled joyfully. Cherry exclaimed, "I wish you'd look at these recipes for war-meals. 'Freedom Meat Loaf,' made out of peanuts and cornmeal."

"Peanuts do have Vitamin B in them," suggested Julia.

"They'd never heard of Vitamin B," Dick said scornfully. "They had to eat peanuts and call 'em meat because our brave allies were buying up all the meat with the money they borrowed and didn't pay back and never did intend to pay back. Do look at that headline—'Every housewife who saves meat and flour in her home is bringing nearer the day of universal democracy!' "

"Do you suppose they really *believed* all that?" Cherry asked in wonder.

Outside, on the balcony, Elizabeth lifted her hands from the arms of the chair and saw that each of the bright blue cushions was stained with a round spot of dampness where she had gripped them. On the other side of the window the children made some fresh discovery and went off into another peal of laughter, gay, mocking, and terrible because it was so utterly innocent. Elizabeth stood up, her muscles tense with impulse. Then she stopped, standing motionless because she did not know what the impulse was. To do something to them—but what? She could not walk in upon them white with anger and cry out, "Yes, we believed it! You inhuman young wretches, we believed it!"

She could not say that because they were not inhuman, and they were not wretches; they were young and well-bred and intelligent, and they would hear her with a pained bewilderment, and answer with the cool logic of their years, "Aren't you ashamed that you did, when you look at the world we're living in?"

And her son—who was seventeen and who did not look at all like Arthur, since he bore no more relationship to Arthur than to the policeman on the corner—her son would ask her, with the same cool logic, "Do you want me to believe it this time?"

How strange it would be if she should try to tell them anything about Arthur. With what incomprehension they would hear her. Her children knew—that is, if anybody had asked them, they could have answered after a moment's reflection—that their father was their mother's second husband. She was not sure they had ever been told their mother's first husband had lost his life in that war they were laughing at. If they had ever heard this, evidently they had forgotten about it. How fantastic it would seem to them if she broke now into their jolly chatter to say, "I know all about that war you find so absurd, and that sentimental nonsense that sent men out to die. I loved a man who died for it."

They would be shocked into uncomfortable silence. Or they might, as they had a right to do, stare at her and ask, "For what?"

This she could answer, for they had told her themselves. He had died for the generation of her own children, to give them the right not to believe in anything. They had told her, as clearly as they could tell her, the futility of his sacrifice. She remembered what he had said to her. "If we win this war, you'll have your children. If we don't, you won't want them." Her children could answer her now, but as she stood within sound of their healthy, laughter-laden voices, Elizabeth knew that she could not answer them.

Indoors the children came across some new monstrosity and broke into laughter again. Cherry finally gasped, "I tell you, my ribs hurt. I haven't had so much fun for ages."

"Oh boy," exclaimed Pudge, "here's another of these things. 'Today, filled with hope and trust, we proudly look upon our great army and our noble allies. Through their sacrifices we are moving toward the victory that will bring triumphant peace to all the world. Bring this glorious day nearer! Work for victory as you never worked before! America is destined to be—' "

"—the prize sucker of all time," Dick finished the sentence for him, with sudden disgust. "Did you ever hear such tripe? Couldn't you throw up?"

"Well—we really ought not to laugh," Julia admitted. "The poor things, they took it so seriously."

"If we don't laugh," said Dick, "we'll all sit down and cry. *We've* got the mess they made."

"Oh Dick," Julia admonished him, "but really, this war is different!"

"Different? Tell that to the Marines. Sure, the Marines who got stuck on Wake Island with a lot of popguns because the Japs were such good customers and they might have got their feelings hurt if we'd fortified it."

"We're a swell bunch of suckers, aren't we?" said Cherry. "To get ourselves born in these times!"

"Well, we couldn't help it," Dick remarked. "But I guess nobody who had anything to say about it would have picked out the twentieth century, any of it."

Cherry gave a low ironic chuckle. "They'll have an easy time remembering the twentieth century when they study it in the history books. A pre-war period, a war, an inter-war period, another war, a post-war period—"

"Don't say post-war too soon, you wishful thinker," Pudge admonished her lazily. "How do you know it won't be just the second inter-war period?"

There was a shuffling sound as they began to restack the magazines, evidently concluding that these had provided as much amusement as they could afford. "This is a fine way for two fellows to be talking," advised Julia, "who'll probably be in the army this time next year."

"No, you don't get it, Julia," said Dick. "I'm not as pessimistic as Pudge, I think the next inter-war period is going to be a lot longer than this last one, why it's got to; by the time this war is over everything will be blown to powder and there'll be nothing left to fight with. But we're a lot better off than those moony-faced laddies who went marching off full of molasses about the brotherhood of man and all that. We won't be disillusioned when it's over because we haven't got any illusions. We know it's all a bloody mess and we're in it because our elders didn't have sense enough to keep us out of it. We'll go into the army and they'll train us to be killers whose business it is to shoot other killers before they have a chance to shoot us first. And that's that."

"But my Lord, Dick!" Julia exclaimed in a shocked voice. "We've got to fight! Don't you hate the Japs?"

"Of course I hate them. I'd like to wipe every one of their monkey faces off the earth. Oh, that's okay by me, I'll shoot 'em and be glad to do it. But that's not the idea. I meant the difference between this war and the last one is that this time we know what we're doing. We're fighting to stay alive, period. We don't expect any brand-new world."

"Lucky we don't expect it," observed Pudge, "because it's a cinch we're not going to get one."

"Mr. Wallace," Cherry said wisely, "thinks we're fighting to provide milk for the Chinese coolies."

Pudge chuckled at her. "Without even asking the coolies if they want any milk."

"You know," said Cherry, "it's really pathetic the way some of the propaganda leaders are trying to sell us on that idea of a brand-new world. Just get this over, and the Russians will love the Chinese and the Chinese will love the British and the British will love the Italians—"

Pudge interrupted, still chuckling, "Just picture anybody actually loving the Italians."

"Oh, but they will," Cherry assured him cynically. "Haven't you read some of these post-war planners? Everybody is going to get along with everybody else, even the Spaniards."

"The State Department," Dick reminded her, "gets along beautifully with the Spaniards."

"Now that Chamberlain is dead," said Cherry, "somebody really ought to send the State Department a lot of umbrellas for Christmas. Oh, it really does make you tired, doesn't it? Ever since I can remember, people have been talking about the next war, and nobody did anything about it except to go on selling the Japs and Germans things to blow us up with. And now that we're in it they're trying to hand us that same old fluff."

"I guess you're right," Julia admitted. "It's—shivery, isn't it?"

"It would be," said Dick, "if anybody believed it."

"Some people do believe it, Dick," Pudge told him seriously. "Nobody our age, of course, but a lot of older people do."

"I don't see how they can. They fell for it once, it doesn't make sense for anybody to fall for it twice."

"Well, does any of it make sense, I ask you?"

Dick retorted, "It doesn't make sense except the way I said it the first time. The Japs and Germans say, 'We're going to kill you and take what you've got.' We say, 'Like hell you are.' So we get up and bang it out. We keep banging till they're so slugnutty they have to let us alone."

"That's not the way it turned out last time," Julia reminded him.

"No it didn't," Dick agreed, "because last time everybody was so full of phony ideals and doubletalk. Why, to read this stuff we've been reading, you'd think the army was a lot of social workers sent out to uplift the community. Those fellows didn't know what they were fighting for. No wonder they left everything in such a muddle. Nobody ever fought a war for any ideals."

"Why Dick, there *are* some ideals in this war!" Julia protested. "You know, the Four Freedoms and all that."

Dick was too polite to contradict her at once, but Cherry was not. "Oh Julia," she said, "don't be so sentimental. You don't really believe anybody in the United States cares whether the Croatians and people like that have any Four Freedoms, any more than they care about us. Nobody fights for anything like that. They just pretend they do while it's going on."

"She's right, Julia," Dick argued. "What they really fight about is property and power. They always talk pretty while it's going on, and then when it's over they get realistic. But as soon as a new war starts they say, 'Oh yes, we know, all the *other* wars were fought for crass reasons, but this one's different, boys, this one's different.'" He became vehement. "Well, this one's not different and I'm thankful we know it. I'm plenty tired of everybody pretending to believe what everybody knows isn't true."

"I wonder what your mother and father would say," Julia suggested, "if they could hear you talk like that."

"Oh, they wouldn't mind," said Cherry. "They're very intelligent people, really."

"They've got some old-fashioned ideas," said Dick, "like everybody their age, but generally speaking they're very liberal for older people. They don't go around being always shocked about things."

Outside, on the balcony, Elizabeth stood with her hands gripping the rail. She was thinking, "Every word they are saying is my fault, mine and Spratt's. They're our children and we taught them to think this way. Or at least, if we didn't teach them to be cynics, we didn't do anything to stop it. We ran away from the last war as fast as we could. In what Spratt called the world's hangover, we didn't say anything but 'never again.' And now there's another war, and Dick will have to fight it—and listen to him! Is that how they all feel? If it is, their children will have to do it again. Oh my God, what have I told him? What can I tell him now?"

Little as she liked to admit it, she knew she had been a coward and that she was still a coward. She had refused to face what was there, and she still lacked the courage to face it. Could she go into the house right now and say to Dick, "This war is a glorious crusade, and you must get into it now. Why wait till next year? They will take you at seventeen. Oh yes, I know, thousands of men have already been killed, but go ahead. What are you waiting for? It's worth it."

No, she could not say it. If she believed this war was worth winning, that was what she ought to say, but the truth was that she simply did not believe it that much. That was what had held them all back during the accumulating horrors of the past twenty years. They knew what war was like, they could let anything happen in the world if only they could keep out of another. She need not blame herself, Elizabeth thought, as though she was the only one. She stood there on the balcony, epitomizing her country.

Turning around, she walked into the house, entering through a hall so as to avoid meeting the children in the den. With the disappearance of the sun the air had grown chilly. A fire might be welcome. She stood by a window in the living room, looking at the darkness as it gathered swiftly over the lawn. A maid came in to turn on the lights.

"Don't you want me to draw those curtains too, Mrs. Herlong?" she asked.

Elizabeth turned. "Why yes, I'd forgotten them. I'll do this window." She pulled the cord that drew the curtains together, and as the maid went out she turned from the window. How well-ordered everything looked, and was. Nothing had happened this afternoon. Nothing had happened except within herself. Everything that had made her feel so strong and happy as she drove home through the canyon was still there. A voice in the doorway startled her.

"Say, mother, we're getting famished. Isn't the boss home yet?"

"Not yet, Dick. He's very busy these days, you know, on the new picture."

"I know, but I'm starving."

"If the boss isn't here by seven-thirty, we'll sit down without him," she promised. "It's getting cold, Dick, will you light the fire?"

"Sure will." Dick knelt down and applied a match to the gas rod under the logs. He glanced at the cocktail tray. "Want me to mix the Martinis?"

"I wish you would."

"Okay." He went first to the door and called the others. "Want to come in here? Fire going."

"In a minute," Cherry called back. "Got to wash our hands first—those magazines were so awfully dusty. Is the boss in?"

"Not yet, but mother says we can have dinner at seven-thirty anyway. So hurry up."

The gas flame sparkled up to ignite the logs piled in the grate. Dick swished the gin and vermouth. Though he was not allowed to drink cocktails himself, he enjoyed the feeling of adulthood it gave him to play bartender. What a nice boy he was, Elizabeth thought as she watched him. Dick asked,

"Like a drink now?"

"I believe I would. I'm a bit tired."

He poured it out for her, and watched while she tasted it. "How's that?"

"Very good. You could get a job."

"I'll be needing one if that physics guy gets much tougher. —Oh hello there," he said as Cherry and the two others came in. They greeted Elizabeth, and Julia said,

"That fire looks wonderful. I wish we had those gas lighters at our house, they start the fire with no trouble at all. You have just everything here, Mrs. Herlong."

"Why thank you, Julia."

"This is the most *comfortable* house I was ever in. We've been having such fun all afternoon."

"I'm getting weak in the middle," said Dick. "I wish you'd ordered some crackers or something."

"I'll have hors d'oeuvres tomorrow night. We're having a guest for dinner—I mean an older guest, from the studio."

"We were all going to ride down to the beach tomorrow night," said Dick. "It'll be all right if Cherry and I leave right after dinner, won't it?"

"For Cherry, but I'm afraid there's another prospect for you."

"For me? What?" he asked in alarm.

Elizabeth gave him an urgent smile. It was a relief to turn her attention to her ordinary day-by-day affairs, to observe her children as normal healthy youngsters hungry for their dinner, to reach for a cigarette and have both Dick and Pudge strike matches for her. She accepted the light from Pudge, and smiled across it at Dick as he blew out the match he had struck.

"Dick, our guest tomorrow night is a Mr. Kessler, from Germany. I've never met him, but he's working on the picture."

"Another refugee?" inquired Cherry.

"Yes, but you'll both please remember not to call him that. Simply say 'German,' if you have to call him anything."

"I get it," said Dick, "but what have I got to do about him?"

"He has a daughter—"

"Oh my Lord!"

"I'm sorry, Dick," Elizabeth continued with sympathy. "But the boss wants to talk pictures with Mr. Kessler after dinner, and you'll have to take care of the girl."

Cherry and the two guests were already beginning to laugh at Dick's woebegone face. Dick groaned.

"Can she talk?"

"I don't know, Dick, but there's a musical show downtown—"

"Mother, please! Honestly, I—what does she look like?"

Elizabeth started to say "I've never seen her," when Cherry put in,

"I bet I know. Two yellow braids around her head—"

The others joined,

"Maybe you could play some Wagner records for her."

"What about *Faust?*"

"Silly, *Faust* is sung in French."

"I bet she's fat and has apple-cheeks."

"She's probably intellectual. Lots of refugees are."

"Talk to her about food. They all like to eat."

"I can't talk to her about anything," stormed Dick. "Mother, I've got a date! Why can't the boss tell Mr. Thingum to leave his daughter at home? Why do I have to—and shut up, all of you. I think you're being unsympathetic and awful."

"Dick, please be a good sport," Elizabeth urged. "This doesn't happen often."

"It does too. You remember that horrible girl from New York who was all teeth that I had to take out when her family had dinner here? But this is worse. A foreigner who can't even talk except to say glub-glub!"

"How do you know she can't talk? Her father speaks English."

Dick groaned.

"Be nice about it, Dick," pled Elizabeth. "She'll probably have a very good time if you'll let her. Remember she's in a strange country, and most of those refugees have had some very unpleasant experiences. Can't you be sorry for them at all?"

"It's easy to be sorry for refugees," said Dick, "when you don't have to put up with them."

Torn between a desire to laugh and tell him he needn't do it, and a realization that Mr. Kessler's daughter must be taken care of somehow if he and Spratt were to have a chance to talk business, Elizabeth did not answer immediately. She was glad to hear the sound of a key in the front door.

"There's the boss," said Cherry, getting up.

"Now we can eat!" Dick exclaimed as though glad to have something to rejoice about. He got up to pour a cocktail for his father.

Spratt came in and greeted them all. "You've no idea what a comfortable picture you make around the fire," he remarked as Elizabeth took his coat and Dick gave him the Martini. "Where's Brian?"

"Having dinner with Peter Stern. Cherry, go to the kitchen and tell them the boss is here."

"What have you been doing?" asked Spratt. "Listening to the radio?"

"No, what's going on?"

"The same, only worse. All hell's loose in Russia. Come on upstairs with me while I get cleaned up," he invited Elizabeth. "Cherry, tell them I'll be ready in fifteen minutes."

"Wait a minute, boss," exclaimed Dick. "I've got something important to ask you. Do I have to take that refugee girl on a date tomorrow night?"

"What refugee girl?"

"The one who's coming here to dinner with her old man. Can't she possibly—"

Spratt drew a long breath and started to laugh. "I forgot to tell you. Kessler's daughter," he said, "is eight years old."

The four youngsters gave long simultaneous whistles. "Oh joy, oh rapture unconfined!" sang Dick. "My life is renewed. I don't have to! Did you hear, everybody? She's eight years old! Why didn't you tell me? What were you doing talking about Russia when all the time you knew that girl was eight years old? Me sitting up here dying and you've got to bring up *Russia!*"

Elizabeth got out of the room ahead of Spratt and ran up the stairs. He followed her. When he came into his bedroom he found her crumpled up in his reading chair. She was laughing uncontrollably.

Spratt stood watching her in amazement. "Elizabeth, what in the world is the matter with you?"

For a moment she could not answer. With an effort she caught her breath, saying, "N—nothing. Only I think—I think that for the first time in my life I've nearly had hysterics."

"Elizabeth, *what*—"

"Please don't pay any attention to me. I'm behaving like a moron. But it is funny, Spratt. We're sitting on the edge of a volcano dangling our legs over the crater, and Dick knows it— I've just heard him talking, so grim and hard he frightened me, and in fifteen minutes nothing was important to him except that that German girl was eight years old and he didn't have to take her out. Oh, that resilience! Did I ever have it, I wonder?" She began to laugh again, this time more softly. Spratt shrugged, went into the bathroom and turned on the water. When he came out Elizabeth, having made herself be quiet, was wiping her eyes.

Spratt stood over her, shaking his head in confusion. "Did anything happen this afternoon, Elizabeth? You can tell me."

"Not a thing. I came home and got dressed for dinner and lay on the chaise-longue in my room till it was time to get out the cocktails." She stood up. "I'm sorry for being so foolish, Spratt. But every now and then—well, maybe sometimes you've got to laugh so you won't scream."

"All right," said Spratt, "leave it at that." He never pressed her for explanations, knowing if there was anything she intended to explain he would get it eventually without asking. "You'd better go and do something to your face. You've laughed and cried it streaky."

"All right, I will." Slipping her hands into his, she stood up. "And thank you for being such a calm person. Most men would either have called me a fool or asked a thousand questions."

With an expression of mingled sympathy and amusement, Spratt kissed her. "You're not a fool. Incidentally, you look mighty well in that outfit."

"It's the hostess-gown you gave me," Elizabeth reminded him as she went into her room to obliterate the tracks on her face.

Spratt was waiting at the head of the stairs. She smiled at him reassuringly and they started down, and he smiled back. They went in to dinner with the others.

"Oh boy," said Dick as they sat down. "Shrimps to start with. I love 'em."

"So do I," said Spratt, and ate the first one. "Quite a sauce, Elizabeth," he observed. "A decent writer on that picture for a change, and a good dinner—" He grinned at his offspring. "What have the millionaires got that we haven't got?"

"Dyspepsia," said Dick.

5.

AT HALF-PAST four the following afternoon, Spratt was winding up another conference with the new writer who had come from Germany. Spratt pushed his chair back from his desk and grinned at his colleague.

"That's all for the present, Kessler. We can go into more detail tonight after dinner. And you'll start writing the story-treatment in the morning?"

"Yes, Mr. Herlong." The new writer smiled back, and though his heavy dark beard emphasized his foreignness to this American office and his customary dignity was such that his smile, unlike Spratt's, could hardly be called a grin, he conveyed his acknowledgment of the comradeship that springs up swiftly when two workers discover they can work together. "When you will read the synopsis—I am sorry, the treatment —you will forgive my awkwardness with the language?"

Spratt chuckled. "In the first place, your language is very rarely awkward, and in the second place I can get a dozen writers who know English grammar for one who can tell a story. I don't mind saying, Kessler, you took a load off my shoulders in our conference yesterday. You understand stories —I wish you could tell me how to make all these English grammar writers understand them."

"Perhaps it is only sometimes viewing situations as other people would view them, and not entirely from the unchanging viewpoint of one's self."

"Am I supposed to tell *that* to the inhabitants of this ego-ridden capital?" Spratt laughed ruefully and shook his head. "Yes, Lydia?" he said as his secretary came in.

"The art department has sent down the sketches of the bedroom and living room sets. Do you want to see them now or are you and Mr. Kessler still in conference?" She glanced toward Spratt's visitor with the respect she gave anybody whose ideas came to the rescue of a befuddled script.

Spratt's visitor answered for him. "He wants to see the sketches, and we are no longer in conference, Miss Fraser." He moved forward in his chair, placed his heavy hand on the head of his heavy cane, and pushed himself into a standing position. It was not an easy movement, but he accomplished it with the skill of long practice. Lydia opened the door for him. A clever girl, she managed to make it look like a gesture of deference instead of necessary aid. Their new writer could not stand without the support of his cane, and since he had only his right hand this made it impossible for him to open a door without pushing a chair toward it so he could sit down. Spratt had risen too, and walked over to the entrance.

"Then I'll pick you up at your office this evening, as close to six-thirty as I can, and we'll go to my home for dinner."

"Thank you, Mr. Herlong." He smiled courteously at Lydia. "And thank you, Miss Fraser."

Lydia went with him to the outer door of the bungalow, then returned to Spratt's inner office with the set sketches in her hand. "A remarkable man, Kessler," Spratt observed as he took the sketches.

"Isn't he? To sink into that script forty-eight hours and come up with a solution. And him half dead, too. Did the Nazis beat him up, or was he in the war, or what?"

"I've no idea. You don't ask about those things, though you can't help wondering. Maybe nothing but an auto accident."

"He does manage to bow from the waist in spite of it. Do you suppose he's going to continue forever calling everybody around here Mr. and Miss?"

Spratt laughed a little, and shrugged. "Probably. Germans are very formal. Never mind. I like him."

"So do I," said Lydia.

Meanwhile the subject of their conversation walked to his own bungalow, which was conveniently located next door, since his power of walking was limited to very short distances. Explaining to his secretary that Mr. Herlong was to call for him later, he went through the reception room into his private office beyond.

Alone, he glanced around the room with approval. It was furnished with only the necessities of his work—a desk with pencils and stacks of paper, a working-chair and an easy-chair, a case holding reference books, a typewriter that wrote only capital letters and required no shift key. He had taught himself years ago to operate such a machine with his one hand. Bare as the room was, he liked it, for it had wide windows bringing in abundant light, and giving a view of the vast hills beyond the studio lot. A mirror on the wall reflected the hills, producing an impression of space and peace. Space and peace, he reflected as he looked around; this was what he wanted now, this was what they still had in America. The Americans took them both for granted. Even now there were some Americans who did not realize how precious they were, and how rare.

This reflection came to him of itself whenever he looked around. It occurred to him now, but he paid hardly any attention to it; he had another concern to occupy his attention. Tonight he was going to see Elizabeth. He was going into her home and see her there, surrounded by all the things she had ever wanted, and the prospect of it gave him a pleasure that was warm and tender, and none the less intense because while she had all these things she would never know that he had given them to her.

He went over to the mirror on the wall and stood there looking at his reflection. It was not possible that she could recognize him. Between them lay not merely twenty-four years, but the wreckage made by that shell at Château-Thierry, which had destroyed him so terribly that it had taken one of

the greatest surgeons in Germany five years to put together
the semblance of a body that he now possessed. A makeshift
that had been uncertain enough in normal times, this frame of
his could hardly, after the effort to which it had been forced
when he had to get out of Germany, be expected to last much
longer. It was only because he was sure he could not last much
longer that he was willing now to let himself see Elizabeth. He
had never expected to see her again. In those frightful days in
the German hospital, he had not wanted to. He had wanted her
to be rid of him, as desperately as he had wanted to be rid of
himself. Even now he trembled when he remembered that slow,
tortured rebuilding, insertion of metal strips to replace shattered bones, stretching of shrunken muscles, inadequate food
and inadequate anesthetics, his own screams and curses at the
man who persisted in keeping him alive when he wanted to die.

How that doctor had kept at him, with implacable hands
that he himself could see only as instruments of horror, forcing
into him the life he did not want, and slowly, through all of
it, giving him against his will life that was really life—not mere
physical existence, but a personality and a will, a re-creation so
profound that it seemed quite natural, when he began to realize
what was being given him, that along with all the rest he had
a new name. Kessler—thank heaven, he had thought then, it
was easy to say, for in those days the new language had seemed
very difficult, though now it was so much his own that when he
first came back to the United States he found that he had half
forgotten the old. The doctor's name was not so easy. Jacoby.
How he had dreaded that man at first!

He remembered Jacoby, in the days when he himself did not
know a word of German, struggling through a scanty knowledge of English to make him understand what was being done
to him, which he did not understand and hated Jacoby for doing, never dreaming then that he was meeting the greatest man
he was ever to know in his life. He shivered with a cold gust
of hate whenever he remembered how the Nazis had hounded

that great man to his death for no crime but the unforgivable iniquity of having been born a Jew, and of being so rockbound in his own goodness that he was incapable of accepting the evil of mankind until it had crushed him beyond escape. There had been little he could do in his love for Jacoby's memory, nothing but get to the United States while there was still time to save Jacoby's child.

His grief and rage at what had happened to his friend, and his terror lest he not be able to bring Jacoby's little girl to safety, had been so great that not until he was on the westbound steamer did he realize that when he got to America he was probably going to see Elizabeth. He knew her husband's name was Spratt Herlong and that he was employed by Vertex Studio, and in his own luggage was a contract signed in the Paris office of Vertex. He would be virtually sure to meet Herlong some day, and it might follow as a matter of course that he would meet Elizabeth. He went into his cabin and looked at himself a long time in the glass, as he was doing now. If there was a chance of her knowing him he would break his contract and make a living as a translator, a clerk, anything that would provide little Margaret with three meals a day without destroying Elizabeth's peace of mind.

But a long scrutiny satisfied him that there was no chance of it. In no sense, except the memory of her behind all that had happened since that explosion at Château-Thierry, could he believe he had any trace of the Arthur Kittredge she had known. He was Erich Kessler, dear friend of the late Dr. Gustav Jacoby, author of books based on case-histories of Dr. Jacoby's patients, and the change in his personality was as thorough as the change in his name. No man who had endured what he had endured in body and spirit could have much left in common with a happy, arrogant youth who did not know what it was to want anything he could not get.

He looked thoughtfully at his image in the glass. Crippled as he was, his appearance was not repulsive. One could see that in spite of his uncertain legs he had been meant for a tall man, and since his torso had to carry his weight the muscles there were powerfully developed. The effect was inevitably one-sided, since his left sleeve had been empty so long, but his right arm was like that of an athlete, and the hand which for twenty years had supported him upon a cane, was strong enough to break a china cup between the thumb and fingers. His face had no visible trace of the wound there except a scar that went upward from beneath his beard in a thin curving line. His hair was still thick, gray like steel; his beard was heavy too, and darker. He had let it grow with no thought of disguise, but to cover the scars that all Jacoby's careful skin-grafting had not been able to eliminate. Now he was glad he had it and was so used to it, for in spite of having seen thousands of Hitler's pictures most Americans still thought of Germans as being professors in dark beards.

She would not know him, but he would know her, as readily as he had known the picture standing on Spratt Herlong's desk. To be sure, he had been looking for it, but he would have recognized it anyway as Elizabeth. She had changed in those years, of course, but her alteration had been nothing more than the well-ordered development from youth into the maturity that could have been foreseen by anyone who had been as intimately acquainted with her as he had. Elizabeth had always known what she wanted out of life, because she was so eminently fit to have it. Physically and spiritually, she had wanted love, marriage, children, a home in which she would be no petted darling, but a versatile and devoted creator. From the beginning she had instinctively known herself capable of bringing all this into being, and so she had looked forward to it with the eagerness of those who have no doubt of their destiny. When he met Spratt, and saw the pictures of Elizabeth in Spratt's office, he felt that the change time had made in her appearance had been no more than the change one observes in the achievement of something of which one has seen the be-

ginning. Now that he could think of her without the pain of
the earlier years, he was glad he had been wise enough to step
aside so that she could have it.

He saw the pictures last week, on the first day he went into
Spratt's office. Spratt had been talking for some time about the
script, and if Kessler's attention had wandered it was no matter,
since he was going to read the script tomorrow anyway. When
Spratt had finished, and he himself had risen to leave, he
glanced at the photograph on the desk, saying with the casual-
ness born of years of self-command, "Your wife, Mr. Herlong?"

Spratt said, "Why yes," taking up the picture and handing
it to Kessler with the proud smile of a man showing his friend
a treasure. "But that's not very good of her—at least, I never
did think those formal portraits were as good as candid shots,
too smooth and pressed-out, if you get what I mean."

"Yes, I understand and agree with you." Kessler was looking
at her face. "But this is very charming."

"Oh yes, so it is, but this one on the wall looks more like
her. Over here by the door. Those are the children with her."

Kessler followed Spratt and looked at the picture on the
wall. "Yes, yes," he said with involuntary eagerness, "that, I
am sure, is more like her."

For it was like her, he knew that without having seen the
original in so long. The picture had been taken somewhere
outdoors, perhaps on a ranch. Either Elizabeth and her children
did not know they were being photographed, or the photog-
rapher was a genius at creating an unposed effect. Dressed in
a sweater and skirt, her hair blowing, Elizabeth sat on a fence
beyond which grew an orange tree; a young girl leaned on the
fence near by, while a tall youth who looked very much like
Elizabeth was standing by the tree, pulling its branches forward between his mother and sister so they could pick off the
fruit, and a little boy, sitting on the ground in front of the
fence, was already peeling the skin off an orange. By accident

or design, all the children were looking at their mother, and they were all four laughing. It was a group of healthy people who loved one another and were very happy about it. No wonder Spratt preferred it to the studio portrait on his desk. That was Elizabeth as she appeared to other people, her private life discreetly concealed behind a pleasant tranquillity of eyes and lips, but this was Spratt's wife as he loved her. Looking at the group, the outsider from Germany knew more profoundly than he had ever known before how much he had given Elizabeth when he had made up his mind to leave her free of his own wreckage. He glanced at Spratt, who was looking not at him but at the picture of his family, and for a moment he hated Spratt so fiercely that he could have killed him. But that passed quickly; long discipline had steadied his emotions as much as his conduct, and after that moment of hatred he felt nothing but gladness that his gift to her had been as great as he had meant it to be.

Today, alone in his office, he let his memory go back to the days when he had realized he had to do this because he loved Elizabeth too much to do anything else. The first days after the battle were nothing but confusion, fever and pain. He was in a place where there were a lot of other men on other cots, and women with pale harassed faces trying to take care of them, but he could not understand anything that was being said or anything that was done. He was strapped up in bandages that were far from clean, and among the people around him was a man gaunt as an ascetic, who came over now and then and did various horrible things to him. He did not know then that in those closing days of the war in Germany there was not cloth enough for fresh bandages or soap enough to wash those that had been used, or drugs to relieve suffering, or that his attendants had white faces and shaky hands because they were not getting enough to eat. Even when he began to discover this he did not care, because by that time he had begun to discover also the extent of the damage these Germans had done to him. He had no doubt that he was going to die, and the only wish he was strong enough to make was that he might die quickly and get it over.

Babbling in the only language he knew, he begged the gaunt cruel man to let him alone. At first the doctor seemed to be paying no attention, but one day his patient observed that he was talking, and after several repetitions the ungainly syllables acquired meaning. The doctor was saying, "Forgive me that I hurt you."

His accent was so thick as to be almost unintelligible, but the fact that he had any English at all gave a flash of hope to the mangled object on the cot. Any effort was torture, but if this fool of a doctor could be made to understand that a dying man wanted nothing more than to be left in peace, it was worth the effort. His own words were muffled because of the bandage on his chin, but he managed to get them out.

"Listen to me. I am not one of your countrymen—you know that, don't you? My name is Arthur Kittredge. I am an American. Your enemy—don't you get that? I am going to die anyway. Why don't you just let me do it?"

The doctor said something. Arthur did not understand it until it had been repeated several times, and when he finally caught the words they were not worth the trouble of listening, for all the doctor said was, "Quiet. You be quiet."

Arthur tried again, desperate with pain and weakness. "Do me a kindness. Give me something to finish it, won't you?— Please listen—I'm talking as plain as I can! Finish it. That's not much to ask, is it?"

Again the doctor said, "Quiet."

"If you don't care about doing a kindness to me, do it for somebody who can get up again—one of your own men. Why should you let me fill up a bed when German soldiers are lying on the floor? Or waste food on me when you haven't enough for your own? Don't keep me—"

His words ended in a gasp of pain. But he still looked at the doctor, too weak to say any more but conscious enough to plead with his eyes. Whether or not the doctor had understood all his words, he had grasped enough to know what Arthur wanted. He shook his head. "No," he said. "No." Exhausted as he was, Arthur could see him groping for more words. Mustering all his strength, Arthur managed to say again,

"I am going to die anyway."

"No, no. You are not going to die."

He spoke with a grim resolution that seemed to typify all Arthur had ever heard about the coldness of Germans and their inability to understand any reason why they might not always be right. Arthur was not able to form any more words, but he looked at the doctor with eyes that Jacoby told him later conveyed all his rage and disbelief. Arthur knew he was going to die and he wanted it over. But Jacoby's thin face had no yielding in it. Jacoby left him then, but he came back later, and this time his bony hand brought up a German-English dictionary out of his frayed pocket. Even with this aid, his English was so poor that he could convey nothing but a repetition of his refusal. Alone in his prison of pain, Arthur thought, "At home they'd shoot a dog that had been smashed by a truck. But this can't last much longer. It *can't*. If I hadn't been so healthy it would be over by now. But good God, have these people no mercy at all? I'd shoot the most heartless German under heaven before I'd let him die a death like this."

He was glad Elizabeth could not see him. She would never know anything about this lingering torment. They would simply tell her he was dead and she would think it had been quick and clean. "He never knew what hit him," they would say to her, and at least it would be easier for her than if she had to know how long it had taken him to die. And of course he did have one thing to be thankful for—if that shell had to hit him, he could be glad it had done its work. He would be dead and done with, and would not have to go back to her a half-human caricature of what used to be her husband. Though that wretch of a German doctor refused to shorten this last phase, though he might be beast enough to enjoy seeing one of his enemies get what was coming to him, even he could not indefinitely prolong it.

But at last Arthur discovered, with a revulsion that he could not have expressed if he had known the whole dictionary by heart, that this was exactly what the doctor meant to do to him.

Jacoby had been trying to talk to him for some days. Arthur had ceased trying to understand him. He had about given up trying to do the only thing that interested him, which was to refuse nourishment and get it over that way, for they fed him through a tube and he was too weak to resist. He hated the sight of the doctor with his gaunt face and thin cruel hands. But though he could not resist him, he did not have to listen to the man's awkward manipulations of the English language and try to make sense out of them.

However, the creature persisted, talking to him with many references to his dictionary. Unable to pronounce Arthur's name, he called him Kitt. He kept telling him something, in a low, insistent voice. He kept at it so long that at last one day the words he had been hearing arranged themselves in Arthur's mind and became an orderly sequence.

Stripped of its grotesqueries and repetitions, what Arthur understood went like this:

"You are not going to die, Kitt. You will be alive a long time. Not as you were. But you have your eyes, your hearing, the jaw will heal and there will be a hand. I think you will be able to sit upright. Walking I cannot promise, but I will try. It will be long and hard. But work with me, Kitt, and I will work with you. Do you understand me? *You are not going to die.*"

Arthur made an inarticulate noise. He looked at the doctor's steely blue eyes. They were fixed on him with a determination that made Arthur feel that this fellow was regarding him not as a man but as the subject of an inhuman experiment. Instead of letting him go, Jacoby was going to keep him conscious for years to come, simply to prove that he could do it.

What was left of Arthur quivered with rage. "You brute," he said, "you damned brute." He continued with epithets worse than that. He had never been addicted to profanity and was surprised to find such language coming so readily to his lips. But the words were there and he used them, and continued using them every time he saw the doctor.

Later he asked Jacoby if he had understood anything of what he had been saying then. Jacoby smiled with the grim humor Arthur had learned to recognize. "Not the vocabulary. But I did not need the vocabulary to understand what you were saying to me, and just then I did not blame you."

But at that time Jacoby paid no attention to the protests. He simply left Arthur there to contemplate his shattered body and go wild with the prospect of being forced to live in it. There was nothing else Jacoby could do. He was working eighteen hours a day, on a pittance of food that in pre-war Germany would not have been thought enough for an idle old man. Besides, since he knew so little English and Arthur knew no German at all, he had to let Arthur go on believing what he believed.

There was no way then for Jacoby to explain that four years of this war had almost annihilated his faith in the human soul. There was no way for him to say that he too was on the edge of despair, searching desperately for some reason to believe that men could be saved from the evil they had wrought.

Before the war, Jacoby had never doubted the essential worth of the spirit. He had not thought mankind was perfect or likely to become so, but he did respect his fellowmen because he thought that for the most part they deserved it. He had no patience with those contemptuous pessimists who shrugged at the human race as though they had looked it over and decided that it would never amount to much. To them he had been accustomed to say, "Most people have a lot to put up with and most of them put up with it very well. I know some of them are fools and scoundrels, but there's a lot of courage in the world, and a lot of quiet unostentatious nobility. People in general are all right, and you'd find it out if you'd take the trouble to know them better."

That, expressed in homely language, was his faith in the fundamental value of life. He had believed in it. But that was in the pleasant days before the war.

Then came the four years he had just lived through. The physical wrecks brought to him had been dreadful enough, but they were not the worst. Some of those he could heal and some he could not. But he had been appalled, sickened, and at last reduced almost to hopelessness as he saw the disintegration of humanity. He had seen men turned into brutes incapable of any emotion but hate, he had seen it over and over, so often that he wondered why he should be trying to save their lives when they had nothing left that made them fit to live. The fury and terror around him had come close to uprooting all the confidence he had ever had in men's being fundamentally better than this. He wanted to believe they were. If this was all they were good for, the sooner they destroyed themselves the better. It was very hard, in this last year of the war, to go on believing in anything.

Arthur had been brought to him when he had begun to feel himself giving in to a brutal cynicism. When he examined Arthur, he suddenly felt that here was a man who could prove the ultimate test, not of a human body to recover, but of human courage to overcome disaster. When this American realized what had been done to him his mind would be black with hate and horror, even if it had never been before. At first he had wondered if he had the right to prolong such a life as this. But after several of those examinations under which Arthur had screamed and cursed at him, Jacoby had convinced himself that with labor and patience he could guarantee that his patient would not be helpless. Arthur would have something to work with. If he could be made to use what he had, and with it regain any wisdom or generosity in spite of what he had lost, Jacoby promised himself that he would take it as meaning that humanity could do the same. As he worked with him, as he saw Arthur's fury and despair, Arthur became to him a symbol of the world's wreckage. If this shattered American could come back, there was hope. The damage of the war was done to the world as it was done to Arthur, but if Arthur could be made to go on, could be made to want to go on, there was a reason for living. By this time Jacoby was not sure that there was. But he was going to find out.

Arthur still hated him. He had ceased to doubt that Jacoby meant exactly what he said: Jacoby was not going to let him die, but was going to restore as much as he could of what had been lost. That there was so much he could not restore made no difference to his eagerness. Much of the work was necessarily experimental. "But it's the sort of experiment he looks for," Arthur told himself bitterly. "It's not often he finds a patient who simply can't be any worse off, no matter how many mistakes he makes. When he gets one like that he gives him the works. One man is better than a thousand guinea pigs. I can see the reasoning. Only I never thought of its happening to me."

When he did have a chance to talk to Arthur again, Jacoby's difficulty with the language was so great that he could tell him very little. But after many attempts he managed to say,

"When you were begging me to let you alone, I was trying to make sure you would keep your right arm. Believe me, Kitt, if you had lost both arms, or if there had been blindness with all the rest, I should have done what you asked me."

Arthur said angrily, "Why don't you do it now?"

Jacoby gave him a look of real surprise. "Do you still want me to?"

"Yes. I do *not* want to be a subject for vivisection."

"Kitt, do you still think that is what I am doing to you?"

"You know it is."

Jacoby shook his head. He fumbled for words. He said, "I watched you for many days. I fought a battle. I cannot say it well. Perhaps in English I cannot say it at all. You are a man, Kitt, but also you are mankind. You must live. You must want to live. You *must*—do you understand me?" He spoke so intensely that he was almost fierce. "Kitt," he exclaimed, "let us try!"

Though he did not realize it then, Arthur remembered later that his own resistance was gradually being worn away by the power of Jacoby's determination. As time went on, he came to recognize the enthusiasm Jacoby was feeling. He had felt it himself when there was some almost impossible job to be tackled. "If I can do this, I can do anything." He knew what it meant to roll up his sleeves, saying that.

What he did not realize at the time was that this was not what Jacoby was saying. Jacoby was saying to himself, "If *he* can do this, I can do anything."

The first time he began to understand that Jacoby was not merely a cold scientist was the day when Jacoby came to his bedside with a slip of paper and a pencil.

"Kitt, if you will tell me—spell it slowly—the name of the woman you kept talking to when you were delirious—?"

Arthur groaned. His impulse was to grip Jacoby's hand, but he could not do this. He could only say, "In God's name, Jacoby, be merciful! If you've made up your mind to do this to me I can't stop you. But don't do it to her."

Without looking at Arthur, Jacoby said, "I thought it might be possible to get her a message. Through the Red Cross."

Arthur did not answer. After a pause Jacoby asked,

"You do not want to tell me who she is?"

Arthur said, "She is my wife."

Jacoby turned his head toward the bed then, involuntarily.

He knew no words to speak and even if he had been using his own language there could have been nothing to say so eloquent as the pity he could not keep out of his eyes.

He crumpled the slip of paper in his fist. There was a silence. At length Jacoby said, "Very well." He turned and went away.

But in the depth of his own despair Arthur felt a stir of astonished warmth. "My God, the man is a human being. There are some things even he can't take without a shudder."

After that, slowly but unmistakably, he began to discover that Jacoby wanted to be his friend. He began, dimly at first, through those days and nights of desolation, to grasp what Jacoby had meant when he said, "You are a man, but also you are mankind." It was a hard realization, and at first he was doubtful that it had any meaning. "He can make me stay alive," Arthur said to himself wearily. "But can he make me find any reason for doing it? Can anybody? I don't believe it."

Jacoby came back to his bedside often. He never again mentioned the woman Arthur had called for in his delirium. But there was more work on the arm, more on the jaw; the rest had to wait on the patient's strength and the doctor's opportunities. Arthur still had very little hope. Now that he understood Jacoby's purpose, he tried to sympathize with it, but he found this hard to do.

For after all, even after years of labor and pain, even with the highest success, what was the utmost Jacoby could give him? Power to use his right arm; power to sit up and write a letter; possibly, after a long time, power to hobble from place to place with a crutch. Power to look on hopelessly while healthy men and women went ahead with their healthy affairs, doing useful work and enjoying the rewards of it. Not even Jacoby's genius could restore him the sense of knowing he could take care of himself no matter what happened, the old happy forthrightness of being able to look the whole world in the face and tell it to get out of his way. Jacoby could never restore him his marriage. He could never give Elizabeth the children she wanted, or even the security and companionship she had had with him. Lying in a helpless huddle on his cot in the intervals of being fed and washed by strange hands, Arthur had nothing to do but look ahead into the sort of life-sentence he would be giving her if he let Jacoby communicate with her. No doubt he had been reported missing in action. When they found him, the Red Cross would have means of notifying Elizabeth he was still alive. After the war, as soon as Jacoby had repaired him sufficiently to make it possible for him to go home, he would have to go.

And then? Elizabeth would offer him everything she had. She was too loyal, and she loved him too much, to dream of doing otherwise. She would work, and use everything she could earn for his support. She would spend her life nursing him, amusing him, taking care of him, himself a broken wreck of a creature who could give her nothing in return except a doglike gratitude. Her splendid vitality would be spent in a twilight of half-living until she was dry and withered like fruit that had been broken off the tree before it had had a chance to ripen. As he thought of it he knew more and more surely that no matter what would become of him, he could not let this happen to her.

His decision was not entirely unselfish. Arthur was too clear-headed to imagine it was. Not only could he not do this to Elizabeth, but he could not do it to himself. Bearing his tragedy alone would be easier than requiring her to share it.

He knew, almost as if he were with her, what she would suffer at being told of his death. But that would not last for-ever, though at the time she would undoubtedly think it was going to. She would pick up the broken pattern of her life and set about putting it together again. Elizabeth was young, vital, alert, and there would be another man who would find her as lovable as he had found her. She would have again the sort of mating she should have. He tried instinctively to clench his fist with decision, and the pain that went like a bayonet-thrust into his shoulder, reminding him that he was not even able to make such a simple gesture, served to strengthen his resolve. When a man dies, he told himself, with more fierceness in his mind since there could be none in his body, it is like taking a teaspoonful of water out of a river. The water closes up, it is gone, and after an instant nobody notices it any more.

When Jacoby came in again, Arthur told him what he had decided to do. He had to speak slowly, repeating often and waiting until Jacoby's intelligence had limped through to comprehension. The effort to make Jacoby understand took his attention away from the bleak import of what he was saying.

"I will make you a promise, Jacoby, if you will do one thing for me. Do it, and come back and tell me you have done it."

"I understand you. Go ahead."

"When I was brought in here, you found the metal tag of identification? And other things, maybe? Take those to the International Red Cross. Tell them your stretcher-bearers brought in an American who died of his wounds. You do not know his name. But you took these objects from his body. You will sign a death certificate, or whatever you have to sign. The American army will take care of the rest. If you will do this, and bring me some sort of proof that you have done it, I promise you that I will let you do whatever you please to me. But if you will not do it, I swear to you that I'll make you do it because I'll end my life as soon as I have a usable hand to do it with."

Deliberately, further to relieve his attention, he fixed his eyes on Jacoby's eyes, tender as the eyes of a mother; on Jacoby's strong, wise, gentle face; and while he repeated his sentences he noticed again what a thin face it was, the skin showing the waxiness of malnutrition, and guessed as he had guessed before that this man was denying himself part of his own rations to provide more nourishment for the men he was trying to save. At last he said, slowly and carefully, "You understand me? You will do what I ask, Jacoby?"

Jacoby nodded. While he sought for his answer his right hand covered the right hand that could not yet be clenched, friendly across the wall of language. He said, "Yes, Kitt. I will do that."

It was all he could say, but by that time they had learned to do a good deal of communicating without language. Jacoby did not have a wife of his own. Until now his life had been too full of work and war to give him much chance to think of personal happiness. Later he was to find out what it meant to have a woman's suffering mean more to him than his own. But he did not hesitate before Arthur's request. Arthur continued,

"You will not communicate with my wife. You will not try to find her."

"I understand what you are saying. I will not try to find her."

"She will marry again," Arthur said. "Another man will love her, she will have children, she will be happy. Do you get it, Jacoby? She's a splendid woman, I'm going to get out of her way. Oh, you don't get all this, do you?—but I know I'm right."

Jacoby tried to answer. "You are—" he hesitated, reaching into his pocket for the dictionary he always carried now— "you are most completely right, Kitt." He looked down at the bundle of bandages before him, and added, "I do understand."

"You—" Arthur's voice broke in a sob, and the sob came from so deep that it sent points of pain through him and he had to wait till they subsided before he could go on—"you don't understand. You never loved a woman." Again the sob rushed up, and again he had to wait till the pain of it went down. "You never loved a woman," he said, "enough to die for her."

Whether the barrier was language or experience, this time Jacoby did not try to answer. But he went and did what Arthur had asked him to do.

6.

JACOBY used one of the precious night hours when he should have been asleep to rig up a sort of shelf across Arthur's cot, and set the dictionary up on it. "My English is so faulty, Kitt, and I have no time to improve it. Why do you not learn to talk to me?"

He read the first words aloud to him, slowly, so Arthur could begin to learn their pronunciation. While he was taking a hasty meal of turnips and potatoes Jacoby drew rough sketches of various objects in the room, writing their names beside them, and set the sheet up for Arthur to study during the day. Arthur blessed him for it. He was not yet able to push his thoughts forward into what he might be going to do with the future Jacoby was forcing upon him. This occupation was enough for the present. He filled up his mind with German words to keep it from being filled up with thoughts of Elizabeth. When Jacoby came to see him he talked in simple sentences, proudly, and felt a childish delight when Jacoby and the nurses began to understand him.

Long afterwards, when they were looking back on those days, Jacoby said to him, "You did not know how you were encouraging me then." Arthur answered, "Maybe you never knew how often I nearly gave up." "Yes I did know," said Jacoby, "but you did not give up. That is what I mean, Kitt."

To the very end, Jacoby sometimes called him Kitt. If anyone asked why, he said, "Oh no, Herr Kessler's first name is Erich. Calling him Kitt is an old bad habit of mine, from years back."

They were both so used to it they generally forgot it was an abbreviation of his old name. The new name was provided by Jacoby after Arthur had been moved to the hospital in Berlin, while he was convalescing from another of the surgical operations Jacoby inflicted upon him. He had been very ill and Jacoby had given him a blood transfusion. When he was better and tried to express his thanks Jacoby retorted, "My blood isn't good enough for gratitude, Kitt—made of nothing but turnips and a carrot or two. But I have something else for you, more important." He produced a document, offering it with an air of triumph. "Here is your birth certificate."

Arthur laughed at that. Birth certificates had not been important in the United States before the war. He had never had one. But Jacoby was a German and thought like a German, and to him his beloved Kitt's physical welfare was no more essential than the records which the Germans demanded even in their most chaotic days. Jacoby explained,

"Listen carefully, Kitt. From now on your name is Erich Kessler. I have lost sleep over wondering how you could identify yourself, until one morning about three o'clock I found the solution. When I was a child, my parents knew a couple named Kessler. They had a son named Erich. While the boy was still a baby, the Kesslers went to the United States. They lived in a town called—" he consulted his notes, and pronounced incorrectly—"Milwaukee. You have heard of it?"

Arthur nodded. "Yes. I grew up in a town called Chicago. They are very near each other."

"You have been to Milwaukee?"

"Frequently."

"That is good. While he was still a small child, Erich Kessler died. I know that, because his mother and mine used to correspond. But there is no official record of that in this country, because the Kesslers stayed in the United States and were naturalized. For all I know they may be there to this day."

"Making beer, perhaps?"

"Why? Do you know them?"

"Never heard of them. But I know Milwaukee. Go on, Jacoby."

"I have obtained Erich Kessler's birth certificate. I have recorded that Erich—you—naturalized without his knowledge or consent when his parents were naturalized, was drafted into the American army. The rest follows. You have returned to the land of your birth, and can stay here now until you want to leave."

"I shall not want to leave, Jacoby."

"I hope not. But anyway, this makes you a German and at the same time takes care of your American accent. However, please listen to me and try to speak like me. Erich Kessler would have heard his parents speak German at home and would pronounce it better than you do."

"I'll do my best. Correct me whenever you please."

Almost automatically, Jacoby was massaging the muscles of his patient's right arm. "These are flabby," he observed. "While you are lying in bed, for a few minutes at a time, clench your fist slowly and relax it slowly. Slowly, remember? That won't tax your strength, and you must take care of this arm. You will need it."

"For a crutch?" said the new-made Erich Kessler, with a note of his old bitterness.

"I hope there will be a crutch," Jacoby answered quietly. "Remember, I've promised nothing about your legs except to do the best I can with them."

"All right, all right, I know. A man isn't hoping for too much in this world when he hopes for a crutch, is he?"

Jacoby addressed him sternly. "My friend, until you can face what you're up against *now*, you aren't fit to try to go further."

There was a long silence. At last the patient said, "I get it, Jacoby. And—ah—thank you."

Jacoby stood up. "Thank *you*, for not being angry with me."

"Oh, shut up, will you?" He felt like changing the subject.

"By the way, Jacoby, this Erich Kessler—me—am I a Jew like you?"

"No, why? Were you a Jew at home?"

"No, that's why I asked. I thought if I was to be one here you'd better teach me something about the religious rituals. But if I'm not, then it's not important."

Startling to remember now that there had been a time when one could say "It's not important," so carelessly, and then forget about it. There was nobody then to tell him that Erich Kessler's not being a Jew was going to be so important later on that it would enable him to save Jacoby's child.

When he was up in a wheel-chair, he went to live with Jacoby. It was almost like living in a hospital. Jacoby had his own laboratory and surgery as part of the Berlin hospital. Patients came and went all day and half the night. There was still lack of food, drugs, trained assistants. Jacoby worked like a demon. Watching him work threw Kessler into dark periods of dismay at his own uselessness. When he spoke of this to Jacoby, he received one of the quiet, direct replies he had learned to expect from his friend.

"Kessler, no man who genuinely wants to be of use in the world is ever useless for long. But that is a question you must answer for yourself. If I tried to answer it for you, I should be doing you an injury greater than any you have suffered. I should be telling you that it is no longer necessary for you to be responsible for your own conduct, and that is a crime I won't commit against anybody."

Still trembling from the storm that had shattered him, Kessler found this hard to take. Later on he blessed Jacoby for having made him take it, refusing to let him sink into the childish dependency which at first seemed so comfortable a cushion for his tortured spirit. But since Jacoby did refuse, and his own bodily lassitude made his mind eager for activity, he had to search for a place he was capable of occupying. His first suggestion was made timidly.

"Jacoby, I don't know a thing about medicine or surgery, but if there's one thing I do know it's chemistry. Do you think I could learn to do some of these routine analyses that take up so much of your time? Blood-counts, and things like that?"

"Why not?" Jacoby returned eagerly. "If you only knew how much I need a technician! I'll be back in a minute."

He hurried off, and came back with an armful of books which he dumped by the table he had rigged up to match the wheel-chair. "Start with this one. If you have trouble with the vocabulary let me know."

Kessler felt a tingle of returning vigor. This would not be much, but it would be something toward repaying Jacoby. The prospect of making any kind of return was an immeasurable impetus.

He went to work. He worked as hard as Jacoby would let him. Within a couple of weeks he was surprised to find his study interesting for its own sake. "I always thought I was burning up with curiosity about the universe," he said to Jacoby, "but I'm ashamed to find how I neglected my own species. You don't know how glad I am you're letting me do this."

Jacoby shrugged. "Where did you get the impression I was 'letting' you do it? I need you. One of these days, when the country is normal again, maybe I'll be able to get enough technicians. But now—!"

Though at first Kessler undertook only the simplest routines in the laboratory, they absorbed all his energy. He was still far from strong. The work was new, his reports had to be made in a language he still found unwieldy, and learning to make one hand serve the purpose of two required a thousand adjustments. But it meant that he was back in the sphere of active men, doing something that needed to be done, and occupation relieved him of leisure for brooding.

Much of Jacoby's practice at this time dealt with reconstruc-

tion of wounded soldiers, and he got into the habit of coming
to the laboratory for advice, at first to bolster his analyst's returning assurance and later because he needed his counsel.
For as the embittered wreck Arthur Kittredge gradually
turned into the confident scientist Erich Kessler, the youthful
violence of the first changed to the gentle wisdom of a man
who had sunk into the ultimate hopelessness and had come
back. Arthur Kittredge had wanted to die; Erich Kessler, after
a long hard battle, wanted to live. Kessler wanted to live
because at last he found other people more important than
himself, and this came about because he found, at first to his
own amazement, that he had something valuable to give them.
While he still had to be carried to his wheel-chair and lifted
out of it, his efforts to be of some use to Jacoby widened into
his being of use to a great many others.

As he progressed from elementary routines into tasks of
more complexity, Kessler began to act as amanuensis for Jacoby
as well as technician. He sat in a corner during Jacoby's inter-
views with his patients, taking notes of their symptoms. As he
never said anything, his presence came to be accepted like
that of the furniture in the consulting-room. Then, gradually,
he fell into the habit of letting the patients talk to him if they
called when Jacoby was otherwise occupied. He began to
learn how many others there were besides himself who had
to recover from the impact that physical disability had made
on their lives. Jacoby had profound wisdom for these people,
but sometimes, looking at Jacoby's healthy body, they did
not believe it. When they looked at Kessler, still limp in his
wheel-chair, they knew he knew what they were talking about.

So they talked to him, bringing him their own experience
of despair. As he listened to all these men and women who
wanted to die he began to see with startling clearness how
little reason many of them had ever had for wanting to live.
They had never been interested in anything but their own
sensations. In a world sick with confusion, they were aware

of nothing but their personal despondency, and they angrily resisted being made aware of anything else. As he heard them he thought he heard himself, bounded by tremendous trivialities, crying out against a destiny that forced him to look beyond these for a reason to stay alive. So many of these people could expect far more bodily power than he could. So many of them could take a real step in the march of civilization if they could first be persuaded to carry their own burdens. He tried to tell them this.

Often he failed, for he learned that there were a great many men and women in the world who would literally rather die than admit that their own characters had room for improvement. But sometimes he succeeded, and when he succeeded he felt the ecstasy of creation. Even when he was allowed to stand up, with a crutch on his right side and Jacoby's arm supporting him on the other, and he actually walked a couple of steps on legs that had been idle four years, his sense of triumph was not as great as when he had managed to convince another human being that there was no real defeat except that of giving up the battle. He had not won his own battle yet. He never would win it completely. By this time he had become reconciled to the knowledge that no matter how he fought there would be periods when he would sit alone in his room sobbing like a child that he couldn't take it; but he knew also that these periods were temporary, and that he could take it.

When Germany had entered into a season of quiet that deceived innocent persons like himself and Jacoby into believing that it was recovering from the war, he got in touch with a private investigating agency and found out what had become of Elizabeth. He was told that she was living in California, married and the mother of a son. The news hurt him a great deal more deeply than he had thought it would. Was it conceivable, he asked himself, that he had expected her to spend her life remembering him? Yes, it was conceivable; that was exactly what the primitive, possessive part of himself had wanted her to do, and now this part of himself was leaping up from where he had buried it, enraged that she had accepted her freedom. He tried to bury it again, though it was a long time before he succeeded in doing so. But during that time, pretending to himself that he had done so helped him go on about his business.

This business had become writing case-histories of the patients whose lives had come under his own and Jacoby's care. Disguising their personal circumstances, he had drama enough for a thousand volumes. His only experience of writing had been in putting out technical pamphlets for the oil industry, but he had learned from this to say what he had to say plainly enough to be understood. Without any literary genius, he had learned to think clearly, and fortunately his present subject required clearness rather than rhetoric.

His books were widely read in Germany before Hitler had the power to order them burnt, and two of them were bought for motion pictures by French studios. With his hospital consultations and his writing, Kessler had more work than he could do. He was not as happy as he had been. This he did not expect, but he had the triumphant knowledge that he had built a worthwhile career on the ruins.

In the meantime Jacoby had married a brilliant girl named Ricarda. Much younger than her husband, Ricarda was already showing a devotion to science equal to his, and after their marriage they worked together. She and Jacoby were passionately in love. Though sometimes the sight of their happy marriage made Kessler feel like a pauper standing in the snow to look through a lighted window, he tried not to let them suspect it. They had been his friends before their marriage, and afterwards they remained so.

They knew there was an Austrian fanatic named Hitler, but beyond laughing at his bad German when they heard it on the radio they had been too busy to pay much attention to him. None of them had ever been interested in politics. It was easy to see now that they should have been. But they were not, and when they heard Hitler's fantastic threats it did not occur to them to believe him. When Jacoby and Ricarda finally realized the persecution directed at them, it was already full-grown and too strong to be escaped.

They had tried to escape. But it was too late. They who had saved so many others could not save themselves. The force of evil closed around them so tight that at last it crushed even their gallant spirits. The Nazis succeeded in doing to Jacoby what the war had not been able to do: they destroyed his faith and with it his courage. So today the great Dr. Jacoby and his wife were only two more of Germany's uncounted Jewish suicides.

Kessler had not been able to save them, but through the connivance of some of Jacoby's friends who were risking their lives along with his to help him, he had managed to save their little girl. He got Margaret into France, her surname changed from Jacoby to Kessler on the passport, and a French representative of Vertex Studios met him at the frontier with tickets to Paris. Once in France, he discovered that the American studios were hiring writers, directors, actors and producers from Germany as fast as permits could be obtained in Washington, with a grimly gleeful "Thank you, Mr. Hitler!" as the finest cinema talent of the Old World poured into Hollywood. It was not difficult for him to get an American contract.

Two weeks after he left Ellis Island he was working in New York. A little while later he and Margaret came to California. As his own language returned to him, he taught her to speak English. She was a happy little girl now, going to school, though she had not forgotten Germany. He wished it had happened when she was younger. But he had learned not to look back. If a man was to keep any sanity in these times, the only view was forward. He did not know what was going to become of Margaret. It was scarcely possible that his own overtaxed strength could hold out as long as she would need him. But he had learned too that though one only looked ahead, one did not need to tax his powers with apprehension.

Through the windows of his office Kessler watched the late sun on the hills beyond, glowing on the slopes while the folds between filled with purple shadow. Dry odors of dust and sagebrush blew in toward him. Around his bungalow were the friendly noises of the day's end, doors closing, cars starting, voices calling "See you tomorrow!" In a few minutes Spratt Herlong would come for him.

Surprising, how simple it was now, to be about to see Elizabeth. He had expected never to see her again. He had made another life for himself without her. But now that the Nazis had smashed that life, taking away his work and his friends, forcing his frail powers to the effort of still another beginning, it did not seem too much to ask that at least he might find Elizabeth in happy possession of all he had made possible for her. When he had seen her, tranquil and assured as she was meant to be, he would know that he had accomplished something in his lifetime. He could be satisfied that neither war nor Nazis had conquered him completely.

He wanted to see her now; for a long time he could not have said that. Even as lately as ten years ago he would not have cared to undertake it. But there was such a thing as having moved beyond resentment, beyond envy, beyond any demand of his own ego. There was a certain austere happiness in having mastered himself so completely. A cold happiness it was, to be sure, and a lonely one, but at least it did mean peace.

7.

"THERE'S the car," said Elizabeth. "Remember, both of you, not to take any notice of his misfortunes."

Cherry laughed at her reproachfully. "Mother, we're not savages! We don't stare at cripples."

"I know, dear, but sometimes the best of us give a little start when we see persons very different from ourselves. We don't mean to."

Cherry and Dick promised to be models of good behavior. Elizabeth got up and went to the door opening from the living room into the entry. She hoped Mr. Kessler would have a comfortable evening. Entertaining Spratt's business associates was a duty they were all used to, and the older children adapted themselves to it well enough. Brian begged to be let off when there were strangers in to dine, so as usual he had had his dinner early and was now upstairs in his room pottering over his natural history collections. Spratt opened the front door, saying,

"Here we are, Kessler. And here's my wife. Elizabeth, my friend Erich Kessler that you've already heard so much about."

Elizabeth looked up with the smile that Spratt characterized as the masterpiece of the accomplished hostess, "not bright enough to look insincere, but not strained enough to look dutiful. Just in between, gracious."

Mr. Kessler's physical handicaps had threatened to make this occasion difficult, but Elizabeth's initial glance dispelled her apprehension. He was badly crippled, but he did not appear resentful; he faced the world before him with a grave acceptance, as though all the fault he had to find with destiny had been got over long ago. As their eyes met Elizabeth was struck with an impression that she had seen Mr. Kessler somewhere before.

It also seemed to her that Mr. Kessler was looking at her with an unusual interest. His eyes went over her swiftly and inclusively, taking in her hair, her face, her dress, every detail of her as though it were important that he should know all about her as soon as possible. It was the way a man might have looked at a famous personage he had long been eager to meet, or a woman so astoundingly beautiful that he wanted to impress her forever upon his memory. Elizabeth was not famous, and while she was not ugly she was no ravishing beauty either. She thought it might mean that they really had seen each other somewhere, and he like herself was trying to identify the recollection. If her own sense of familiarity persisted she could ask him about it later on.

All this was only a quick flutter in her mind, pushed aside in an instant while her attention turned itself to its immediate concerns. She took in his appearance quickly: a big man of more powerful build than she had expected, bent over a heavy cane with a dependence that told her instantly that she should not expect him to shake hands; iron-gray hair receding at the temples, a thick beard, a scar that rippled up his right cheek, dark eyes with a line of concentration between the eyebrows and crinkles of kindness at the outer corners, and a pleasant smile—what she could see of it between the whiskers—a very pleasant smile indeed. If he had any idea that this was not their first meeting he gave no evidence of it, for all he said to her was, "How do you do, Mrs. Herlong," with the stateliness she had learned to expect from Europeans. Elizabeth indicated the room beyond.

"Come in by the fire, Mr. Kessler. These are my children."

Dick was standing, with that mixture of assurance and awkwardness that made her find boys in their teens so eminently kissable just when they most resisted being kissed by their mothers. Cherry, with fewer years but more social graces than

Dick would acquire for another decade, sat smiling a welcome to the newcomer. Elizabeth introduced them, and again it seemed to her that Kessler was regarding them with an attention extraordinary in a man who could hardly be supposed to have any interest in them. There was an alertness in the way he spoke to Dick and Cherry, as though he had decided in advance that he was going to be fond of them and hoped they would respond. He said, "Your father has told me a great deal about you, and has shown me your pictures. I am so glad to see you."

Dick, who had already said "How do you do," tried to look pleasant without knowing what else to say, while Cherry, a shade too adept at social fibs, answered, "He has told us *lots* about you too, Mr. Kessler," with such a bright smile that Elizabeth privately reminded herself, "I've got to warn Cherry about that sort of thing, if she isn't careful she's going to be an intolerable gusher before she's twenty." Kessler appeared to be finding them the most attractive youngsters on earth. While she was offering him the chair she had intended for him, arranged with a little table at its side so he could set down his glass when the hors d'oeuvres appeared, she added to herself, "Spratt must have led him to expect a most remarkable pair of children, he really shouldn't—or is Mr. Kessler as charming as this with everybody?" Spratt, evidently pleased at the good impression his offspring were making, crossed the room to the door leading upstairs, explaining that Kessler had had time to wash up in his bungalow before leaving the lot, but he himself had not, and if they'd forgive him he'd go up and make himself presentable. "I'll leave you with the family, Kessler," he concluded.

Kessler gave him a smile and a slight formal bow. Elizabeth returned to the fire. "Now we'll have a cocktail. Dick, will you bartend?"

Dick would; he was always glad of this to occupy him during his first minutes of encounter with a stranger. Everything became quite as usual. Dick mixed the Martinis, and as the war had reduced the number of their servants Cherry brought in

the hors d'oeuvres. "These are liver-paste, Mr. Kessler, and
these are smoked salmon, and these thingumbobs on toothpicks
—I don't know what they are, something she made out of an
old lampshade." But as Elizabeth and Kessler picked up their
glasses and their eyes met across them, she felt another twinge
of familiarity. "I have met this man before, I know I have, and
he knows it too. Or doesn't he? If he doesn't, why is he looking at me like that? Maybe it's just because I keep looking at
him—for pity's sake, I do believe I'm staring. Behave yourself,
Elizabeth." She was relieved to hear Cherry say,

"Have you ever been to the United States before, Mr.
Kessler?"

He turned to her at once, and Elizabeth thought, "He's as
relieved as I am to have that look between us broken, or if he's
not, then I'm letting my imagination go haywire." He was answering Cherry,

"Yes, Miss Herlong, but that was many years ago, long before this country was brightened by your existence."

"Say, that's very good!" Dick exclaimed with a grin.

Elizabeth flashed him a teasing glance. "You will, Oscar."
They all laughed, and Dick said to Kessler,

"You speak awfully well for a man who's just been here once,
and that so long ago."

"It has been three years since I left Germany. Besides, I have
visited England and Scotland. We have more chance to practice
foreign languages in Europe than you have here."

"Oh yes, of course you do," said Cherry. "We don't have
any. We take French, and learn to say 'Have you seen the garden of my grandmother's cousin?' and then school is out for the
summer and we forget it. At least, I always did."

Kessler continued talking with Dick and Cherry. He asked
them what they liked to study at school, and what they wanted
to do when they had finished, so that they loosened up their
company manners and began to talk readily. Their experience
with representatives of the picture business had been that most

of them were so engrossed by their work that they rarely attempted any conversation about anything but the picture they were working on now or the one they had just finished, and they had been prepared to sit in polite boredom. They were surprised and delighted to have a guest who took an interest in their affairs. At first Elizabeth thought it was very good of him to do so, and she wished more of their visitors were like this; then it occurred to her that Kessler was concentrating on the children in order to avoid talking with her.

He had drawn them out skilfully. Dick was telling him the rules of football, and Kessler had nothing to do but listen with the interested appearance of a foreigner who wanted to learn about a native institution. "Am I just seeing things that aren't here," Elizabeth asked herself, "or is it on purpose that he hasn't looked at me once since that curious tense moment across the cocktails?" It seemed to her now that when their eyes had met and held each other so strangely it had been as though Kessler was about to say something, and at the last instant had caught himself back from saying it, grasping at Cherry's question as a means of saving himself. She did not understand what it was all about, but at any rate the dissertation on football had given him time to recover his equilibrium, and he now turned to her with a calmness that made her almost believe all this was merely an exaggeration of her fancy, saying,

"Haven't you three children, Mrs. Herlong?"

"Why yes," said Elizabeth, "but Brian is only eleven, so he had his dinner early." But she could not help asking, "How did you know there were three?"

"Mr. Herlong told me, and showed me a picture of you all. Brian isn't asleep yet, is he?"

"I'm sure he isn't. Do you want to meet him too?"

"I should like to very much, if it's quite convenient."

Elizabeth laughed a little. "Mr. Kessler, you should know it's never inconvenient for a mother to display her jewels. Dick, will you run up and get Brian?"

"Sure, but you'd better warn Mr. Kessler that he'll be all smeared with glue and bugs. Brian's mounting butterflies, does it all day and night, and he'll talk your ear off about them if you let him."

"I should like that. Tell him to bring his specimens down and show them to me."

"There are thousands," Cherry warned, but Kessler showed no dismay. He only said,

"Then tell him to bring a few, and don't make him brush his hair, or he'll dislike me before he sees me." He and Dick exchanged a look of understanding. As Dick went out Kessler turned to Elizabeth. "I hope I'm not upsetting a domestic arrangement, Mrs. Herlong, in asking that he come in. But your two older children are so entertaining that I couldn't help wanting to see the other."

"Aren't you nice!" exclaimed Cherry.

"Thank you for saying so," answered Elizabeth. "Of course, their father and I think they are, but we love having other people agree with us."

"I'm sure other people do. You should be very proud, Mrs. Herlong." He glanced around him. "When one sees a home like this, one knows who is responsible for it. I don't mean the physical furnishings of your house, attractive as they are—I mean its atmosphere. It's not by chance one achieves such confidence and vitality."

He spoke sincerely, obviously meaning what he said. Elizabeth felt a glow of pleasure. It was like what she had felt when she sat on the balcony yesterday afternoon, before she heard the children talking in the den. She wondered what Kessler would say of them now if he had heard that conversation.

She said, "I hardly know how to answer such a compliment, Mr. Kessler. Has it occurred to you that perhaps we have too much confidence, a good deal more than is justified by the world we live in?"

"Oh yes," he replied instantly. "That's true of nearly all

Americans—at least, it seems true to anyone who comes to the United States from Europe. But surely," he added smiling, "you can't hold yourself guilty when a man long surrounded by terror comes into your home and feels encouraged at the thought that this, and not the other, is the normal state of living?"

His words made her feel better than she had felt all day. Now that the two of them seemed to be back on a normal basis from which a friendship could be started, it occurred to Elizabeth that perhaps Kessler, fresh from Nazi Germany but evidently not part of it, could tell Dick more clearly than she ever could something about the issues at stake in this war he was going to be asked to fight. Much as she loved Dick she could not disguise from herself the fact that he was more superficial than she would have liked him to be, so occupied with girls and football that he was glad to accept clichés that relieved him from being occupied with more troublesome matters. Dick was a nice boy, but mentally he was a rather lazy one, and neither she nor his father was quite capable of coping with him. Spratt was inclined to believe he would begin to take life seriously when the time came; Elizabeth thought the time had come for it. Sometimes it happened that a friend was better at this than the parents who had spent so many years being more indulgent than they should have been, or who at least had emphasized details of socially acceptable behavior at the expense of the much harder job of making a boy think for himself.

Her thoughts were interrupted by the opening of the door from the hall. Spratt and Dick came in with Brian, who had a glass-topped box of specimens under his arm. "This is Mr. Kessler, Brian," Spratt said. "He wanted to meet you so he could know the whole Herlong family."

"How do you do sir," said Brian, all in one word, and held out his hand. Fortunately Kessler was sitting down instead of leaning on his cane, and so could give him a handshake. Brian stood uncertainly, one foot curled around the opposite ankle.

"Your brother tells me you are interested in natural history," said Kessler, "and I asked him to tell you I should like to see some of your specimens. Is that what's in the case?"

Brian nodded. "Butterflies. Want to see them?"

"Look out," warned Dick, and Cherry said simultaneously, "You don't know what you're getting into, Mr. Kessler." Paying no attention to them, their guest already had his head close to Brian's as they bent over the butterflies together. Dick poured a cocktail for his father, and saying, "You'll need another one too, Mr. Kessler, if you let him get started," he refilled Kessler's glass. Kessler appeared to be deeply interested in Brian's butterflies. Brian was chattering.

". . . that blue one is easy to get, they're everywhere except where it's too cold for them. The name is Lamp—Lampides something, I forget, but I've got it written in my notebook. This is a monarch butterfly, they fly north in the summertime like birds. The copper and black one, you've seen thousands like it, it's a viceroy."

Spratt sat down by Elizabeth. "Good fellow, isn't he?" he said under cover of the other dialogue.

"Yes indeed. But we mustn't let Brian wear him out."

"I think he likes it," said Spratt. "One of these men who's interested in everything."

Elizabeth glanced at Kessler, almost ready to believe that her impression of self-consciousness on his part had been mistaken. Certainly their exchange of remarks before Brian's entrance had not suggested it. When the maid came in to announce dinner neither Kessler nor Brian heard her. They were deep in conversation, Brian sitting on the floor with his case in his hands, this time listening instead of talking.

". . . one of the ugliest objects in the world, but strangely fascinating," Kessler was saying to him. "It looks like a man with his hands spread out, but they are tremendous hands, many times larger than his body. The first time you look at one you feel a cold shiver run down your spine."

"What on earth are you talking about?" Spratt demanded.

Brian started and turned his head. "The skeleton of a bat. Mr. Kessler says if we can get hold of a bat he'll help me mount the skeleton."

"If your mother doesn't mind," Kessler amended.

"Of course I don't mind," said Elizabeth. "But Brian, Mr. Kessler is a very busy man, and you mustn't use up too much of his time."

"Mother, Mr. Kessler says I can come over to his house and we can take the bat apart there, and Peter can come too. He's got time for it, haven't you, Mr. Kessler?"

"I shouldn't have offered if I hadn't. Will you let him come, Mrs. Herlong?"

"Certainly, and it's very good of you. Brian, we're going in to dinner. Won't you move so Mr. Kessler can get up from his chair?"

Brian scrambled to his feet. "Mother, couldn't I come to the table?"

Recalling Brian's usual eagerness to avoid company dinners, Elizabeth was astonished. Kessler had won him, evidently, as he had won the others. She let him come in, pausing to remind him in an undertone that he mustn't monopolize Mr. Kessler's attention. Brian nodded solemnly. As Kessler stood up, Brian watched the procedure with undisguised interest, for hitherto he had only seen him sitting down and had not been warned of all his new friend's handicaps. Elizabeth felt a moment's embarrassment, until she reminded herself that Kessler must have had to bear many stares from children and would understand that Brian did not know he was being rude. She was not sure she had been right in permitting Brian to bring a chair to the dinner table. Though she had planned the menu with special reference to his disability, Kessler might nevertheless be awkward about eating with one hand.

But here she was immediately relieved. He was so skilful that she concluded he must have lost his arm many years ago to have learned so well how to make up for the lack of it. But still, he puzzled her. He did not talk very much, though he listened to what was said and answered readily enough, but now and then he glanced at her and looked away, as though he could not trust himself to pay too much attention to her. Once, while Spratt was telling a studio anecdote, she turned to speak to the servant and had the feeling of somebody looking at her in a crowd. She turned back to the table, to find Kessler studying her with an expression she could not define. He shifted his eyes instantly when she saw him, so quickly that she might almost have doubted that he had been looking at her at all. When Spratt had finished his story, Kessler, as though to assure Elizabeth that his scrutiny had been an accidental glance that meant nothing, turned to her and commented, "How well Mr. Herlong's secretary gets rid of nuisances like that. She is a very clever young woman—I suppose you know her, Mrs. Herlong?"

He did it so deftly that he almost erased her earlier impression. Elizabeth answered yes, she knew Lydia very well and thought Spratt was fortunate to have her. While she was answering she was thinking that there was probably nothing more to this than that Kessler like herself was plagued with a recollection of their having met before. She would ask him about it before he left, and get these cobwebs out of her head.

Except for her fancies, which she was inclined to call absurd, it was a very successful dinner. They all liked their visitor and he evidently liked them, and Spratt was glad to find his family and his friend getting along so well together. They had coffee in the living room. Over the coffee Kessler said to her, "Your household is exactly what I most hoped to find in this blessed country, Mrs. Herlong. I can't tell you how much I have enjoyed meeting all of you."

He spoke this time with a simple friendliness, as though quite unaware that there had been any odd glances between them. Elizabeth said,

"Now that you know us, I hope you'll come back to see us again."

"Thank you," he answered. "I should like to very much."

That was all they said to each other. Spratt got up and suggested that he and Kessler go into the study and talk over their story problem. The children said good night with a cordiality very warm compared to their usual routine of politeness toward adult guests, and Brian went upstairs. A few moments later Pudge and Julia came to call for the two older ones. "Get through dinner all right?" Pudge asked with a sympathetic grin.

"Pudge," said Cherry, as though conveying momentous news, "he was *nice*."

Pudge scowled incredulously. "A refugee?"

"Sure," said Dick, "but he's okay."

"Not a single remark," Cherry continued, "about what a godawful country this is."

Elizabeth could not help laughing, but she said, "You haven't much tolerance, any of you."

"We've got just as much as most of them deserve," Dick retorted. "One foot off Ellis Island and they start weeping for dear old Europe. They give me a pain in the neck."

"Yes, I know, Dick, and sometimes they give me one too. But they have gone through a lot, you know, and some of them can't help being bitter. Mr. Kessler isn't, as you noticed."

"No, he's different. I liked him. We're going now, mother."

"All right. Be back by eleven."

Elizabeth went upstairs to say good night to Brian. He was enthusiastic about Kessler and the promise of help in mounting the skeleton of a bat. "You know what he told me about bats, mother? He said if we had ears as good as theirs we could hear a fly walking up the wall. He said a bat was one of the most mysterious creatures on earth, we just didn't understand them a bit. That guy sure does know a lot."

The initial sense of familiarity returned to tease her. But

whether or not she already knew him, Kessler was a fine fellow, she reflected, and she was glad Brian liked him.

Brian turned over in bed. "Mother, I just thought of something. Peter's a Jew."

"So what?" asked Elizabeth.

"Mr. Kessler's a German, and you know how they are about Jews. He said I could bring Peter, but I didn't tell him—"

"If Mr. Kessler had approved of that sort of thing he'd have stayed in Germany, Brian."

"Maybe Mr. Kessler's a Jew," Brian suggested hopefully. "Is he?"

"I don't know, but you needn't worry about it. He's not stupid enough for that foolishness."

"I guess not," Brian said, relieved. "I sure do like him."

"So do I." She reflected that Kessler's enjoyment of a happy domestic scene might mean he was lonely in a strange country. "Brian," she suggested, "since we like Mr. Kessler so much, let's prove it by doing something for him. Let's ask his little girl to bring some of her friends over to go swimming."

"Oh, rats," said Brian. One thing he could not understand about his big brother was Dick's liking for girls.

"Brian, suppose we had to pack up all of a sudden and go live in Germany. Wouldn't you be glad if other children made friends with you instead of making you play all by yourself?"

"Well—do we *have* to?"

"Not at all, and Mr. Kessler doesn't have to help you with the bat, either. Come on, Brian, be a sport. We'll have a good party with lots to eat, sherbet and one of those big cakes from Delhaven's, and all you'll have to do is be polite. You can ask Peter over and she can bring her own friends."

Brian sighed. "It'll be awful," he objected.

"All right, let's put it this way. If you go over to Mr. Kessler's and he helps you put a bat's skeleton together, you can play with his little girl one afternoon by way of saying thank you. If you don't go over there, you needn't do it."

Brian mournfully considered the alternative. It was a struggle, but at last, after she had tried again to tell him the value of give-and-take in the world, he yielded. As she closed the door Elizabeth drew a long sigh of her own. "I don't wonder so many parents let their children grow up to be monsters of selfishness," she thought. "It's so much easier. But then they grow up to grab, grab, grab, until they turn out to be fascists grabbing for the whole world."

She went into her own room. Glancing at the radio, she wondered what fresh disasters she would hear about if she turned it on, and did not turn it on. She sat down at her desk and got ready to write some letters.

"Maybe my children are pretty self-centered anyway," she was thinking. "Oh, for pity's sake, why should I be discontented with them? They're not malicious, disobedient, untruthful—they're simply hard, and it's the age they live in. We've tried to make them a decent lot, Spratt and I. But no parents can contradict the age they live in, because they're a product of the age themselves." Elizabeth turned to the desk and began writing an order for some tools needed for the Victory garden. She had finished this and several other notes when she heard Dick and Cherry come in. Going to her doorway, she watched them scamper up the stairs, enjoying the healthy windblown look of them. "Did you have a good time?" she asked.

"Oh yes," said Cherry. "The sea was just beautiful and we all had a hot dog and Dick ate two egg sandwiches besides."

"Meat shortage," Dick explained. "They wouldn't give us but one hot dog apiece."

"I don't know why you don't kill yourself," Elizabeth exclaimed.

Dick said he felt fine, which he evidently did. They said good night, and Elizabeth went downstairs. Spratt and Kessler should be finishing up their conference by now if they expected to go to work in the morning. They did appear in a short time, Spratt saying he didn't know why Kessler insisted on taking a taxi when he'd be glad to drive him home. Shaking his head with good-natured insistence, Kessler said,

"I'm sure Mrs. Herlong will agree with me. I can't drive, but it's one of my principles not to let my friends drive for me if I can help it. It may be convenient tonight, but there will be times when it isn't. Am I right, Mrs. Herlong?"

How sensible he was, Elizabeth thought, to accept his handicaps so frankly. "Yes," she answered, "though either of us would be glad to drive for you, in principle you're quite right."

"Thank you. And now, since I don't know where the telephone is, will you stop arguing and call a cab for me, Mr. Herlong?"

Spratt chuckled and complied. Kessler turned back to Elizabeth.

"Mrs. Herlong," he said earnestly, "I can't tell you how happy you have made me."

It seemed a great deal to say in return for a pleasant evening, but he sounded as though he meant it. "We were all glad to have you, Mr. Kessler," she answered. "You have quite won the hearts of the children."

"They are delightful, all three of them. What a joy it is to see a home like yours. Your mode of living is so clear that it leaves no room for doubts. No one who spent an hour here could go away asking, 'Are they happy? Are they free? Do they love each other?' The answers are obvious."

Elizabeth stood up to face him. "Are we really like that? Would you say it just to be pleasant?"

"Indeed not. You should be very proud of such an achievement."

"It hasn't been all mine." She glanced at Spratt, who was returning from the telephone. "I've had a great deal of co-operation."

Kessler's eyes followed hers, then came back to her. "Yes, that is easily seen. I congratulate you both."

He was no longer unsure of himself with her, or if he was,

she was too much concerned with what he was saying to observe it. "You told me tonight," she answered thoughtfully, "that we had a great deal of confidence. Sometimes I'm afraid my children have too much. Too much confidence in themselves, I mean, and too little in the intangible virtues."

"Don't let that distress you." Kessler glanced at Spratt and Elizabeth together. "Isn't adolescence the time when we doubt everything we can't see? Don't you remember?"

"Yes," said Spratt with a short laugh, "I shouldn't like to go through the teens again. But sometimes I feel like Elizabeth —I seem to remember that we had a few beliefs in those days. This younger generation has never seen anything but disillusion."

"Our generation," said Kessler, "began with expectations and underwent despair when the world didn't live up to them. Maybe it's better to begin with nothing, because then when you do come to believe in the higher potentialities of humanity, it's because they've been proved to you."

"You almost frighten me, Mr. Kessler!" Elizabeth exclaimed. "Because that means, doesn't it, that it's up to the older generation to prove them?"

"Could we ask for a better job?" he inquired smiling.

Elizabeth and Spratt both smiled back at him gratefully. Elizabeth wondered at their talking like this to a stranger. But just now Kessler did not seem like a stranger. From being a newcomer among them, he had subtly changed into a friend who made her comfortable with the security of mutual understanding. Whatever memory he had stirred within her, it must be some old experience of peace. Since overhearing the children yesterday she had felt unsure of herself and of them, but now, hearing him speak, it was as though she had slipped back into some forgotten period of long ago when everything was safe and right. He was saying to them,

"Your children can afford to be cynical about themselves because they don't know how superior they are to most of their fellowmen. They believe in the obvious because they've found it good. When you see people deliberately clinging to a belief in abstractions they don't know anything about, you can be pretty sure they need to do it, because everything they do know about is unsatisfactory."

"How cheering you are!" exclaimed Spratt.

Elizabeth was looking up at Kessler. She asked,

"Mr. Kessler, have you and I ever met before?"

He started. For a moment he looked down. She looked down with him, and saw his hand tighten on his cane. She was to learn that he did this often, making an unconscious gesture toward his physical means of support when his spirit felt undefended.

But he hesitated only for a moment. His self-discipline had been learned in a long hard school. He answered,

"Before tonight? If we had, Mrs. Herlong, I can't believe I could have forgotten it. No, I am sure we have not."

He had looked up, and was regarding her steadily. Elizabeth did not know that letting his eyes meet hers just then was one of the hardest achievements he had ever accomplished in his life.

He did it so well that she nearly believed him. "Maybe I'm wrong, then," she said. "But tonight, as soon as you came in, it seemed to me that I had seen you somewhere and I couldn't think where it was."

"Maybe," suggested Spratt, sitting down and taking up the cigarette-box from the table, "you two saw each other at one of those big cocktail parties where you see hundreds of people and don't get to know any of them."

"Very likely," Kessler agreed readily, turning toward Spratt as though welcoming his suggestion. "I've been forced against my will to attend several of those. Or possibly," he added, "you saw me at the studio. You come there now and then, don't you, Mrs. Herlong?" He glanced at her an instant as he spoke her name, and then became occupied with watching Spratt blow smoke-rings. "You might have caught sight of me walking from my bungalow to a projection room—chance glimpses like that sometimes tease our memories unmercifully."

"I suppose it must have been something of the sort," said Elizabeth. But she was still not satisfied. She continued, "But do you know, Mr. Kessler, when you came in I thought I knew you, and I thought you gave me a sort of startled look, as though you knew me too. You didn't?"

"If I stared at you rudely, I hope you will forgive me, Mrs. Herlong." He spoke lightly, almost humorously, as though it were a trifling matter. "I hope you will remember that I had been looking forward to meeting you, more eagerly than you realize. Attractive women have not been a great part of my life recently, or happy homes either. In the life of an exile they assume an importance that you do not understand, and I hope will never have to understand."

Elizabeth thought, "He protests too much," but Spratt was agreeing, "Yes, I should think they would. Is that your taxi pulling up, Kessler?"

"I believe it is," said Kessler. "Good night, and thank you both again."

Spratt walked out to the taxi with him. Elizabeth took a cigarette from the box on the table and stood looking down at the remains of the fire. When Spratt came in she turned around.

"Spratt, I don't care what that man says. I *have* seen him before tonight."

Spratt shrugged. "Wherever it was, you went there without me. I've been with Kessler every day for the past couple of weeks, and it never entered my head I'd seen him before. Probably a cocktail party, Elizabeth, or rambling about the studio."

"It wasn't. I tell you, I *know* him."

"All right, all right, you know him. He doesn't know you. He said so. I'm going to sleep on my feet. We talked and talked, and didn't get a thing done."

"You didn't? I'm sorry."

"His mind wasn't on his work. He kept bringing himself back from a great distance and repeating something he'd said fifteen minutes ago. I never saw him like that, he's usually sharp as a whip. Tired, I suppose—working all evening after working all day never is a good idea."

Elizabeth laughed a little. "Maybe I'm a moron. But I still have a notion that his mind wasn't on his work because he was thinking about me."

Spratt was puzzled. "I don't get it. If he thought he remembered you, wouldn't he have said so when you asked him?"

"Oh, I suppose he would." She threw her cigarette into the fireplace. "Maybe he just reminds me of somebody else, and I'll wake up in the middle of the night remembering who it is."

"Probably some fellow who kept a German delicatessen in Tulsa," Spratt suggested. He yawned, and Elizabeth added,

"Go on up to bed, darling. Would you like to have me bring you a highball?"

"I would indeed. Thanks."

Spratt was already in bed when she came up with the drink. He was tired and sleepy, and they did not speak of Kessler again. Now that she had talked about it to him, her impression had begun to seem rather silly.

Long after Spratt and Elizabeth were both asleep, Kessler sat up in his apartment, thinking about her. He had seen Elizabeth, he had been into her home among those she loved best, and now that it was over he wondered why he had gone. Had it made him any happier to do this? He could hardly answer. He had seen what he wanted to see, Elizabeth the central figure of a happy home, and all he had said to her about it was true. But was he glad he had seen her there?

Certainly, at the beginning he had not been glad he had come. Though you prepared yourself for an event ahead, when it happened you found that you were not as ready as you thought. When he met Elizabeth at the door all his carefully rehearsed formality nearly went down before her. He had managed to get through those first minutes without betraying himself, but she would never know how close he had come to doing so. He had planned so many remarks to make to her, casual-sounding statements that would lead her to telling him all about herself, and he had not been able to make any of them. Thank heaven her children were not shy, and had chattered until he could recover a semblance of self-possession.

And then, in spite of all his efforts, he had nearly given himself away at the end. "Haven't you and I met before?" The question had come just when he had begun to feel at ease with her, and was talking to her like the friend he had dreamed of being when he went there. Its very frankness had taken him aback, leaving him no defense but a bare denial. He wondered if he had satisfied her. He could not be sure, but at least he had satisfied himself that though she might find him oddly familiar she had not suspected who he was.

Now the part of wisdom would be to let her alone. She had made her life without him and was content with it. She had, perhaps, more than he could have given her if he had returned uninjured from the war. He would never have made Spratt Herlong's income, for he had not that flair for material success. As for the rest—hard as it was to admit, the rest was none of his business. Elizabeth and Spratt were husband and wife. Their marriage had endured for twenty years and he was not going to endanger it now. He had come here from Germany to save Margaret, not to bring trouble to Elizabeth.

He could say all this to himself, but all the time he knew he was not going to ignore Elizabeth because he had not the power to make himself do so. She was there; he could see her whenever he pleased, and her children, who drew him nearly as strongly because they were hers. Spratt was the only one of them he would have been glad to ignore if he could, and he had to work with Spratt because he had to make a living. But he wanted to see Elizabeth again. Though he had left her such a little while ago, he already wanted it.

Then what could he do? He could keep away from her for awhile, until their next meeting would seem a casual one. He could keep himself better in hand than he had tonight, and if she still thought him familiar he could persuade her his memory was blank of the subject. And if she ever needed him—if there was ever any support or advice or consolation that he could give her—it hardly seemed possible that there could be, but if she needed him, he would be there.

After all, was it too much to ask? He wondered if she would ever know what it was to be so vastly lonely as he was now. Her life was so strong and copious—if he asked now and then for a crumb from the table, an hour of her time, an occasional assurance that he was her friend and she trusted him, was that very much?

He did not know. But he did know that right or wrong, he was going to ask it.

8.

FOR several weeks Mr. Kessler did nothing about getting a bat for Brian, a reticence that both Spratt and Elizabeth admired. They had had experience of persons who wanted to move in on their lives and had started by trying to load the children with attentions. As they all liked Kessler she invited him to dinner again, and Spratt brought him in two or three times to have a drink on their way from the studio, so when Kessler had had time to be quite sure the Herlongs were accepting him as one of their friends he brought up the subject of the bat again, to Brian's great delight. Two days later he telephoned that he had obtained the bat, and made a date for Brian to come to see him.

It was very kind of him, Elizabeth thought, and she was glad to see her children's increasing friendship with him. Kessler never patronized them, and he had a great talent for minding his own business. He rarely mentioned the war unless somebody else brought it up, and when he did refer to national affairs he refrained admirably from making adverse criticisms of the President and from telling them what he thought Americans ought to do about anything. In fact, he listened to them a good deal more than he talked, though none of the children realized it. "He's swell," they said of him.

Kessler said to Elizabeth, with a touch of wistfulness, "There is a great deal of you in all your children." Occasionally she wondered why he seemed more interested in finding her characteristics than Spratt's. He and Spratt were good friends and Spratt frequently said his work on the picture was proving invaluable. But when he came to their home it was primarily to see her, a fact that Spratt observed with a sort of proud amusement. He liked other men to admire his wife.

Brian and Peter Stern visited Kessler so often that Elizabeth was sometimes afraid they were going to be nuisances, though Kessler insisted they were not. Brian saw little Margaret and announced grudgingly that she was not bad, so Elizabeth suggested the party. The next time Brian went to see Kessler she went by to get acquainted with Margaret. Kessler's modest street-floor apartment was kept for him by a motherly woman who came in leading Margaret by the hand and telling her to speak nicely to the lady, which Margaret did. She was an intelligent-looking child, with big blue eyes and two fat pigtails, shyly polite; as Elizabeth rarely had any trouble getting along with children, their acquaintance began without difficulty. Margaret had learned the English language very well. Oh yes, she said, she went to school and she was learning to swim, and when asked if she would like to have a party with her school friends she nodded eagerly. When they had got that far in their conversation Kessler came in, having left Brian and Peter blissfully occupied with the bones of the bat. "I'm going to have a party!" Margaret announced to him.

Kessler looked down at her and smiled fondly. Again Elizabeth felt a flash of recognition. "I've seen him somewhere, I know I have," she thought. "Maybe he doesn't remember, but I'm sure of it." However, she did not mention the subject, for Margaret was talking, and by the time they had arranged the date of the party and other details she felt it was time to go.

On the way home she made up her mind that though he might think her foolish for persisting, the next time she happened to be alone with Mr. Kessler she was going to ask him to rack his brain and figure out where it was she had met him. There was no good reason why it should seem so important to her to remember, since it must have been a very casual meeting to have escaped her so thoroughly, but these occasional twinges of recollection teased her. Just for the instant when he had looked down at Margaret with a tender little smile, not only the expression of his face but his whole attitude had been so familiar that she had felt as though she was watching someone she had known for years. Then it was gone, and now she could not remember at all.

Since Margaret's party was going to strain their already over-taxed problem of household help, Spratt suggested that he bring Kessler over that evening, leaving him there while he drove Margaret and some of the other guests home, and then that he, Kessler, Elizabeth and the two older children go out for dinner. Elizabeth agreed gladly. She had managed to keep servants so far, but she wanted to give them no grounds for complaint. The party went very well, for Margaret was not shy among friends of her own age. They played in the pool, gobbled sherbet and cake without noticing that war exigencies had made it impossible to get ice cream, and were happily tired when they were finally coaxed back into their clothes and their parents began to arrive to take them home. Margaret came over to Elizabeth.

"Thank you for the party, Mrs. Herlong. We had a very good time." She spoke with careful politeness.

"I'm so glad you enjoyed it. We want you to come over often —tell your father I said so."

Margaret was evidently glad to hear this. "Thank you, I'll tell him. Mrs. Herlong, may I pick one of those purple flowers on the fence?"

"Why of course. But the stems are strong—wait a minute and I'll get a pair of scissors." When she brought the scissors Margaret was waiting. "We can cut a lot of them if you like," Elizabeth offered. "There must be thousands of blossoms here on the fence."

"The yellow ones are the same sort of flower as the purple ones, aren't they?"

"Yes, and the deep orange ones too."

"The dark ones have yellow centers. That's pretty. What do you call them?"

"Lantana."

"Lantana," Margaret repeated. "I've seen a lot of them here, but I never knew the name. They bloom all the year round, don't they?" She gathered the bouquet into her hands. "You must like flowers," she suggested, looking around, "you have so many of them."

"I do like them. We used to have some beautiful beds there on the other side of the pool, before we put in the Victory garden. You enjoy flowers too, don't you?"

"Oh yes." Margaret nodded vigorously. "Do you like to put them under a microscope and see how they're made?"

"I don't think I've ever done that. Where do you have a microscope? At school?"

"No, at home. My father shows them to me. He knows all about flowers. We put lots of things under the microscope at home and we look at them. It's fun."

"Your father certainly knows a lot. But he was some sort of doctor in Germany, wasn't he?"

"Not exactly a doctor. He worked in the laboratory. But my real father was a doctor."

"Your real father? Isn't Mr. Kessler your father?"

"Oh no," said Margaret, her blue eyes serious across the lantana. "My real father died. And my mother too, and I was very sick. That was a long time ago when I was little. But I remember being very sick, and before I was well we left the hospital, late one night, and we rode a long way in an automobile in the dark, and I started to cry. I don't cry now, I'm too big, but I was little then and I cried, and he—you know, my father, Mr. Kessler—he said he would give me something to put me to sleep so I wouldn't be so tired, and he did, and I went to sleep, and when I woke up he told me I was his little girl now. That's how he got to be my father."

"I see," said Elizabeth. Not wanting to push Margaret into details of what might be a Nazi atrocity better forgotten, and which was none of her business anyway, Elizabeth went on, "I'm sorry your real parents died. But isn't it fortunate you could get another father right away? And such a fine father, too. You must love him very much, don't you?"

"Yes, sometimes I don't remember at all that he isn't my real father. I like him better than some girls like their fathers. He plays with me."

"You must have a lot of fun together."

Margaret nodded. She had begun to tell more details of their games when they caught sight of Kessler and Spratt walking down the driveway toward the back lawn. As she and Margaret went to meet them Elizabeth watched Kessler's slow limp and the wise, kindly expression of his features, and thought what a battle such a man must have had to show no evidence of resentment toward life for what it had done to him. No wonder Margaret liked him better than some girls liked their fathers. She was a fortunate child to have such a guardian.

Margaret had run ahead of her. As Elizabeth met them she was talking to Kessler.

"We had the best time! I can swim all the way across the pool, the short way, not the long way. And look, these are named lantana and they grow on the fence."

"I should have warned you," Kessler said to Elizabeth, "that Margaret would demand a sample of anything she saw that was unfamiliar to her. Either she was born inquisitive or I've infected her with my own curiosity."

"I like children who ask questions," Spratt commented. "How are they going to learn anything if they don't?"

"Margaret's been telling me," said Elizabeth, "how you encourage her with a microscope."

He laughed, and then said soberly, "I'm glad she enjoys that. In these days—or for that matter any days—we can't foretell what children are going to live through, but we can be pretty sure it won't all be pleasant. But nobody is utterly desolate if he's learned to appreciate the world around him."

"That's a good reason for knowing something about science," Spratt approved. "Not that I know much about it myself." He began to chuckle at a sudden recollection. "That reminds me—a couple of years ago when Elizabeth and I were in Chicago we went to the Field Museum of Natural History and looked at the dinosaur skeletons. I'd never thought much about dinosaurs, but we were reading in the guidebook how these creatures had ruled the earth for a million years, which is a lot longer than human beings have ruled it, and all of a sudden I burst out laughing, because it occurred to me right there, 'Who the hell does Hitler think he is?'"

"We laughed all the way back to the hotel," said Elizabeth. "It was the first time either of us had ever thought Hitler was fundamentally funny."

The garden had grown chilly. Spratt gathered up Margaret and several others whom he had offered to take home, and Kessler said he would occupy himself with a book while Elizabeth changed for dinner. She went through the den, where Dick sat by a table agonizing over his lessons. Dick was evidently in the throes of struggle. His papers strewn on the floor and table, he sat holding his head between his fists, his hair wildly rumpled and his forehead wrinkled with anguish. Elizabeth paused at the door.

"What's the trouble, Dick?"

He groaned without looking up. "Mother, did you ever get through physics?"

"Not very gloriously, and I'm afraid I've forgotten most of it."

"I liked physics in high school." With an effort Dick untangled his hands from his hair. "I still like it, but every now and then you get a problem that simply will not make sense—" He shook his head, looking at her through a fog.

"I wish I could help you!" Elizabeth exclaimed.

"Oh, I'll get it. It's always the same. You can't do the problem—you try everything and you can't make it, you go nuts, and then you see some tiny little detail you've already seen a thousand times but you never noticed it, and there it is, click-click like a safe opening, and the answer is so simple you want to kick yourself around the block for not having seen it in the first place." He laughed at himself. "Then when you go to school the next day you say, 'That third problem was a humdinger, wasn't it?' and the dumbest guy in the class says, 'Why, that's the only one of the whole bunch I could work.'"

Elizabeth laughed too. "I remember it used to be like that with Latin translations. Why don't you stop till after dinner? We're going to Romanoff's."

Dick gave his head a violent shake as though to stir up his brain. "Think I will. Evening paper come? I'll read the funnies."

"It should be here. I'll see." She went out to the front lawn, Dick following her. In front of the house Spratt and Kessler were shepherding the little girls into the car. Dick picked up the Hollywood *Citizen-News* from the grass and moodily began to open it. Black war-headlines went across the front page. Elizabeth glanced around, thinking how little Beverly Hills had the look of being in a country at war. The dancing flowers, the damp odor of grass, the noise of carpenters repairing the house across the street, all seemed so ordinary. Margaret, about to get into the car, paused and looked up at Kessler.

"Why do you see those men hit with the hammers before you hear them?"

He smiled at her. "We always see things before we hear them, because the noise comes to us by sound-waves and the sight by light-waves, and the light-waves get to us faster."

Margaret frowned, puzzled.

"I'll explain it better when I get home after dinner, if you're still awake—" Kessler had begun to say, when Dick shouted, "Holy Jerusalem!"

He had shoved the paper untidily under his arm and was laughing at their astonished stares.

"It's that physics problem. It's about sound-waves and I was figuring with the speed of light. Oh, such a dope, such a dope —thank you, Margaret!" He was off into the house.

Elizabeth explained what Dick was talking about. As the children drove off with Spratt she was wishing her own problems had so ready a solution. That was why physics and mathematics were such satisfying studies, the answer was there to be found, no matter how hard you had to look for it you knew it was there all the time, and when you found it there was no doubt of its being right. She waved goodby to the children, and Kessler expressed thanks for Margaret's happy afternoon.

"Are you tired?" he added. "Wouldn't you like to rest for a minute before going up to dress?"

"I'm not really tired, just a bit breathless. But it might be pleasant to sit down for a minute or two. What shall we do?"

"It's about time for a news broadcast."

"I'm losing courage to listen to the radio," Elizabeth confessed. "All it brings is news of more calamities."

For an instant Kessler did not reply. She had said nothing to him about her dread of Dick's going away, but she saw him give a glance toward the house and suspected that he had guessed it. Leaning heavily on his cane, he turned back to her, saying, "Mrs. Herlong, will you forgive me if I tell you something?"

"Certainly." Then, as she saw the gentle gravity of his eyes, she added, "If it's a rebuke, go ahead. I deserve it."

"Yes," answered Kessler, "you do." He smiled, and went on. "Mrs. Herlong, talking about one's personal troubles is unforgivable unless one has learned something from them that is worth passing on. You and your family are so kind about ignoring my handicaps that I feel almost unkind to refer to them. But I have learned something from them."

"Yes, go on," she said earnestly. "I know you've had to face life in a way that I haven't. Tell me."

"It's simply this," said Kessler. "There is a rigorous joy in facing a battle even when you have very little chance of winning it. The worst experience on earth isn't tragedy that comes from outside. That may be dreadful, and it frequently is, but it's almost pleasant compared with the experience of being ashamed of yourself."

Elizabeth lowered her eyes. They showed her his thick right hand grasping the cane, and she looked up again. "You can tell me that better than anyone else I know," she said in a low voice, "because—well, you've never said anything to me about your past life, and I'm not asking you, but I know you aren't referring only to physical distress. Such a disaster as yours doesn't just change your bodily powers, but everything else. You had to face spiritual tragedy as well, didn't you?"

"Yes, I did."

"And you did face it," she went on. "Instead of becoming resentful and bitter, you became so wise and kind and understanding that everyone who sees you feels the presence of a great man. You have suffered terribly, but you have no reason to be ashamed of yourself."

"Neither have you, Mrs. Herlong."

"How do you know?"

"You haven't told me anything about your past life either," he returned smiling. "But as soon as I came into your home the first time, I knew I was meeting a mature and courageous woman. It's impossible for anyone to live as long as you have—"

"Forty-four years," she said with a little laugh. "I'm not sensitive about the passage of time."

"Very well, it's impossible for anyone to live forty-four years without experiencing a good many unpleasant events, things you either have to face or run away from. When you meet a woman whose husband adores her, whose children are intelligent and uninhibited, whose domestic affairs run like invisible clockwork, and who goes about with a serenity suggesting that all these things just happened that way—you can be sure that she achieved it by meeting each crisis as it came. Some people's lives are like wastebaskets, so cluttered up that nobody can find anything there but trash that should have been disposed of long ago."

"I have tried to keep things clear," she answered simply. "I can't say I've always been successful. But looking back, I can say I've tried."

"When I left your home that first evening, I told you that being there had made me very happy. Perhaps you thought I was too intense in what I said. But I had seen so much clutter, so much wretchedness that could have been avoided, that it did make me happy to see so much unobtrusive richness of living. I had hoped I should find you like that."

"You had hoped? Why did you care what you'd find?"

He bit his lip as though he had said too much. But he answered, "Was it too much to hope for? I had left a continent full of torture and despair, for one thing; for another, I liked and admired your husband, and he had shown me your photographs. You have a good life, Mrs. Herlong, because you have made it a good life. Don't lose it now by being afraid."

"How can I help being afraid?" she exclaimed. "Yes, I have a good life. I've said so myself a thousand times. And I *have* worked for it. As you said, there are plenty of occasions in anybody's experience when he's tempted to sit down and quit trying. But when you do achieve a good life, when you feel that now at last you have what you want and can enjoy having it, and then when you see it about to be blown to pieces by circumstances you aren't responsible for and can't control—how can you help being afraid? I'm sick with fear. I look over it all—Spratt bothering about his pictures, Brian with his bats and bugs, Cherry excited about a party dress, Dick struggling with his lessons, and I think, 'How much longer?' I love them so, I've been so proud to know I was important to them—but now!" She stopped. "Why on earth am I talking to you like this? It's the first time I've been so frank about it to anybody."

"You couldn't talk to anybody who'd be more interested," Kessler answered. "It's good now and then to confess our fears. Of course you're frightened. You see the war coming closer, you don't know what it may bring—"

"I do know," she interrupted sharply. "I don't live in a tower looking down on two conflicting ideologies! Oh, it may be a noble struggle, fought for a better world, but I don't see it that way and I can't. I don't see it in terms of anything but my son."

"I wish to God there were something I could say to you," he told her in a low voice.

Elizabeth had clasped her hands and was moving them against each other restlessly. "I don't know why I feel so much like talking to you. Maybe it's just that if I don't talk it out pretty soon I don't know what will become of me. Do you mind listening?"

"I want to," he answered, with such simple sincerity that she could have no doubt of his sympathy. He hesitated an instant, then asked, "Can we sit down, Mrs. Herlong?"

"How stupid of me!" she exclaimed. She hurried to lead the way to two deck chairs placed on the lawn, at the side of the house. Cherry had left a sweater on one of them, and Elizabeth put it on, for the evening chill was blowing in from the sea. "We aren't just courteous about not noticing your limitations, Mr. Kessler," she remarked as they sat down, "we're usually not even aware of them."

When he answered it was in a matter-of-fact voice. "This is one of the things I found hardest to get used to," he said. "I mean, asking for a chair. I had always been so healthy that I was the one who had to be reminded not to expect too much of other people. Please don't be embarrassed—I'm not."

"Are you cold?" asked Elizabeth.

"No. What was it you wanted to tell me?"

"I'm glad it's getting dark," said Elizabeth. "Talking in the dark is easier for some reason. It's about the war, about feeling it coming close, about this unbearable sense of helplessness. I've always thought of myself as a rather strong person, one who could take things as they came and go on somehow. But this time I feel beaten before I start. My husband is afraid of what we're up against too, but he's taking it much better than I am. You see, there's a difference: when you don't know what you're facing, and when you do."

She heard Kessler move his cane against the grass, but he did not answer. She went on.

"I can't tell him. In fact, I don't want to tell him—why should I? But I'm shaking with terror because I've had a tragedy of war before. And if it should happen again like that—when I say I'd rather die than get another of those telegrams from the War Department, I'm not speaking lightly."

Kessler's cane was poking at a tuft of grass. Nobody had turned on the lights in the rooms on this side of the house and it had grown dark outside. She could not see him, nor did she try to; she could barely make out the end of the stick, restlessly attacking the grass, but she did not turn her eyes toward him as she continued.

"Spratt is my second husband—you didn't know that, did you? It's not important in any personal sense between us, it never has been important and it wouldn't be now except that my first husband was killed in the last war. I loved him very much. Of course, now, looking back on it, it's easy to say it shouldn't have mattered so much, I was a young girl with all my life before me, and as it happened I met Spratt and everything turned out as you've seen it. But at the time there was no way for me to look forward. When I remember it—" She stopped.

After a moment Kessler asked, "Did you suffer so horribly?"

"I can't tell you what it was. It wasn't anything anybody could understand except somebody who had been through it.

I had loved him so, and then all of a sudden he was dead. It was —anyway, I never went through anything like it before, and I never have again. Of course, it's all over—I don't even think of it very often, but now—" She stopped again.

There was a silence that seemed to last a long time. At last Kessler said, in a voice so low she barely heard him, "Yes? But now?"

"Don't you understand? I can't take it again. I can't. I thought there never would be anything else like that. It was over and done with. My world had been shot to pieces, and I picked up the pieces and made myself go on living, and I was rewarded more than I ever dreamed of expecting. But I can't do that another time. Even if I had the strength, it's too late. I was twenty when I lost Arthur. God knows it wasn't easy to go on then. But now I'm forty-four. If my world is shot to pieces again, it stays that way. I can't go back and start over. And why should I be expected to? Life can't be all beginnings and no fulfillment!"

As she broke off Kessler asked, "What is that exquisite scent that's suddenly here all around us?"

"Night-blooming jasmine. Sometimes it blooms till late in the year. Are you listening to me?"

"If I hadn't been listening I shouldn't have asked about the flowers. I was just thinking, in a world so full of possibilities for pleasure, why should anyone have to say what you are saying to me?"

"Yes, why should we?" exclaimed Elizabeth. "Why should it be like this? I don't know and I'm tired of asking. It's too much to demand of us. It's as though destiny were saying, 'The world is all broken up, start over and build a new one. Hurry and get it done so it will be all ready to be demolished again. We'll give you just enough rest between strokes to make sure you're quite conscious and sensitive to feel the next one. We won't start the next war until your firstborn son is just old enough to be carried off. You thought you'd felt the last limit of pain, but you may find that you haven't. If this happens, it will be worse."

"It would be worse?" Kessler asked her. His voice seemed to have a thickness, a slight unsteadiness, that was unlike him.

"Yes. Because before, there was only myself. If I had cracked, if I'd ended my own life or had lived on like a useless shadow, it really wouldn't have mattered to anybody. But now it's different. There are people who count on me. There's Spratt— oh, I know Spratt goes striding around the studio lot like the most self-sufficient creature alive."

"I have sometimes wondered," said Kessler, "if you knew how much he depends on you."

"Yes, I know. There's a lot between us that I shan't discuss. Say I'm his best friend and let it go at that. And there are the younger children. They need me so much more than they realize—if I weren't equal to it they'd know then what they had lost. Don't think I'm trying to say I'd be the only one who'll be hurt by this war. Spratt loves Dick as much as I do. As for Cherry and Brian, heaven only knows what the war will take away from them. But what I do mean is that in the midst of anything that may happen, I'm the one who'd be expected to stand like a pillar. When you said I was the center of this household you were right. I've made it that way. I've wanted them to need me. I've done my best to make them feel that no matter what happened, trivial irritations or the most vital disillusionments, I would always be there to listen and understand. And now I'm about to fail them. They don't know it yet—or maybe Spratt has guessed it in spite of me—but already, before we've been hurt at all, I'm cracking inside because I'm afraid."

Again there was a silence. It lasted a long time. After awhile Elizabeth turned her head toward him. Kessler was sitting very still. By the starlight she could just make out the lines of his figure, lying back in the deck chair. He was no longer poking at the grass with his stick. It was resting at his side, his hand on it.

"You're not answering me, are you?" she said. "There isn't any answer. But thank you for listening." After a moment she went on, "I can't tell you what a relief it has been to say all this. I believe saying it to you has got it out of me so I won't pour it all out to Spratt. That's why I'm grateful." She reached her hand out and laid it over his, as it rested on the head of his cane. To her astonishment, she found that instead of lying there lightly as she had thought, his hand was gripping the cane with such violence that the muscles were hard and the knuckles were like rocks. Elizabeth drew away quickly and sat up. "Mr. Kessler! What have I done to you?"

"Nothing," he answered sharply, and sat up too, as though startled. "What is the trouble?"

"Why couldn't I keep quiet?" she demanded of herself contritely. "Here I've been babbling like a child who thinks nobody has anything to do but listen—"

"But I wanted to listen!" Kessler exclaimed. "You're not sorry you talked to me!"

"Not for myself, oh no. But I was so absorbed in myself I didn't realize how I might be affecting you. Have I brought back something that's better forgotten? Forgive me, please forgive me, if I've tried you too far."

Kessler stood up abruptly. He turned and moved a step so as to face her. She looked up at him standing between her and the stars, a black figure that gave an impression of strength in spite of the crippled body.

"I feel more like asking you to forgive me, Mrs. Herlong," he said, and again he was speaking with the steadiness of tremendous control. "You were right in suggesting that there is a chapter in my life that is not easily remembered, and what you said did reopen it. There is no reason why I should not tell you it concerns the last war."

"It was the war that crippled you?" she asked. She began to laugh in ironic anger. "Funny, in those days we never thought of its striking the Germans too. We always thought of the Germans as the fiends who were doing it to us."

He did not answer that. He continued as he had begun. "My own disaster, like yours, would be easier to bear if we could look now upon a fresh new world and feel that what we went through had helped bring it to pass. But there's no fresh new world, there's only more of the same, and worse."

"I told you not to try to answer me. Please don't try. There's no answer, for me or for you."

"Yes there is," he exclaimed decisively. "For a moment, sitting there, you had me almost believing that there wasn't. You said it was too late for you to start over. You are not required to start over. But you are required to keep going. Remember, your responsibilities are of your own creation. You aren't responsible for what's happening in the world, but you are responsible for how you take it."

"I told you I couldn't take it. I can feel myself breaking at the prospect. I *can't* take it."

"Yes you can," he said sternly, "and you're going to."

His force was like a stimulus. Elizabeth exclaimed, "Do you believe I can, Mr. Kessler? You seem to know me pretty well by now—do you believe I can?"

"You can," he returned earnestly, "because you've promised it, by every action of your life. Nobody required you to get married, or to have children, or to live so that you would be essential to their wellbeing. If you had wanted to, you might have been one of these whining creatures who takes to her bed at every annoyance and becomes the center of her little universe by demanding attentions she's too useless to get any other way. But you didn't do that. You outlived your own early grief. To do it you had to strip your character down to its core of strength, so that this is what they have seen of you, this is what you have taught them to expect. They believe in you. They need you, and they're going to need you more. In God's name, don't fail them."

Elizabeth drew a long breath. Her chest felt tight. After awhile Kessler resumed his chair. He turned to her, saying,

"Right now, you are beginning to fail."

She started. "Is it as obvious as that? Already?"

"Why don't you stop looking at this entirely from your own viewpoint?" he asked. "You wonder if you can take it—has it never occurred to you that Dick is taking it very well?"

"Dick? He doesn't seem to think very much about it."

"He doesn't seem so to you, maybe. But he is thinking about it."

"How do you know?" She was startled. "Has he said anything to you?"

"No. But I know he is, because I've been there."

Elizabeth exclaimed, "Yes you have. Tell me what it's like!"

"It's a torment of bewilderment," he returned. "You don't say much about it because everybody seems to understand it better than you do. You don't know the reason other people aren't explaining it to you is that they don't understand it either. You go around wondering how you're going to act like a brave hero because God knows you don't feel like one. You do a little blustering to cover up how scared you are. You're angry, mad as hell about the whole thing, you think you ought to feel like a killer but you don't—you keep telling yourself you're not a coward, you'll go out and do what you have to do, but all the time you keep wishing to God somebody would tell you why you've got to do it. That's what it's like, Mrs. Herlong."

Elizabeth was sitting forward, her hands tight on the arms of her chair. "My God, that's what's going on in his mind! But why hasn't he told us? Mr. Kessler, why doesn't he ever *say* so?"

"I suspect it's because he knows what's going on in your mind, a lot better than you think."

"You mean," she said bitterly, "he knows his father and I

aren't fit to be told. Because we have failed him, terribly."

"Have you? Do you know you have?" He asked it quietly.

"Yes, I do know it!" she exclaimed. "If Dick has no idea what the war is about it's our fault. We were two of the people who thought we could avoid another war just by not wanting it. We always thought we were tolerant, broad-minded persons; we didn't hate anybody, we just wanted to be let alone. We were the people who read about Hitler and hoped we wouldn't have to do anything about him. Then Pearl Harbor, and we were angry. Dick was angry too. I was astonished at how angry he was. But all I could think of that day was 'This means Dick.' I suppose I was so engrossed with it I didn't stop to realize Dick was there at the radio thinking 'This means me.' He was mad. I thought he was mad with the Japs. I didn't know then—you're just beginning to make me know—that he was mad with us too, for letting this happen without making any of it clear to him. It's not clear to him now. He doesn't understand it and I can't tell him. I'm beginning to see the issues at stake, but I'm still inarticulate about them. Maybe I'm so frightened I'm paralyzed." She broke off, and added more quietly, "There now, I've said it."

Kessler said in a low voice, "I understand."

"You do, don't you?" she pled.

"Would you believe me if I told you I loved your son, Mrs. Herlong? I do love him. He's so much like the son I used to think I might have."

"You never had any children, did you? Margaret told me this afternoon you adopted her after her parents died."

"No, I never had any children," he returned steadily. "That was another of the things the war made impossible."

"Oh," she said faintly. After a moment she exclaimed, "Yet you have conquered, Mr. Kessler. You have gone on living, living well and nobly, in a world that left you absolutely nothing to live for. How did you do it? It seems strange that I who have everything should turn to you who have nothing, and say

'Please help me.' But I do. Because right now it seems that it is you who have everything and I who have nothing. Will you help me?"

He asked, "Do you want me to try to tell Dick what he's being asked to fight for?"

"Yes! Can you? Will you?"

"I'll try. I'll do my best."

"Thank you! You can do it better than I can. You've seen it. And you are so wise, so gentle, so—how can I say it? I mean you're the only man I know I'd trust to do it well."

There was a brief silence, then he said, "And you?"

"I'll take it, Mr. Kessler. Forgive me for being such a coward."

"Yes, you'll take it. You aren't a coward. A great many of us think we are until the time comes to be one, when we find we aren't. And incidentally," he continued, "don't let me meddle with your affairs, but whenever you feel like telling somebody how difficult it is, won't you talk to me?"

"Isn't it very hard for you to listen? It was tonight."

"Suppose it is? That makes no difference. You and I understand something these others do not. We know what it means to be alone in the universe. Knowing that, it may be that we can give each other courage now."

"Each other? I wish there were some way I could be of use to you."

"You have been, Mrs. Herlong."

"Why, how?"

"Don't ask me to explain. There are no words."

"I don't know what you mean. But there's one thing I do know—I'm a lot farther from a crackup than I was when I began talking to you this evening. Thank you for being my friend, Mr. Kessler. I needed you."

He did not answer her, and there was another long silence. At length Elizabeth said suddenly, "Mr. Kessler, we have met each other before. When was it?"

"You've never met me before this fall, Mrs. Herlong."

"Then why do I keep thinking I have? I'm not given to visions and superstitions! I don't believe you were a king in Babylon and I was a Christian slave."

"There weren't any Christians when there were kings in Babylon," he retorted.

"Don't laugh at me. If we've never met before this fall, why do I keep this curious illusion that we have? Why did I feel that sense of recognition the first time you came into my house? When you were telling us about teaching Margaret to appreciate the world around her, it was as though you were repeating something I'd heard you say already. Just now, while you were talking to me, it was as though you were an old friend I knew I could count on because I knew you so well. Nothing like this has ever happened to me."

Kessler answered her as though brushing the matter aside. "Sometimes two persons do understand each other very well from the start because they have congenial minds. When that happens a friendship grows fast, as ours has. That's all, Mrs. Herlong."

"All right," she yielded unwillingly. "I've got to accept that because I can't explain it any other way. At any rate, I'm glad to have found such a friend."

"Can you go to dinner with the others now," he asked gently, "and let them think we've been talking about the flowers?"

"Good heavens," she exclaimed, springing to her feet, "I forgot about dinner. Spratt will be back any minute, famished, and I haven't started to get dressed. Come on indoors, Mr. Kessler, it's really grown very cold here. I'll be down in a few minutes."

She heard him laugh softly as he got up. "You do feel normal, don't you?"

"Yes, I do. Isn't it lucky life keeps calling us back with little things?"

They went indoors, and Elizabeth ran up to her room. She

felt better than she had felt for many weeks. Kessler had given her the only possible answer, she told herself as she got a dress out of her closet. When you had to do the impossible, you went ahead and did it, that was all. Spratt and her children were going to need all the fortitude she had. Spratt had never failed her, and no matter what happened, she was not going to fail him now.

9.

KESSLER was her friend, and he remained so. But during the next few weeks this very fact made it impossible for Elizabeth to lose her curious sense of this friendship's being an old intimacy renewed.

She tried to tell herself not to be foolish. You saw somebody by chance, you remembered without knowing you remembered, and when you saw him again you knew this wasn't the first time and it worried you until you could recall that earlier meeting. It was a common experience in Hollywood to look up in a restaurant and catch sight of a familiar face at another table, and give a nod and smile before you recognized the face as that of some actor whom you had seen a dozen times playing those obscure roles in pictures which everybody saw and nobody remembered. That happened so often that many professional bit-players habitually smiled and nodded at anybody they saw looking at them with that puzzled I've-seen-you-somewhere expression, just so as not to appear discourteous.

If that happened with actors, why not with other people? She might easily have seen Kessler in a theater lobby, in the Brown Derby, on the streets of the studio lot, not once but many times before the night Spratt brought him to dinner. Elizabeth was annoyed with herself for being unable to accept this as the answer.

She liked Kessler so much, and yet he had for her an almost irritating attraction. His wise sympathy never ceased to delight her. Yet with it there was always the bothersome sense that she had done all this before. Though she tried to ignore it, and laughed at herself for it, the feeling would not down. It kept returning, like the teasing involuntary search for a name, a line, or a tune long ago forgotten and too unimportant to be worth remembering, but which lay so close to the surface of her consciousness that no matter how much she tried to ignore it, it kept trying to push through, troubling her in the most unexpected places by knocking on the door of her memory and demanding that it be let in. She would have been glad to let it in and so be rid of it, but this required opening a door to which she had long since lost the key.

She was ashamed to keep asking Spratt to help her remember. She had tried that several times, and he only laughed and shook his head. "Wherever you saw him, I wasn't there. And if you'll forgive me, my dear, I suspect Kessler wasn't there either. He certainly doesn't remember you."

All of a sudden one day it occurred to her, "Is it possible that I can't remember because I don't want to remember?" The idea was startling, but the longer it stayed with her the less startling it became. She had read about the thoroughness with which the mind rids itself of matters it does not want to remember.

And then, without any more effort on her part, the question ceased to annoy her. She did not deliberately put it aside; as long as she had tried to do that she had been unable to achieve it. But for some reason, as soon as it occurred to her that she had forgotten something she did not want to remember, the question simply ceased to exist. Queer, she thought, how it had pestered her in the beginning. As if it mattered. He was a splendid friend to have. Both she and Spratt, as well as the children, were drawing into closer intimacy with him, and now she could be glad they had all found so excellent a companion without worrying about whether or not she and Kessler had previously exchanged a glance at the Brown Derby. Kessler enjoyed coming to their house. Spratt often brought him in after work, when he would advise Brian about mounting his specimens or discuss school and the day's events with Dick and Cherry. Kessler had not yet said anything to Dick about Dick's approaching part in the war. He was too wise to walk up to him with a peremptory "I want to talk to you," without first making sure Dick was ready to listen. But the subject of the war appeared one day unexpectedly.

Margaret was going to have a Christmas party for some of her schoolmates, and Elizabeth suggested that she and the two older children come to Kessler's apartment one afternoon to decorate the Christmas tree. As it was hard to buy ornaments in the stores they brought their own, part of an abundance left over from earlier holidays. Margaret was there, jumping with excitement while Kessler looked on. He liked Christmas, and enjoyed her pleasure in it. While he was showing Elizabeth the silver fountain pen Spratt had given him as a Christmas present, Dick was dragging in a ladder, and calling to Elizabeth to move out of his way. "We'll start at the top," he said, setting up the ladder by the tree and beginning to climb. "You hand me the junk, Cherry."

With Elizabeth's assistance, Cherry handed up the junk. Margaret helped, her arms full of tinsel and her eyes wide and joyous. "It's just beautiful," she kept saying over and over. "It's just *beautiful*."

She got close against the resplendent tree and looked up through the branches. "I can see you up there, Dick! Look at me."

He bent down, scratching his face on the branches. "Sure, I see you. Hello." As he leaned over, a collection of glass balls slipped out of his hand and smashed on the floor at her feet.

"Oh!" Margaret cried in dismay.

"It doesn't matter," Cherry reassured her, "there are plenty more."

"You've hung up about all it will hold, anyway," Kessler observed as the door opened and the housekeeper came in to tell Margaret her supper was ready. Margaret shrank back against the tree, looking down at the broken glass before her.

"I—I'm scared," she confessed. "I might fall down and get cut."

"Yes, so you might," Elizabeth agreed. "Come give her a lift, Dick."

"Okay. Wait a minute, Margaret."

Dick scrambled down from the ladder. Remarking that he had jolted some lights out of place, Cherry climbed up to adjust them. Dick reached across the broken glass.

"Put your arms around my neck and hold tight so I can lift you, Margaret. There you are. She'll be along in a minute," he said to the housekeeper, and as she went out he swung Margaret across the pile of glass and set her down. "Right?" he asked her.

She nodded. "Right, thank you. I'm always scared of falling down on broken things. I fell down once, and got a bad cut on my neck. See?" She drew the collar of her dress aside.

Dick bent to look at the scar she showed him. "Why, you did get a bad cut. How did that happen?"

"A man kicked me," said Margaret, "and I fell down."

"*What?*" said Dick.

The eyes of them all turned to her—Elizabeth, her hands full of tinsel, Cherry on the ladder adjusting the lights, Dick standing beside Margaret at the foot of the tree. Kessler, sitting in his chair near by, said nothing. But Margaret appeared not to realize the start she had given them.

"What man kicked you?" Dick demanded, and stopped, absorbing the idea of men who kicked little girls.

Margaret answered without any excitement. "The man who killed my mother."

She said it as matter-of-factly as a German child in a happier era might have said, "The Three Bears." For an instant the others around the Christmas tree stood immobile, frozen with a horror the more shocking because Margaret seemed unaware that there was any reason why they should be surprised.

Elizabeth could not say anything at all. She was thinking, "We hear of these things. A thousand anonymous deaths, ten thousand of them, and we're blunted. But hearing it, like this, this makes it sharp again."

Cherry was the first of them to catch her breath. Standing on the ladder by the tree, she gasped, "But Margaret—where were you? When was this?"

"In Germany. A long time ago—oh, a long time ago," Margaret answered, looking up at her. "I was very little." She glanced at Elizabeth. "I told you, didn't I, Mrs. Herlong? I told you my mother and father were dead."

"You told me they were dead," Elizabeth said with difficulty. "But you didn't tell me what happened to them." She glanced at Kessler. He was looking at Margaret, his mouth tight with pity, but he did not try to stop her.

"They came looking for my father," Margaret explained. "He wasn't there, and my mother said he wasn't there, but they wouldn't believe her, and they broke things up looking for him. They were terrible men, the Nazis, they used to push us off the street, and my mother would not take me out. They broke things up, and they hit her, and I was scared and I cried, and the man kicked me out of the way and I fell down, and when I saw the blood I got more scared than ever. It was dreadful." She shivered. "Nobody does things like that here in Beverly Hills. But my mother bandaged up my neck and made it stop bleeding. She was a doctor and she knew how to do things like that. She didn't cry at all. I don't cry either now, I'm too big. The Nazis were gone then. She made me take some medicine. It tasted awful, but she made me take it, and I went to sleep. But I know they came back while I was asleep, because they killed her, and they killed my father too."

Dick swallowed and wet his lips. He had heard stories like

this before, but hitherto they had been something that happened to people who had the far-off quality of anonymity. Hearing it reported as a matter of course by a little girl in his own home town was something else again. He looked at Kessler, and back at Margaret. Cherry, who had sat down on top of the ladder, was looking at Kessler too, as though they both wanted him to say it hadn't really happened like this.

"Come here, Margaret," said Kessler gently.

She went to him, and he put his arm around her.

"It was dreadful in Germany," said Kessler. "But we aren't afraid any more."

She looked up at him artlessly. "Oh no, of course not. Not here."

"Nobody does things like that here," said Kessler. "There aren't any Nazis in America."

"Oh no," Margaret said again. She laughed at a recollection. "When we first came here," she said to the others, "I was scared of the men in uniform. But they were just policemen and soldiers. They didn't bother anybody."

"No, everybody is safe here," Kessler went on. "Nobody comes into a house without being asked. If they want to come in they ring the bell, and if you tell them not to come in they stay outside. Nobody is scared in the United States. Margaret used to be scared, but she isn't any more."

"It's different here," said Margaret.

"And your supper is getting cold," Kessler suggested. "You'd better go eat it."

"All right."

"And aren't you going to thank Mrs. Herlong and Dick and Cherry for helping you with the tree?"

"Oh yes! It's just wonderful. Thank you so much."

"We're glad we could help," said Elizabeth. She took Margaret's hand and went with her into the dining room where her supper was ready. Margaret started to eat with a healthy appetite, evidently not appalled by the story she had told.

When Elizabeth returned to the front room Dick was still standing by the tree and Cherry still sat on the ladder, apparently too horrified to move. Kessler was speaking to them.

"If it seems cruel to let her go on talking, it's less cruel than making her shut it up inside herself. I thought it was easier on you to listen than it would have been on her if I had told her to stop."

"But what sort of cattle are they?" Dick exclaimed. "We hear a lot of things about them, cruel and vicious and all that, but not just going around kicking little girls!"

"I told your mother once," said Kessler, "that your only fault was that you didn't realize how superior you were to your neighbors."

"To my neighbors? But I don't know anybody like that!"

"No, *you* don't know anybody like that."

"Good Lord," said Dick. He went over to another side of the room and sat down.

"Why did they kill her parents?" Cherry asked breathlessly.

"They didn't. Her parents killed themselves."

"Ah!" Cherry let go her breath audibly.

"Margaret thinks the Nazis killed them. They killed so many others. I haven't tried to tell her any differently. She doesn't understand suicide."

"But why?" exclaimed Cherry. Then she added apologetically, "I'm sorry. I guess it's none of my business."

"There's no reason why you shouldn't know," Kessler answered. He glanced at Elizabeth. "Shall I go on, Mrs. Herlong?"

"Yes, if you can bear it. After all, Mr. Kessler, we've heard it before. It's been in the papers and on the radio."

Cherry said what they had all been thinking. "But it's different when it happens to somebody you know! You mean it happened to Margaret's family like what we read about?"

"Why yes, the same old story," Kessler answered. "She and her mother were shoved off the sidewalk, she didn't have enough to eat and even when her parents went without there wasn't enough for her, they saw other children beaten and starved and knew there was nothing else in store for Margaret. Their old friends crossed the street when they saw Margaret's parents coming because they were afraid to be seen speaking to Jews. They tried and tried to get away and every door was shut against them. They stood it as long as they could. They were a brave and gallant pair. But that day Margaret told you about, her mother's spirit broke. She tried to kill Margaret, and she succeeded with herself. She was a doctor and there were still a few drugs in the house. The only reason she didn't succeed with Margaret was that she wanted the child's death to be quick and easy, and she gave her too much."

Cherry was staring at him, unconscious that there were tears in her wide-stretched eyes.

"And her father?" Dick blurted.

"He and I came in together. We had been out to buy food. We had to stand in line to buy it, and I tried to help him, because as I am not Jewish things were easier for me. But I can't stand in line very long, or carry any parcels except what I can put into my pockets. We used to do the buying, it was too frightful for Margaret and her mother on the street. When we came in we thought they were both dead. We knew the house had been searched because it was in such disorder. Jacoby—Margaret's father—knew they would come back for him. With Margaret and her mother gone he had no more reason to keep trying. He was like an insane man. He had no gun— they had taken that long before—so he stepped out of the window."

"But Margaret?" Elizabeth exclaimed as he paused.

"God knows how I ever realized, just then, that the child wasn't dead. I knew something about first aid, and I did the best I could for her, and got help from a doctor at the hospital where her father had worked before the Nazis took over. We worked with her, asking ourselves every ten minutes why we were doing it. We almost agreed with her mother that it would be better to let her die. But I managed to get a letter to the French studio that had bought two of my books, and they gave us help. That was just before the war began. A few more weeks and it would have been too late."

There was a moment of stricken silence. Then Elizabeth demanded,

"How can you talk about it so quietly! Your friends driven to death, a mother trying to kill her own child—and you might be talking about the weather!"

"You have to learn to talk about it like that," Kessler said. "If you don't—" He shrugged.

"Was he a very good friend of yours?" Dick asked.

"My best friend. He saved my life after the last war, and made it possible for me to walk instead of spending these years in a wheel-chair. He was a very great man."

Dick considered a moment, scowling at the rug. When he looked up, he said, "You know, I never have been able to get this business of suicide. People do it, but I never did understand how they could. But I guess over there, you do understand it, don't you?"

Kessler nodded. "Yes, you understand it. People take their own lives when they've lost their faith in living. That's what happened to Jacoby. He had already been pushed close to the limit of endurance. Then when he came in and found his wife dead, and thought Margaret was dead too, and knew there was nothing ahead for him but slow torture in a concentration camp, he had nothing left. The terrible tragedy of it was that after he had given faith to so many others, he lost his own."

Dick said, as if forgetting his mother and Cherry were there, "You mean he was really a great man, a famous doctor, and all this happened to him?"

"He was one of the most famous surgeons in Germany. And more than that, he was, as I said, a very great man. Through the worst disasters—and there were plenty of them in Ger-

many after the last war—he had clung to his belief that no
matter what happens there is always something worth saving,
in one's self and in humanity. Then when he had lost everything else he lost that too. I'm not blaming him for it, but I'm
sorry for it."

"I don't *get* it!" Dick exclaimed abruptly. "I hear about
such things and hear about them, but I don't *get* it. Why were
Margaret's parents treated so?"

"Because they were Jews, for one thing."

Dick shook his head, as though the room had got dark and
he was trying to see. "But I still don't get it, Mr. Kessler. It
doesn't make any sense at all. Even if you were brutal and
anti-Semitic and all that, why should you want to kill a doctor
who might save your life? You might get sick and need just
what he could do for you—don't they ever think about that?
It doesn't make sense," he said again.

Kessler did not try to tell Dick that he was asking a question that half the human race had already asked. He only replied, "It doesn't make sense, and I don't get it either, Dick.
The Nazis and their babble, and then a child like Margaret."

"A nice sweet helpless little girl!" Cherry exclaimed.

Kessler turned toward her, and spoke earnestly. "It's not
only that, Cherry. There are people in the world who haven't
your sense of humanity toward helpless little girls. But it's
what Dick said—even if you had no sense of humanity, why
should you do that to yourself?"

"To yourself?" said Cherry, puzzled.

"Why yes. Why should you want to destroy your own
hope in the future? Margaret's heredity includes two of the
finest minds in Germany. If parents give their children anything of themselves, and we know they do, the chances are a
hundred to one that Margaret is a genius. Only God knows
what she's capable of becoming, but they tried to destroy her."

"Gosh!" said Dick. "Mr. Kessler—you mean that kid's liable to do something like discover radium, and she nearly got killed?"

"That's exactly what I mean. I don't know that Margaret's a genius, it's too soon to tell. But I know that in this mad killing of theirs the fascists from Berlin to Tokyo *have* destroyed genius, and they're still doing it. They're destroying their future, and yours. That's the real tragedy of our time. It's so terrible we don't often think about it because we can't bear it. Margaret's parents had at least had a chance to contribute something to the world. But she's never had any, and those other children who didn't escape had never had any. And what it amounts to," he said clearly to Dick and Cherry, "is that your children may die of loathsome diseases because the scientists who could have saved them were killed when they were four years old."

"Oh, my Lord!" cried Cherry from the top of the ladder. Her hand caught at her throat. "That's what they're doing. I never thought of that till this minute. That's what it's about."

Dick stood up. "Holy smoke," he said slowly. "It's ghastly. You're right—it's too awful to think about. You just think of kids as kids, but golly—when you do think about them as growing up, or not growing up, I mean the important ones—suppose the Germans had blitzed England fifty years ago and had got Churchill, I mean, and now we'd never know."

Elizabeth put her hands over her eyes. It seemed to her that she could suddenly see them, little boys like Brian, little girls with fat pigtails like Margaret, the Einsteins, Chiangs, Curies of the future, going in a horrible procession to annihilation. Suppose the bombs had dropped fifty years ago. She thought of sulfanilamide and the Four Freedoms, television and cargo planes, vitamins and the Panama Canal. Her generation had these because the men and women who brought them into being had been allowed to grow up. She could hear Kessler's voice, passionate with a great grief.

"That's the real horror of fascism. We are sick at what they are doing today, but this is such a little part of it. Their awful crime is what they are doing tomorrow. We don't know what they've already destroyed—a cure for cancer, a new philosophical system, a rocket to the moon. Margaret got out, but the others who didn't get out—my God, the books that will never be written, the work that will never be done. They're destroying tomorrow, and tomorrow is forever."

For a moment nobody answered him. They were looking at what he showed them, and it left them stricken. At last Dick spoke, slowly, as though to himself.

"Tomorrow is forever," he repeated. "I guess that's right. We'll never know what we might have had but for them. Nobody will ever know."

After he had spoken none of them said anything else for what seemed a long time. Elizabeth looked up at the bright Christmas tree. Cherry moved restlessly, stirring the branches; the ornaments tinkled and glittered as though laughing at the world's pain. Margaret came in.

"Mrs. Stackworth is making some tea for you," she announced.

They all looked at her, without answering; she was suddenly a rare and precious symbol left standing above a vast destruction. Margaret continued,

"She's making some sandwiches too, and she says tell you they'll be ready in a minute." Margaret looked up at Cherry. "What are you still sitting up there for? Isn't the tree done? Why don't you come down?"

"I—I guess I forgot about it," Cherry returned lamely. "We were—we were talking."

"What were you talking about?"

Elizabeth got up and went over to Margaret. She bent down and took Margaret's hands in hers.

"We were talking about what a dear girl you were, and

how glad we are you came to this country to be with us. We hope you're going to have a wonderful Christmas."

Margaret smiled at her, shyly. "You're sort of like my mother," she said. She hesitated a moment, and then, conquering her diffidence, she put her arms around Elizabeth's neck and kissed her.

10.

SEVERAL days after the turn of the New Year, Kessler received a letter from Dick:

DEAR MR. KESSLER,

I guess there is no use trying to tell you how shocked I was at what you said the other day. My sister felt the same way I did. I do not write very well and it is hard to say what I mean. But this is what I am getting at. I know you are a very busy man but if there is a day, maybe a Sunday, when you have some time to spare would you let me come over and see you? I did not want to bother you until after Christmas, but there are some things I have been thinking about and I would like to talk to you anyway. You seem to understand our family very well and I know they like you and would not mind anything I said to you. Let me know if this would be convenient.

Sincerely yours,
RICHARD SPRATT HERLONG, JR.

After he had read Dick's letter, Kessler sat for some time thinking, his forehead resting on his big thick hand. These months in Beverly Hills had been more difficult than he had thought they were going to be. Most things were, when you came down to them.

In the beginning Elizabeth had frightened him when she said he looked familiar. But she had not mentioned it again for some time, and by the time she did bring up the subject, the evening after Margaret's swimming party, he had discovered that she needed him. Elizabeth thought she understood disaster. Looking back on what he had learned, Kessler knew she had only a small conception of it. As for Spratt, keen-witted, successful, humorous, devoted Spratt, he had none at all. But Kessler knew what it took to keep going in this world. He had a great deal to give them and he intended to stay here and do it. By this time Elizabeth appeared to have given up the idea of having seen him before; if she said anything about it again, there was nothing for him to do but convince her she was wrong. But as long as she needed him as she did now he was going to stay.

She and her children were asking more of him than they knew. Even if he had wanted to, it would have been hard to explain to such vital persons the strain they were placing on his emotional and physical powers. But if he was wearing out it did not matter very much, except for Margaret, and he would take care of her somehow. What did matter was that he could be of use now to Elizabeth and the people she loved.

When he came to Beverly Hills, it had not occurred to Kessler that she would have any need for him. He had wanted to see her secure. He had not realized that she would not be secure.

Odd, he reflected, that when you thought of persons you had not met for a long time, you thought of them as being still like what you remembered. You never grasped beforehand that time had affected them as it had affected yourself. It was not merely that you were surprised to find them older—though you usually were, absurdly enough—but you were surprised to find that they lived, not in the world where you had left them, but in the world of today.

At first Elizabeth had seemed to be all he had wanted to find her—poised, serene, beloved, mother of children who had no faults except the over-assurance of young ignorance. He had been so absorbed in watching the outer manifestations of this fullness of living that he had not at first realized that it covered what he should have known it did cover, the trembling uncertainty of the age Elizabeth lived in. Everything she had was a potential source of danger. Perhaps, he thought wearily, it might have been just as well if he had come back from the last war and let her wear herself out taking care of him. Then at least, today she would have nothing to lose.

He jerked himself back angrily. He had given her the chance to be happy and she had used it; if happiness brought its own penalties that was not his fault or hers. She had a great deal to lose. Nobody knew what the war might do to this country before it was over, and the whole fabric of her life and her children's future might be ripped to shreds in the days to come. She had made that clear to him when she said, "If my world is shot to pieces again I can't go back and start over. I did that once." Elizabeth did not suspect that when he heard her say that he had nearly burst out sobbing with defeat. He had been so sure, back in 1918, that when he gave her the chance to start over it was the chance to build for permanence. Now he had no consolation to give her, or to give himself—nothing but a desperate courage. There was nothing to do but go on telling her what he had already tried to tell her: that in the final analysis life consisted mostly of doing things one did not want to do, and the only way to keep any self-respect through the whole wretched business was to look squarely at what had to be done and then go ahead and do it.

Now he had to tell Dick the same thing. Not tell him to go to war, that Dick was ready to do; but he could understand from the boy's awkward little letter that now Dick wanted to be told what it was all about. It would be so much simpler if Dick could be left with the idea that it was merely a matter of killing Japs and Germans before they killed you. Or it would be very simple to tell Dick what the men of his father's generation had been told, that he was going to come back into a new civilization of innocence and glory. But Dick would not believe him, for Dick had never seen the world except when it was looking back on one war or looking forward to another, and to any such statement he would retort, "Are you a fool or do you think I'm one?"—which was exactly what it would deserve.

Then what could he tell him? The truth, as he saw it, which might be wholly wrong or at best only an approximation of the whole truth, but which was the only thing he could say that had any meaning. And if it was hard to do, he could at least be glad that by this time he was used to knowing that the business of living was not easy.

Kessler turned to his typewriter, holding the paper with his thumb and forefinger while he turned the platen with the other three fingers, made steady by the pressure of his palm. He wrote:

My dear Dick,

Can you come around Sunday afternoon about three? Margaret is learning to skate and will be at the ice-rink with her playmates, so we can count on not being interrupted. I'll be very glad to see you.

> Your friend,
> Erich Kessler.

He signed the letter with the silver pen Dick's father had given him for Christmas.

Dick arrived at ten minutes to three. They did not waste any time on preliminary courtesies. Dick had a lot to ask and he immediately started asking it.

"You see," said Dick, "I'm just about to be eighteen, and as soon as I'm eighteen I'll get into the service. Maybe I'll join up before then. I kind of like the Marines. That's okay—I'm not saying I'd join the Marines if there wasn't a war, but there is a war, so that's what you do, the Marines or whoever will have you. But there are some things—" He hesitated.

"Yes, Dick, I think I understand, but you tell me so we can be sure we're thinking together. What things?"

"Well—" Dick looked down, frowning at his hands. He was sitting in his favorite ungraceful position, straddling a chair, his arms crossed on the back of it so he could look across at the person he was speaking to as though leaning on a fence. To Kessler he looked very innocent and very young. "Poor kid, he is having a fight," Kessler thought. "I remember, I had one too, but I was ten years older than this. Why do these things have to happen? Even if I had no interest in her, I'd understand what his mother feels. Dick's a nice boy. He's too thoroughly a nice boy to conceive of what his civilization is up against. That's the trouble with all of us. We can't imagine what goes on in the mind of a moral imbecile."

"Well, you know, Mr. Kessler," said Dick, "it comes as a sort of shock to a fellow the first time he notices that his mother is smaller than he is." He looked up shyly. "You know what I mean?"

"Why yes, Dick, I know."

"I guess you do. Gosh, it's good to get this off your chest to somebody who's older. At school they hear about complexes and they think they know it all, I mean it gets so a fellow might as well say he's got a complex as own up that he likes his mother. But I do like her, Mr. Kessler. I like her and I like the boss too. They're all right. They take a lot of interest in me."

He paused again, but Kessler only nodded without interrupting him. Dick went on.

"I know a lot of things about them they don't think I know. I know they don't want me to get mixed up in this war. They haven't said a word, they've been awfully good sports about it, but here lately I can see that it's mighty hard on them. At first I didn't notice it. We all talked about it—the fellows I mean—and we knew we'd get into it and we sort of took it for granted, I mean we got sort of impatient, it seemed silly to stick around doing algebra and things with so much going on. The day of Pearl Harbor I was so mad I could have lit into every Jap gardener I saw and it burned me up to think I couldn't do anything about it. I just wanted to kill them. I still do. The Japs, I mean. I never did get that excited about the Germans, I guess it was because they were going after other people but it was the Japs who had tried to sink the whole Navy when the Americans weren't doing anything to them. The Germans—I don't mean because you're a German, anyway you never do seem like one—but I'd been hearing about Hitler practically all my life and I guess I'd got kind of used to him."

"I suppose you would," Kessler observed thoughtfully. "You were eight years old when he burned the books."

"Was I? I don't remember it. The first thing I remember —I think it was the first thing—was something about a pogrom. The boss read about it in the paper, and he laughed. I suppose that sounds strange to you, but he did, and my mother too. The boss said, 'Imagine his thinking he can get away with anything like that in this day and age,' and my mother said, 'Oh, the man's insane, Spratt.' I asked what a pogrom was and my mother said, 'There are some people who think so highly of themselves that they want to exterminate everybody who isn't exactly like them.' I was just a little boy then. I had forgotten about that, but I remembered it the other night when you were telling us about Margaret. That night I couldn't go to sleep for thinking about it. I thought that was the trouble with my folks, they're too decent, they're so decent they're innocent, like children who don't know anything can happen to them."

"They are, Dick. All civilized people are. I was thinking the same thing a few minutes ago."

"Well, I was pretty innocent myself until just lately," Dick confessed with confiding wisdom. "I thought wars were just wars, because somebody had to run the earth and it had better be your side than their side, and mostly wars were fought to take care of trade and profits and it was principally the Morgans who got us into the last one, and we'd never have been in this one if the Japs had minded their own business. Now I see that's not right, you can't go along letting things happen the way they are happening, things like Margaret I mean. But what I want to know is, what can I say to my mother and father? I can't just go off and have them smiling and shriveling up inside the way they are doing. Don't think my mother has said anything to me, Mr. Kessler! She hasn't. She won't either. But I can't just go off grinning and let them think I don't know anything about it. You see, there's something else I guess you don't know," Dick continued, regarding his friend so seriously that it gave him a pucker between his eyebrows. "The boss is my mother's second husband. She never says anything much about the other guy, just occasionally when she's had to fill out a legal paper and give all the names she's ever been known by, or something like that, in fact it was so long ago I suppose she's more or less forgotten about it. But anyway, he was killed in that other war." Dick suddenly began talking very fast. "I never had thought about that, but I got to thinking about it the other day and I thought it might have been pretty tough for her at the time, because she didn't know then she was going to meet my father. But that guy was killed—and now me—you know, we don't say much about it but you were in the other war yourself and you know a man does think about that sort of thing when he's about to get into a uniform."

He laughed a little, as though embarrassed to have mentioned the subject, and went on talking fast, more to be talking than to get anything said. "Funny how she happened to mention his having been killed, I mean it would seem funny to you since you haven't been around Hollywood very long, but you know how people are always getting divorced here, children take divorces for granted in a way they don't most places. It was years and years ago, Cherry asked her—Cherry couldn't have been more than six or so—we were all in the living room and there was something on the radio about some movie star getting a divorce, and Cherry said, 'Mother, have you and the boss been divorced or are you the only husband and wife you ever had?' Mother said no, she had been married before but she'd never been divorced, her other husband had been killed in the war, and the boss said something about what a place this was to bring up children, they didn't think there was any way to terminate a marriage except in court, and it never would have occurred to him to ask his parents such an idiotic question when he was a little boy in New York. Funny, isn't it?"

"Why—yes, yes," said Kessler. "It's funny."

"Well, I don't suppose I'd ever thought about her first husband five minutes at a time in my life, but just in the past few weeks, when I got so close to military age, all of a sudden I thought about him, and I thought, well, she never says anything, but it must be tough on her, another war. You know it must be."

"Yes, Dick," Kessler said slowly. "It must be, and it is. I've come to know your mother rather well since I've been here. She's a brave woman, but she's not finding any of this easy. You'd like to make it easier for her. So would I."

"And we can't. Can we?" Dick exclaimed with unconscious appeal.

"No, we can't," Kessler answered without hesitation. "Leave me out of it. You're the one she's interested in. There's just one thing you might do, if you can do it."

"What?" Dick asked eagerly.

"Let her and your father understand that you know what you're doing. Don't let them believe that you're going off grinning, as you express it, just to put an end to a lot of toothy villains because mass hatred happens to be the emotion of the moment. It's not merely that they have a right to think better of you than that. But if you expect them, and the rest of the decent people in the world, to get anything from this war except more destruction and suffering, if you want it to be something more than just another war, you've got to have an idea of what you want it to bring about. Even if you know what you want you may not get it, but if you don't know, this certainly won't be anything but just another war."

"Well, what do we want to get?" Dick demanded. He

laughed uncomfortably. "I guess you think I'm pretty silly to ask that, don't you? I guess you think I ought to know."

He stopped to listen. His attention was itself a demand. Dick had spent his life in a world where everything was in its right place, so he knew of chaos only by hearsay. The turbulence of his century had reached him by newspaper and radio, and from remarks made by refugees he had met occasionally, but it had been such a long way off that it had never had as much reality as the week's football game. His habitual tolerance of mind had developed, not in response to opposition, but partly in reflection of his parents' attitude and partly because he lived in a corner of the earth where there was enough for everybody and hence no reasonable objection to anybody's having a share. Now that he felt himself confronted with the necessity of plunging into the confusion beyond his safe island, he felt bewildered. Having begun to understand that his arrogance had been that of an amateur who thinks a problem easy because he has never tried to solve it, he felt his confidence turning to humility. This war, involving a country that had assured him it was never going to have another war, was an enigma he wanted explained.

Letting his cane drop between his knees, Kessler rested his elbow on the table and regarded Dick thoughtfully for a moment before he spoke.

"No, Dick, I don't think you're silly not to know. We who are older than you ought to be wiser, but sometimes we feel we don't know any more than you do. I'll try to tell you how it looks to me. That's all I can tell you."

"Go ahead," said Dick. He added with an embarrassed grin, "I guess I've been talking a lot. But now I'm listening."

Kessler turned his cane under his hand and looked at it, then raised his eyes again.

"Dick, the sweep of history doesn't take much account of individuals. That's hard for us to realize, because we are individuals and we can't think except in terms of ourselves.

But suppose you could stand aside and look at the current of six thousand years."

"Holy smoke," said Dick.

"It is difficult. Just at the moment you aren't seeing anything but today. You're seeing the persecutions in Germany, and the Japs using their prisoners for bayonet practice, and you are revolted, you want to kill them thoroughly and fast."

"You're damn right I do."

"But suppose you were watching all of recorded history at once. If you were, you would notice that there was a time when nobody was revolted by such conduct. It was taken for granted in the ordinary course of things."

"Wait a minute. Is that right?"

"Certainly. You've studied ancient history, only like most schoolboys you memorized the dates and forgot them, and didn't think much about its actually having happened to human beings no different from you. But you know, for instance, that the Babylonian kings flayed their enemies alive. Flay—that means peel the skin off, in strips. They did it for no reason but the pleasure of doing it. Nobody was shocked. In fact, they were proud of it—the reason we know about it is that they left drawings on their monuments boasting of it. And you know it was the accepted practice to sell the people of conquered countries into slavery. Nobody questioned its being right or wrong."

Dick nodded. "Sure, now that you say that, I do remember."

"And when the ancients weren't busy with a war, they were no better. You know how the pyramids were built, by millions of slaves who were quite literally worked to death, in order to feed the vanity of some preposterous nincompoop who happened to have been born in a palace. Nobody questioned that either. It never occurred to them that the slaves who built the pyramids were human beings just like the kings and queens whose bodies were going to lie in them."

"I guess it didn't," Dick acknowledged. "But Mr. Kessler, what's that got to do with us?"

"A great deal, Dick. Have you ever thought about how very recently it did occur to anybody that human beings were human beings, no matter where you found them? It's hard to make a man like you understand what a strange new idea that is. We're all likely to assume that what we take for granted, everybody else takes for granted too. You see, you know a laborer living in a cabin is not necessarily inferior to an aristocrat living in a mansion, because you grew up with the story of Lincoln." Kessler leaned forward, speaking slowly. "It's hard for you to understand that as recently as a hundred years ago men were still writing in the English language that So-and-so came to a bad end because he bought a book and concerned himself 'with subjects too complex for the mind of a peasant.' Or that such a statement provoked no comment, because it was generally accepted as true."

"That peasants didn't have minds?" Dick asked with a puzzled frown.

"They generally took it for granted," Kessler answered, "that the minds of peasants were fundamentally different from those of aristocrats—that the difference between ignorant laborers and cultured ladies and gentlemen was not the result of education, but an inherent difference in the way they were made. One of the favorite subjects of old stories is the duke's child who was lost in infancy and adopted by a shepherd, but who grew up finer than his supposed brothers and sisters because he had noble blood in his veins."

Dick began to chuckle. "Gee, Mr. Kessler, I don't know why you limit that tripe to olden times. Some people believe it this very minute."

"Do you believe it, Dick?"

"Of course not," Dick said scornfully. "Lincoln isn't the only poor boy who made good in this country. But you know —or maybe you don't know, being a foreigner—that there are still a lot of legends going around about Lincoln's father having been some Virginia planter, because such a great man must have had 'good blood' in him."

Without saying whether or not he had ever heard this explanation of Lincoln's excellence, Kessler reminded him, his mouth quivering with amusement, "Even Shakespeare hasn't escaped the suggestion that if the courtier Bacon didn't write the plays, some other courtier must have wandered into Stratford nine months before Shakespeare was born. We have a great talent for finding reasons to believe what we want to believe, Dick. The rich and powerful want to believe in their right to be rich and powerful, so they justify it by saying they are inherently superior to the poor and lowly. So when somebody born poor and lowly proves himself to be as good as they are, they explain it by some accidental infusion of blood or influence from their own ranks. Then everybody's happy except the rest of the poor and lowly, who can't talk back anyway. What do you think about it, Dick?"

Dick considered. "Well, some people are stupider than others, that's a fact. Aren't they?" he exclaimed, and waited for confirmation.

"Certainly. But go on. I want to know what you think."

"But they aren't stupid because they're poor, I'm sure of that. Take our class at school. We've got some first-class dopes from some mighty good families, and a couple of the brightest fellows—" he hesitated an instant—"are Negroes. Mr. Kessler, what do you think about Negroes?"

"What do you think?" asked Kessler.

"I think they're all right!" Dick retorted, almost defiantly. "Aren't they?"

" 'If you prick us, do we not bleed?' " Kessler quoted smiling.

"That's what I think!" Dick said in relief. "But you'd better not say that around some people."

"Why not, Dick? If you don't say it, and act on it, what are you fighting for?"

"Wait a minute," exclaimed Dick. "I don't get it. Maybe I'm

slow. Let's go back. We were talking about Babylon, and people being skinned alive and sold into slavery and nobody minding, and the pyramids and everybody's thinking it was all right for a thousand slaves to be worked to death to please one king, and people just lately thinking aristocrats and peasants were born different like human beings and apes. And then about white people thinking they're superior to Negroes. And now we're back to the war. We've gone pretty deep, haven't we? Do you mean we're no better than the Babylonians?"

"No, Dick, I mean we're a great deal better than the Babylonians. The very fact that you and I are sitting here talking like this proves we have come a long way." He smiled at his listener. "For example—you're a very fortunate young man, you know."

"Am I?" Dick asked with artless astonishment.

"Why yes. You've had all the advantages your civilization can give you. Which means that in the United States you occupy a position like that of a prince in Babylon."

"Holy cats," said Dick.

"And no prince in Babylon ever sat down as a matter of course to say that the people born in the cabins of Babylon were quite as good as he was, and as entitled as himself to life, liberty and the pursuit of happiness. Certainly if any of the princes did, he left us no record of it. All they ever thought worth writing about was how they made slaves of anybody they could lay hands on, and made them build monuments and temples to prove the superiority of their overlords. No, Dick, we've gone a long way. But we've taken every step of it through blood and torture and hell, and we're in this war because we haven't gone as far as we'll have to go before we get peace."

"Go on. I'm listening. I don't think I ever listened so hard in my life."

"If you look at the sweep of history," Kessler went on,

"you'll notice that there are certain currents that appear as almost invisible little ripples, and they grow, and move forward, and finally push away everything in their path. Some of these are minor alterations in social customs, others are tremendous new philosophies that overturn nations and change the lives of millions. Every one of them has the same course. It starts as a ludicrous notion that gets no attention but occasional jokes, it grows until it's called an attack on law and order and revealed religion, and at last, sometimes after a revolution or a war, it becomes the normal way of thinking and everybody says, 'I told you so, I knew it all the time.'"

"Like what, for instance?" asked Dick, still puzzled.

"Let's take some small examples—they're easier to see. What about the revolution in bathing suits?"

Dick started to laugh. "You do think of the damnedest things," he commented.

"You're not old enough," continued Kessler, laughing too, "to remember when men's swimming suits had shirts with sleeves to them, or when women went into the water wearing corsets and petticoats, but you must have seen pictures. Anybody who suggested anything different was a fool. Everybody knew a man would get sick if he exposed his body unprotected to the summer sun. And as for women, everybody knew their muscles were too weak for them to stand up without whalebones to support them."

"Honestly?" Dick exclaimed. He laughed incredulously, and Kessler laughed too, thinking of Dick's lean sunburnt body and the strong young figures of Cherry and her friends.

"Honestly," Kessler assured him. "So naturally, only a lunatic would think of any change. At last when a few lunatics did begin to adopt scantier suits, the suits were called indecent, contrary to Scripture, an insult to womanhood and a threat to the home. The scantier the suits got the more the uproar increased."

Dick found this very funny. "Of all things," he commented.

Kessler continued, "However, if you've noticed, uproar against a new idea, and laws to prevent anybody's accepting it, nearly always can be regarded as a signal that the new idea is just about to be taken for granted."

"You mean that? Why?"

"Why, as long as nobody thinks of trying to do some particular thing, why go to a lot of trouble to prohibit their doing it? There's no law to prevent the citizens of Beverly Hills from climbing up to hang their laundry on the telephone wires."

Dick nodded slowly. "Say, wait a minute. You know, I believe your idea is true. Wait a minute, let me think." He scowled, his mind fumbling among the scraps of his knowledge. "The anti-evolution laws were like that, weren't they? I mean, they didn't start making laws to prohibit the teaching of evolution until everybody was about to take it for granted."

Kessler nodded. "They were like that. So were the old church dignitaries, threatening to put Galileo on the rack unless he'd stop saying the earth moved around the sun. It didn't occur to them to insist that the earth was the center of the universe until just before everybody was about to stop believing that it was."

"I've often wondered," said Dick, "why the old dopes didn't get some telescopes and go out and see what moved around what before they did anything about it."

"Why Dick," said Kessler, laughing again, "you don't notice Hitler asking for scientific tests to show that Nordic blonds are superior to Jews, or the Japanese trying to prove their descent from the sun-goddess, or the white-supremacy school of Americans favoring intelligence tests for themselves in competition with Negroes. Hell hath no fury like a fanatic asked to find a reason for what he's doing. He simply wants to do it, and generally he wants to do it because he observes, often unconsciously, that something new is coming into existence and he doesn't like it, and he's going out with fire and sword to hold it back."

"But it comes into existence anyway?" Dick asked eagerly.

"Yes, Dick, it does. When a new idea is about to be born, nothing under heaven can stop it. Sometimes the fire-and-sword opponents can put it off a generation or two. Jefferson did lose his fight to get slavery out of this country, you remember. It was one of his hardest defeats. But looking back on those days, we moderns can see that even in Jefferson's time slavery was doomed and no power on earth could have kept it here much longer. Incidentally, you might remember that the proponents of slavery didn't go to war to keep it until a time when machinery was making it not only morally wrong but economically impossible. It would have gone without a war, conquered by tractors and push-buttons. When a particular change is on the way, not even a war can do more than delay it; sometimes as in the case of American slavery the war speeds it up, because the side of the future destroys the side of the past."

"And sometimes," Dick suggested thoughtfully, "the side of the past destroys the side of the future?"

"Yes, as the Persians destroyed the Greeks at Thermopylae. But they never did succeed in establishing Oriental despotism in Greece, because while Greek democracy was a long way from what we call democracy now, it was still the side of the future. We're up against something of the same sort today."

Dick nodded, thought a moment, and asked, "What would you call this current that's coming in now?"

"We call it by a lot of high-sounding names—the Four Freedoms, the dignity of the individual, postwar security. But essentially it's the idea that nobody is born with a natural right to beat up anybody else and take over the products of his labor. It's the idea that everybody—not merely the persons of your own family, or your own race, or your own nation, but everybody—should be allowed to develop whatever brains he was born with and do whatever sort of work he's capable of doing. That's the new idea, the one you and I believe in. Our opponents are fighting to re-establish the past."

"Gee, don't stop!" Dick exclaimed when Kessler paused. "Just how do you mean—re-establish the past?"

"Well, as the Nazis worked it out in Germany, and as the Japanese have set it up too, it's the resurrection of feudalism. The Nazis' purpose is a feudalism modernized by having the great industrial corporations take the ruling place that used to be held by the great landed estates. Those not born to power are to work as servants of the rich, regardless of what intelligence and energy they might be born with, just as in the Middle Ages the peasants served the lords, regardless of the fact that a peasant might be brighter, more honest and more excellent in every way than his lordship. Is that clear?"

"Holy smoke, Mr. Kessler—but that won't work! It doesn't make sense in these days—it won't *work*."

"It did work for a long time," Kessler reminded him.

"But that was years ago," Dick protested. "You can't do that to people now. They're too smart. They won't take it."

"No, they won't take it. There's your answer. And there's the war."

Leaning on the back of his chair, Dick studied the wall in front of him. "Do those bums really think they can get away with that?" he asked after a moment.

"Of course they do. If they didn't think so they wouldn't be fighting for it." Kessler regarded him almost apologetically. "I know it sounds absurd to you, living in a country where every child is taught that his chance to rise in the world depends on what he can do, and not on his family's social position."

Shrugging, Dick gave Kessler a faintly cynical glance. "That's the idea, Mr. Kessler, but don't fool yourself that it always works. Being a foreigner, maybe you don't know it, but it's not true that all Americans have a chance. I know they're supposed to, and they ought to, but they don't."

"Why no, they don't, Dick." Kessler smiled at him earnestly. "I never said there weren't any backward thinkers in this country, did I? Or that there weren't any liberal-minded persons in the Axis countries. But the prevailing ideal of the United States is individual freedom, and that is not the prevailing ideal in Germany or Italy or Japan. Your ideals in this country are better than you are—what would be the use of them if they weren't?"

Dick frowned, thought, and nodded. "I get it. You mean it's like what the boss always told us kids—if a fellow tries to do the right thing he doesn't always do it, but he does better than if he wasn't trying. You mean it's like that with countries."

"Exactly. Don't get too discouraged about your country, Dick. The United States has a standard it's trying to live up to —of course you haven't reached what you're aiming at, but you're closer than you used to be. Look back and you can see the idea coming—slowly, painfully, cruelly, but always on the march. The American Revolution was part of it and the French Revolution another part. They went as far as they could, but not as far as the idea was destined to go. The American Revolution was a war for liberty, but it didn't finish the fight— haven't you ever read about the howls that went up in this country, long after the Revolution, at the suggestion of free public schools for all children?"

Dick shook his head. "I thought they always wanted schools in this country."

"Not for everybody. There were opponents who said compulsory schooling would break up the home by taking children away from their parents and putting them under control of the state. There were others who said it would destroy the ordained order of society by making the working classes dis-

satisfied with the position in which God had placed them. But
the schools came, because they were part of the current toward
human equality."

"Gee," said Dick. "You know, you're encouraging. The
place is getting better, isn't it?"

"Of course it is. Whenever you're tempted to believe it isn't,
you might remember that it was in 1870, a good deal less than
a hundred years ago, that the State of Massachusetts was hailed
as an enlightened leader of progress when the legislature passed
a law that children under twelve should not be allowed to
work in factories *more* than ten hours per day."

"Good Lord," said Dick. "Is that true, Mr. Kessler?"

"It's absolutely true. Some day when you've nothing better
to do, look up some of the expressions of horror that greeted
the notion of universal suffrage, in this country." He shifted
his position to face Dick squarely. "Every proposal leading
toward more freedom has been opposed, and defeated again
and again. But we have come forward, Dick. It's been a long
hard march and it isn't over. People who believe in the idea
go down. But the idea moves on."

Dick nodded slowly. "I'm beginning to see it." He wrinkled
his forehead, and exclaimed, "But right now, I don't mind telling you, that big idea sure is up against a lot."

Kessler nodded too, in agreement. "Suppose I try to tell you
why it's up against so much right now. Shall I?"

"I wish you would."

"Well, you see, a few years ago the idea had gone so far that
in several of the most powerful nations of the world, people
were actually asking one another if any commonwealth was
benefited by keeping part of its citizens in compulsory degrada-
tion. In cases where they were still doing so—as with the Negroes in this country—they were ashamed of it and made ex-
cuses for it. The march toward human freedom seemed to be
going along very well. But then, certain persons, more farsighted perhaps than their neighbors, looked ahead and saw

what we were headed for. The result was a long, long way ahead, so far ahead that most of us never thought about it, but for those who did visualize it the very suggestion was so dangerous, such a threat to all nations and all established institutions, that something simply had to be done to stop the march, and quick."

"Gosh, go on!" exclaimed Dick. "What's that suggestion you're talking about?"

"Can't you see it? It's very logical—simply the suggestion that if a country could be improved by releasing the talents of its people, might not the world be improved by releasing the talents of *all* its peoples? That's a terrible idea."

"Why?" Dick asked with ingenuous defiance.

"Don't be so simple-minded, Dick! Why, that contradicts everything we're used to. It takes away our colonies. It drives us out of places where we've invested our hard-earned money. It means that the coolies no longer have any respect for their betters. It makes us acknowledge we are no longer called of God to meddle with the private lives of the heathen. It turns us upside down and flattens us out and leaves us no better than anybody else."

Dick considered this, slowly and soberly. At length he said, "I believe I get it." He turned it over in his mind again, then ventured, "It means—'*all* men are created free and equal, endowed by their Creator with certain inalienable rights—' it means *all*. Not just us. Everybody."

"Exactly," said Kessler. "You do get it, don't you? Those are beautiful words, inspiring words, until you stop to consider what they mean. That's what has happened in the world —some of us have stopped to consider what those words mean. Just when human freedom began to look like a desirable goal, those farsighted persons we were talking about got a glimpse of what that goal would really be. They felt something had to be done to stop the advance right now. So they set out to stop it. They are called fascists."

"Whew!" Dick gave a long whistle. Settling his elbows on the chair-back, he looked across at Kessler with a broad comprehending grin. "So that's what it's about!"

"I don't pretend to any super-knowledge," said Kessler. "But as I see it, that's what it's about."

"And you mean they can't win!"

"I don't mean anything of the sort," Kessler returned sharply. "They can win. They can't win through the next six thousand years, but they can win in this generation, and this is the only one we have a chance to live in. If they win in this generation they'll push us back to do it all over again."

"If we lost this war, they'd have to fight it all over? People in the future, I mean?"

"Yes, they would. The conflict is here, you see; the current of human freedom is pushing along the flow of history, and we'd better stay on the side of history if we want peace. Do you remember when Chamberlain came back from Munich with 'peace in our time'?"

Dick nodded.

Kessler got up and started to walk toward a low bookcase on the other side of the room. Dick sprang to his feet.

"Let me get it, Mr. Kessler."

"No, I can manage. I know just where it is." He sat down in a chair before the bookcase, and his hand being thus freed, he took out a volume and ruffled its pages. "Did you ever read this?" he asked, and without waiting for an answer he read aloud. " 'I once felt that kind of anger which a man ought to feel against the mean principles that are held by the Tories. A noted one who kept a tavern at Amboy, was standing at his door, with as pretty a child in his hand, about eight or nine years old, as I ever saw, and after speaking his mind as freely as he thought was prudent, finished with this unfatherly expression, "Well, give me peace in my day." A generous parent would have said, "If there must be trouble, let it be in my day, that my child may have peace." ' "

Dick spoke eagerly. "Who wrote that?"

"Thomas Paine, during the American Revolution."

"Gee, I like it. It's reasonable, I mean, it comes out even. All you've been telling me comes out even." He said in a low voice, as though to himself, "We're fighting for the liberation of everybody."

Kessler returned to his former seat. He said, "We're fighting toward recognition of the simple fact that we don't know where the next genius is going to turn up. Toward finally realizing that good minds and noble characters are not so abundant that we can afford to waste them, no matter where they happen to be. That's all."

"Holy cats," said Dick. "That's terrific. That's big. That's worth doing, Mr. Kessler! But why can't they see it?" he demanded. "The fascists, I mean. It's so simple!"

"Most of the important facts of life are very simple, once you make up your mind to look for them, but they're often very hard to accept. Like that business of loving your neighbor as yourself, for instance—it's very difficult to admit that he's as much worth loving as yourself. Most of us hate nothing so much as an idea that threatens our good opinion of ourselves. We don't like owning up to it that if the earth belongs to us, it also belongs to the Chinese coolies."

Dick began to laugh suddenly, then he sobered again. "Cherry said once that Mr. Wallace thought this war was being fought for the coolies. We laughed when she said it. It sounded preposterous. But you mean it really is?"

"Why yes, though not many of us are willing to admit it. But that's what we mean when we say we're fighting for human freedom."

"That's *terrific*," repeated Dick. "That's what I'll be fighting for in the Marines."

Kessler hesitated an instant, then shook his head. "No. Not precisely."

"Then what will I be fighting for?"

"For your country."

"But isn't it the same thing?"

"No. I almost didn't tell you this, but I might as well say it. It's not the same thing. You see, Dick, one of the great tragedies of the human race is that history moves too fast for us to keep up with it. Our ideals are always somewhat behind the facts. Right now our ideal is that each army shall fight for its own nation. We'll co-operate just as much as we have to in order to keep safe. Go ahead and fight for your own flag, you've got to, because if you don't crush the fascist nations your country will go down to barbarism with them, but don't forget—or forget it if you want to—that you're fighting toward a time when you'll have no flag to fight for."

Dick whistled again. This time his response was uncomfortable. "Gee—I'm not sure I can follow you that far, Mr. Kessler. That takes a lot of getting used to."

"You're a very patriotic fellow, aren't you, Dick?"

"You bet I am. What's wrong with that?"

"Nothing, right now. But that's why the ideal of individual dignity is so dangerous. It ultimately denies patriotism."

"I don't get it."

"Don't you? Don't you see that love for your country implies that your countrymen are somehow more worth loving than foreigners?"

"Well, from the foreigners I've seen, I think they are—oh gosh, excuse me, Mr. Kessler. But you don't seem like a foreigner."

Kessler smiled. "That's all right, I'd rather have you say what you think than be artificially polite. But this ideal of nationalism grew up when it was so hard to move around in the world that each little political group could keep to itself. They can't do that any more. Did you read in the paper the other day that a Liberator bomber had crossed the Atlantic in six hours and twenty minutes? You've certainly read these airline ads everybody's been quoting, about no place on earth being more than sixty hours from the airport. The world's tightening up. We aren't used to it. Our hearts still cling to our own spadeful of earth, and we don't realize that the other spadefuls are so close they can fall over our fences any minute."

"Holy smoke," said Dick. "I guess I never thought about that before, not like you say it. I don't believe most other people have either."

"Haven't you noticed," said Kessler with a certain grim amusement, "that this country is still somewhat bewildered about the purposes of this war?"

"You bet I have. I was bewildered too. That's why I wanted to talk to you."

"This country is still uncertain," said Kessler, "because it has gone into the war on the side of history. The people know it's the right side, they're fighting valiantly for victory, but they're frightened at what victory will mean."

"It will mean—?" Dick stopped.

"That Americans will have to go on, marching through more blood and pain toward a goal they are not sure they can bear to reach. You *are* fighting for the coolies, Dick, not because you give a damn what becomes of the coolies but because you care a great deal about what becomes of yourself. You don't dare not to fight for them. They've come so close to you that what happens to them touches you already, and will touch your children even more. Don't stop to think of this now if it's too much. I know it's terrifying. Go on and fight for your country. That's what is being asked of you now."

"I want to think about it," said Dick. "But you don't think I'm a dope because I'm—well, kind of shocked, do you?"

Kessler laughed a little. "Of course not. It's the most shocking conception that has shaken the minds of men and women since they were asked to believe that on the other side of the earth people were walking upside down. If you said you weren't shocked by it, I shouldn't believe you."

Dick rambled among his own thoughts for a moment. At

length he inquired, "How did you come to think of all this?"

"I was pretty badly hurt in the last war," Kessler answered frankly. "When a man's life is so violently changed, he has to do a lot of thinking. At first I thought in terms of individuals, each learning to manage his own problems. But when hell broke loose again I had to start thinking all over, not in terms of individuals only but in terms of the human race. That's all."

Again Dick was silent. He thought, contemplating himself, the world, and himself again. Finally he said,

"Well, I'm going to stick to my own country awhile. I like Americans and you can say what you please but by and large I do think they're more decent than other people. Of course, we'll be liberating the Greeks and Poles and Russians and Norwegians and the rest, but especially we'll be keeping the United States okay. I guess we'll even make it better than it is when we clean up those fascist b—— excuse me, when we clean up those palookas. We'll be that much ahead. We'll get the Four Freedoms anyway, and that's something."

"Be careful, Dick," said Kessler. "Don't expect too much."

"What do you mean?"

"I mean that if you go out with any expectation that when you get this war over anything will be cleaned up for good and all, you'll run into the same disillusion that licked the generation just ahead of you. It's not that easy."

"I don't expect it to be easy! I know it's going to be tough."

"It will be tough, you're right about that. You'll go through the hardest training ever devised for military men; you'll be sent into a desert or a jungle or some frozen island; you'll fight disease and bombs and submarines, because you believe in freedom. Then at last you'll get it over and come home, to your own free, gallant country. And you'll walk right up to a summer resort that advertises 'restricted clientele.' You'll meet another man who went through what you did, because he, like you, believed in freedom, and you'll see him unable to buy a sandwich in a drug store because they don't serve niggers. You'll hear comfortable ladies and gentlemen arguing comfortably that there'd be no unemployment if men would only work. You'll be told that free lunches in poverty-stricken school districts are merely another way of pampering the thriftless. You'll find that nine men and women out of ten don't care what happens to anybody anywhere, don't even notice it unless it interferes with their own personal convenience. And you'll stand in the midst of all the stupidity and cruelty and senselessness of your own country, saying to yourself, 'If this is taken for granted in the freest nation in the world, what can the others be like?'—and you'll remember the bloody horrors behind you and wonder if they were all for nothing."

He stopped, almost sorry he had said so much. Dick was looking down at the rug. Kessler had decided to tell him the truth as he saw it, but now he wondered if he had been right to blurt out all the truth. Dick looked up.

"No I won't," he said abruptly.

He stood up and pushed his chair away, and then, awkwardly, finding that he had nothing to do with his hands he stuck them into his pockets.

"I swear I won't, Mr. Kessler! I *won't* get to believing it was all for nothing. I'll feel pretty bad sometimes—I guess nobody can help that, especially not right out of a war—but if we win this one I'll know it wasn't all for nothing. I'll remember what you've been telling me."

Kessler leaned forward again, supporting himself on his cane. "Will you, Dick?" he asked, his voice tense with eagerness. "Will you promise me to remember?"

"I do promise you. I will remember. About the long hard march you were telling me about, and how we go ahead through history even when we can't see it ourselves. I'll remember about the Babylonian prince, and the pyramids, and the times when it never even occurred to anybody that people were people. I'll know it's better, there is more decency than there used to be, and if I can't see it, it's just because I can't see a thousand years at once."

"Remember it, Dick. It's your only salvation."

"No it's not." Dick started to get red. He looked down at his shoes, and started talking fast to get it over. "I'll tell you something else, Mr. Kessler, about what I'm going to remember, after the war and during it. I hope you won't think I'm being sappy or sentimental or anything—but gosh—I mean—I'll remember you." He turned redder.

"Thank you, Dick," Kessler said quietly. "I'm glad you think I'm worth remembering."

"You are," said Dick. Still looking down, he kicked at a corner of the rug. "I mean—oh I know it's not polite to make personal remarks but I can't say it any other way—I mean for a guy that got shot to pieces in one war and then saw what happened in Germany and should have thought it was all for nothing if anybody ever did but can still talk the way you do —anywhere they send me, Alaska or the Pacific islands or anywhere—I'll remember you."

He looked up then, but his embarrassment would permit his eyes to go no farther than the clock. "Gee, it's late," he exclaimed before Kessler could answer his last speech and tempt him into any more sentimental outbursts. "They'll be wondering what's become of me. I've got to go."

Kessler did not try to detain him. Dick got out a few words about its having been fine to be here, and hurried to the door. They made a few commonplace remarks to each other, and Dick, still abashed by his confession, ran to his bicycle. Standing in the doorway, Kessler watched him swing across the bicycle and scurry off. He wondered if Dick would come back to remember anything, or if he would come back with his strong young body shattered into such wreckage as his own.

"He might have been my son," Kessler was thinking. "Good God, what I've sent him into. If he had been my son, I wonder if I should have said all that to him. I'd have had to send him into it just the same. But he believes me. That's something. He believes me."

His eyes were stinging. He pushed his shoulder against the door and shut it quickly, lest somebody come by and see that he was crying.

11.

DICK announced to his parents that he was not going to finish this year at UCLA, and not going to wait at home until he was eighteen. He was going to join the Marines right now, if they'd have him.

Spratt told him to go ahead. "This is one place where you've got to make up your own mind," he said. "I'm not going to boss you."

To her own surprise, Elizabeth was able to answer him steadily. If it had to happen, it had to happen. She said, "Go ahead, Dick. It's all right with me."

"Thanks," Dick said shortly. But he stood there, evidently wanting to say more. After a moment he pulled up a chair with his foot and sat straddling it. "I was talking to Kessler the other day," he began. "He told me a lot about the war, and all that. He said he thought I ought to tell you—" He hesitated.

"Tell us what, Dick?" Spratt prompted him.

"Well—about making you understand that I didn't want to join the Marines just because I was excited or anything like that. About why this war is something we've got to do. You know it's got to be done, don't you?"

"Yes, we know it's got to be done," Spratt answered decisively. "I don't mind saying I'm sorry you've got to do it, Dick. But since you've got to, I'm glad you want to."

"And this war's got to be different from the last one," Dick persisted. "This time we've got to finish it, not leave everything up in the air the way it was before. You understand that too, don't you?" He looked at Elizabeth.

"Oh yes!" she exclaimed fervently. "I'm not very good at praying, but I feel like going down on my knees a dozen times a day to ask, 'Oh God, make this one different!' "

"That's a coward's prayer," Dick blurted rudely.

"Why—what do you mean?"

"I mean it is. Honestly, I've got a lot of things straight I never had before. Kessler didn't say just this, but I mean— well," he said defiantly, "just asking God to make this one different is being like some squash-bottomed middle-aged dame eating chocolates and praying, 'Please, God, don't let me get fat.' God answered her prayer when he gave her brains enough to know candy would make her fat. The rest is up to her. If this war is going to be different we've got to *make* it be different—don't you see? It's up to us. Unconditional surrender, and then go on from there. Don't you see what I mean?"

He spoke with a pleading earnestness. His parents were hearing him in astonishment. They had never heard Dick talk like this before.

All of a sudden, as Dick went on to tell them something of what Kessler had told him, Elizabeth realized that Dick had grown up. It dawned upon her that this must inevitably have happened whether or not there had been a war. Spratt had understood this better than she had, and it was this understanding, and not merely a smaller realization of the price of war, that had made Spratt less reluctant than herself to let him go. War or no war, they could not have kept him, and if this means of separation was a particularly cruel one, it was still only another way of bringing about what would have had to happen anyway. How much worse it would have been, she thought with a painful wrench, if he had clung to them. Hard as this was, it would have been harder to have Dick try to evade what Spratt had called the challenge of his generation.

But instead of trying to evade it he had tried to understand it, and now, in halting sentences full of clichés and schoolboy colloquialisms, he was trying to make them understand it too.

The future against the past—he was right.

"It makes sense!" Dick was saying. "You do get it, don't you?"

"Yes, I do get it," Spratt answered decisively. "I'm proud of you."

"Well, I didn't figure it out all by myself. I'm not that smart. But in times like this, you do like to know what you're doing." Dick stood up and kicked his chair aside. "I guess you do understand," he said, and gave them a grin that was half embarrassed and half relieved.

Elizabeth came over to him. "Yes, we do. Go ahead, Dick. I mean it." She took his face between her hands and kissed him. It was the first kiss she had given him in a long time, and he kissed her back without minding it.

"I've got to go call up Pudge," he announced. "He and I have been talking a lot about the Marines."

He went out, banging the door so lustily that Elizabeth started. She went over and sat on the arm of Spratt's chair. He put his arm around her and she leaned against him.

"You're a good sport, Elizabeth," he said to her.

"No I'm not. I'm shaking inside. But he doesn't know it."

"So am I," said Spratt, "but he doesn't know it. I think he's a pretty good sport too, if you ask me."

They stayed like that for a long time, but they did not say anything else. How good it was, Elizabeth was thinking, to be married to a man you could communicate with even when you were not talking.

Early in March Dick and his friend Pudge went down to enlist in the Marines.

Elizabeth was in her room, writing checks for the month's bills, when he telephoned her.

"Mother!"

"Yes, Dick? What happened? Tell me!"

"Mother, they took me!"

("This is your chance, Elizabeth," she was telling herself. "Do it right.")

"Oh Dick, they did really? I knew they would!"

"They took us both, me and Pudge both! He's phoning his folks now. They took us both, mother!"

"After all, how could they help it? As if they wouldn't be proud to get you."

"Well, I sort of thought they'd take me, but you know how it is. They said there was nothing wrong with me, and gosh, by this time they'd sure know if there was. You never heard of such an overhauling as they gave us. There's nothing wrong with your son, Mrs. Herlong."

"I knew there wasn't. I'm so proud of you, Dick."

"We'll be going to boot-camp any day now. San Diego. Look, I've got to get out of this booth, there's other fellows wanting the phone, but I just wanted to tell you they took me. You'll phone the boss?"

"Right away. When are you coming home?"

"Pretty soon. We kind of want to talk about it."

"Of course you do. I'll call the boss now. He'll want to know it."

"Okay."

Dick banged up the phone. Elizabeth heard the click and replaced her phone for a moment, then picked it up and dialed the studio. "Extension 269, please," she said. "Lydia? This is Elizabeth Herlong. May I speak to my husband? Spratt, this is Elizabeth. Dick just called from downtown. He's passed his physical. They took him."

"They did? Sure, I knew they would. Nothing wrong with Dick." He hesitated an instant. "And you?"

"Fine."

"You mean it, don't you? You sound like it."

"Of course I mean it. I'm all right, Spratt."

He laughed softly. "Good. Keep it up."

"Can I keep it up?" she wondered when she had put the phone back again. "Of course I can. Nothing we can give up to win this war can be compared to what we'll give up if we lose it. We lost the last one. Nothing would be worse than making Dick's generation do it again after this. Oh God, please give us strength to get it over this time! Don't let them go through it twice!" Remembering what Dick had said about a coward's prayer, she repeated, "Give us strength to get it over."

She went back to her desk and began counting the meat coupons. There should be chops at least for dinner tonight, something in the way of a celebration.

She had to try at three markets, but at last she got the chops, and made it a celebration. Spratt was proud, Brian full of envy and excitement, Cherry a little tremulous but thrilled. "It will be the first time any of us have been separated, really," she said, but she spent half the evening calling up her friends to tell them she had a brother in the Marines. Dick was delighted. "If they had turned me down—gosh, it must be tough on those 4F fellows. Imagine wanting to go and having them turn you down."

After dinner he went off to see Pudge. Elizabeth smiled proudly to herself. Strange, but you really could take it when the time came. That night Spratt came into her room.

"Thought I'd sleep in here with you. Mind?"

"Mind? I was just going in to sleep with you. Spratt—I was all right, wasn't I?"

"You bet you were." They got into bed and he put both his arms around her. "Now you can say anything you please about it. If you feel like crying, that's all right with me."

"You should know by this time I'm not much given to crying. I just wanted to be with you." She put her head against his shoulder. "You were pretty splendid, Spratt. Anybody would have thought going off to war was just what you'd hoped he'd do since the day he was born."

She felt him draw a long breath. "Well, it wasn't. Lord, I wonder if it's this tough on everybody."

Elizabeth felt a pain coming up into her throat. Though she was not, as she said, much given to crying, the pain turned into a sob against Spratt's shoulder. She whispered, "I'm sorry, Spratt."

"Sorry?" said Spratt. "What do you suppose I'm here for?"

Though the days that came afterward were not easy, they were easier than the first one. She seemed to have a great deal to do. There were parties, with Dick rushing about importantly and Cherry engrossed with clothes, for nearly all Dick's friends were going into some branch of the service. Brian strutted. "My brother, you know, the one that's in the Marines. Getting off to boot-camp next week."

Dick left for boot-camp early one morning. Elizabeth was not sure what either she or Spratt had said to him. There was a great deal of, "Lucky it's only to San Diego. You'll be getting in for Sundays sometimes." And Dick, "Wait till you see me in a GI haircut. Won't know me." Spratt shook hands with him, grinning in spite of a faint mist about his eyes. Elizabeth kissed him goodby. As she did so, Dick whispered to her, "You two are swell. Tell the boss I said so. Some of these mothers—the scenes they do put on! You wouldn't believe it."

It was an accolade. Elizabeth got into the car to go home, knowing she had done it well.

Brian and Cherry went to school. Spratt had to go to the studio, but before he left he said, "Let's go out to dinner tonight. There's no sense moping through the first evening. I'll reserve a table at Chasen's."

"Oh yes," she exclaimed, "let's do go out. With some other people."

"The Sterns? Kessler?"

"All right."

"I'll call them," said Spratt. He got into his car again, and waved at her.

Fortunately, she was very busy around the house. It was the day for the laundryman, the cleaner and the gardener, there was a call from the Red Cross blood bank asking if she wasn't ready to make another donation, and another call from a man who asked if she would consider taking a shift at an aircraft observation post. She had no time to stop and think. When Brian and Cherry came in, they were very busy too. Brian had to see Peter Stern about an important Scout meeting for the salvage drive. Cherry said, "It seems queer without Dick around, doesn't it? I've got to go down to the canteen. I may be latish getting in, but Julia's mother will be there, she'll drive us home."

Spratt came in early. "The Sterns and Kessler will meet us at Chasen's. How do you feel?"

"Fine. I'm glad you thought of going out. It is better than just staying around. I'm going to wear that tight black dress and the crystal necklace."

When she was dressed and standing before her mirror, Spratt came in. "You look beautiful. Thank the Lord for a woman who keeps her figure."

"I don't get time to sit down long enough for it to spread. I do look rather well in this dress, don't I?"

"You look rather well, period," said Spratt. He picked up her mink coat from the bed. The fur brushed his cheek as he held it out to her, and he grinned. Elizabeth said,

"Remember when you got raised to a hundred a week?"

"Do I! Never had heard of so much money." He chuckled.

"Neither had I," said Elizabeth. "You came dashing into the apartment like the boy who had just made the only touchdown of the game. You said—" She stopped. What he had said was, "And just at the right time, too! Now we can afford a special nurse when you have the baby!"

Spratt remembered too. His mouth tightened. He said, "I guess we can't help it, can we? But it's no use trying not to remember those things."

"No. We've had such a lot together, and we have such a lot. I'm not cracking up, Spratt. Believe me."

"I believe you. You're all right, Elizabeth."

He put the coat around her. She smiled at him as their eyes met in the glass. "And he's only gone to San Diego," said Elizabeth.

Chasen's was gay and full of noise. Mr. and Mrs. Stern met them there, and Kessler arrived a few minutes later. While he was giving her a compliment on how well she looked, Elizabeth was thinking, "Mr. Kessler knows how tough this is, even better than Spratt knows. Mr. Kessler knows what war is. Spratt, these others, they can imagine it, but they don't *know*."

"Drinks?" said Spratt.

"Yes," said Irene Stern. "I'd like a Manhattan and I feel like having it double."

"So do I," said Elizabeth.

Spratt nodded. Irene put her hand over Elizabeth's. While her husband was saying something to Spratt, Irene half whispered, "I'm just beginning to understand what you've been up against, Elizabeth. Jimmy was seventeen yesterday. He doesn't want to wait to be drafted. Do you think it will be over by next year?"

"I don't know. I know I need that Manhattan, though."

When the drinks were brought, she saw Kessler's eyes on her. He was watching her with a look that was gentle, almost tender. All of a sudden the idea that had not troubled her for months came back with astonishing force. She knew that man, she was sure of it. She was sitting at his right side. Her eyes dropped to his hand, just closing around the stem of his glass. That enormous, strong right hand—sometimes a hand was more revealing than a face. But the hand told her nothing. She looked up at his face again. It must be his eyes, or the way his hair grew. But his hair, though it was still thick, had withdrawn at his temples; if she had ever known him it must have been a long time ago, and no young man's hair grew like that unless he was prematurely bald—not his hair, then, but something. He saw her scrutiny, and smiled.

"Be honest, Mrs. Herlong," he said to her in a low voice. "Do you want to talk about the war, or the picture business?"

"The picture business," said Elizabeth.

He nodded. The others were talking; Kessler said to her, "You are doing this very well, Mrs. Herlong. Keep it up. Don't forget all we said about it. Now I shan't refer to it again unless you do."

She smiled gratefully and picked up her drink. Kessler lifted his, and to her surprise she saw the cocktail trembling in the glass. That strong hand of his was not steady. Odd—she was sure she had never seen it quiver before. He saw her notice it, and when he had set the glass down he said,

"Not tonight, but one day soon I should appreciate having a talk with you. Whenever it's convenient."

"Why of course. About me?" she asked.

"No, this time about me. I have a very great favor to ask of you."

"You know I'd do anything in my power for you, Mr. Kessler. At least I hope you know it."

"I believe you would. You are very generous. That is why I don't hesitate to ask it."

"Tomorrow? Or will you be busy at the studio?"

"I'll be at home tomorrow. Will you call me?"

She promised, and picked up her drink again. A cocktail never did any real good, of course, but it did quiet one's nerves and help keep up the pretense of being a good sport. "I'm glad Mr. Kessler is here," Elizabeth thought. "It's a bracer to have somebody around who knows just what I feel like. But I won't crack up. I'm probably going to drink too much, but we're all going to; we don't do it often, but tonight I think we will. But I won't crack up."

Spratt ordered another round of drinks, and dinner. Irene said to Elizabeth, "Look at all these boys in uniform. Good heavens, most of them are *children*. They ought to be at home doing their lessons. Damn Hitler. Damn Tojo. I'm not as brave as you are, Elizabeth. When Jimmy goes I'll be a shivering wreck."

"No you won't. You think you're going to give way, but you don't. You don't think you can take it, but you find you can."

Irene shrugged. She turned abruptly to Spratt.

"Spratt, I see by the *Motion Picture Herald* that *April Morning* grossed a hundred and fifty per cent of average its first week in New York. I'm proud to know you."

"More than we ever expected," said Spratt. "But you can't judge by New York. Wait till it gets to the sticks."

"The only modest man in Hollywood," said Irene.

"Don't you believe it," said Mr. Stern with a grin. "He's not modest, he's just whistling past the graveyard. In case the sticks slap him down, you know."

Everybody laughed good-naturedly. The party became gay and usual. They were good friends; it did not matter that each one was playing a part and the others knew it. They had come to Chasen's for the chance to do so. "If you still have your shoe-coupon," Irene said to Elizabeth, "I saw some beautiful walking shoes at Bullock's-Wilshire."

"Smart and comfortable at the same time?" Elizabeth asked. "That's what I need now—shoes wear out so fast with all this walking."

"Remember how we used to take the car out every time we wanted to go three blocks?"

"Do I! It's probably going to do wonders for us, walking and bicycling instead of driving everywhere, and all these vegetables from the Victory gardens."

"Yes, I suppose we'll stay young and beautiful forever. They say the English are really getting a more balanced diet now than they did before the war, though it's frightfully monotonous. They never were as vitamin-crazy as we were."

Spratt was saying, "But you can't cast Blakeney as a juvenile, Stern! Those pouches under his eyes."

"They're learning to do a lot with gauze since the army took all the young ones. We're testing him tomorrow."

Kessler chuckled. "Gauze won't help that face. A thousand up-all-nights have left tracks on it."

"Aren't there any pretty juveniles," exclaimed Mr. Stern, "with just a slight heart-murmur?"

"The army takes 'em for desk duty," Spratt said sadly. "Why not rewrite the script to make him a romantic lover of forty?"

"You'd think," Irene said to Elizabeth, "those men would get fed up with pictures *sometime*."

"They never do. You should know that by now. It's like eating, one meal is hardly over before you want another. I have a brilliant idea, but nobody will listen to it."

"What?" asked Kessler.

"Shakespeare had to present all his plays without any women. It's no sillier for a girl to play Romeo than for a man to play Juliet. If the war lasts two more years you'll be driven to it."

They found this so funny that two aged waiters paused to glance at their table wistfully, wishing that they had heard the joke so they could repeat it to a columnist dining in another booth, who was known to pay liberally for quips by well-known persons.

"Real French brandy," Mr. Stern observed with appreciation. "Not much of this left."

"We won't suffer too badly when it gives out," said Spratt. "Some of the California brandies are very good."

"I wonder if the Japs are rationed stiffly," said Irene. "I hope they are."

"They don't need to be," said Spratt. "They never ate much besides rice and dried fish, did they?"

"Serves them right," said Mr. Stern. "I detest meat rationing. I never did learn to like fish. We always had such a lot of meat at home. We would, of course, being there in one of the meat capitals of the world."

"Where was your home, Mr. Stern?" asked Kessler.

"Kansas City. Those Kansas City steaks!" he sighed reminiscently. "Have you ever eaten steak in Kansas City, Mr. Kessler?"

"I believe not. That's one of the pleasures I'll look forward to after the war."

"You probably got one on the train, on your way to California," suggested Mr. Stern. "Coming from New York you must have changed trains in either Kansas City or Chicago. Which was it?"

Kessler tasted his brandy. "Chicago," he said.

Something clicked in Elizabeth's head. He had pronounced it *Chicawgo*. A hot summer day in Tulsa, herself by the pool, the extraordinarily vivid young man on the grass beside her. "Chicawgo. I can't seem to say it any other way. It's like a birth certificate, isn't it?"

"My God," she thought, "am I drunk or is this the way you feel when you're about to faint?"

The others were still discussing ration points. Their words were a bumble of sound around her. Talking to them with his habitual unobtrusive geniality, Kessler was giving her no particular attention. Elizabeth's eyes clung to him, her lips slightly parted and her whole body tense as she stared. All the details of his appearance suddenly fitted into a pattern, so evident that it was as though some voice within herself, unheard by the others but loud in her own ears, was crying out *Arthur*.

She saw, as though for the first time, the way his eyebrows grew, those crinkles about his eyes, that vertical line above the bridge of his nose, which had been very faint when she knew him. She saw the way his finger stroked the handle of the cup while he talked. She heard his voice, thicker and deeper than it used to be, the words spoken with a faint German accent, but Arthur's voice.

Arthur had died in a German hospital. But there he was, so close that she could have touched him. She did not touch him, for in that first moment of recognition she was paralyzed into immobility. What a fool she had been—for six months she had been seeing him and hearing him speak, and she had not seen him or heard him. But there he sat at her elbow, Arthur who had been dead for nearly twenty-five years.

Chicawgo—what a tiny key to unlock such a tremendous door! She remembered Dick and his problem in physics. "You can't do the problem, you try everything and you can't make it, then a tiny detail, and there it is."

Had she ever before heard Kessler pronounce the name of Arthur's native city? That first evening at their house something had been said about his trip from New York to California—had he mentioned then that he had come by way of Chicago? She could not remember. But she had heard it now, it had fitted with everything else that hitherto had been a puzzle, and now she knew.

Kessler was making a casual remark to Spratt, something about being nearly ready to submit the treatment of a new story.

"He doesn't know I know," Elizabeth was thinking. "He has lied and lied to me. I asked him if we had met before, and he said no. Good heavens—is it possible that he *doesn't* know? Is it conceivable that Arthur, who was my husband, doesn't know me? I didn't know him. But I have changed a great deal less than he has. I'm not crippled or bearded, I haven't got so used to speaking a foreign language that there are traces of it on my tongue. Of course he knows me. He said he didn't, but he does. How did he stay alive? Why didn't he tell me then? Where has he been? Aren't we ever going to get out of this place? I've got to get away from here, I've got to think. Shall I tell Spratt?"

The thought of Spratt gave her power to move. She changed her position slightly, and glanced across the table at him. Giving superficial attention to something Mr. Stern was saying, Spratt was watching her with an inconspicuous but unmistakable expression of concern. His eyes were saying, "Careful, you've had too much to drink."

Elizabeth nearly laughed out loud. Too much to drink—that would be his interpretation. Possibly he was right. Those Manhattans had amounted to more than she generally took in an evening. She had to behave normally now, for Spratt's sake as well as her own. There was nothing he detested more than noticeable conduct in a public place. She had to move, to say something.

"This can't last forever," Elizabeth told herself desperately. "Somebody will suggest that we leave, we aren't going to sit here all night. I can get out soon, I can speak to him, but not now. For the next few minutes I must be ordinary. If I've had too much to drink so have they all, we had the same cocktails, their attention is a bit blurred too and they won't notice me as much as if nobody but me had had those Manhattans—except Kessler—Arthur—he didn't have the second round. He may notice."

She picked up her coffee and took a sip from it. The coffee was nearly cold. Evidently it had been quite a while since the waiter brought it. She drank the coffee quickly, hoping it would sharpen her attention, and with a great effort she forced her mind to focus on what they were saying.

"When it's today in America is it yesterday or tomorrow in Japan?"

"Yesterday."

"Tomorrow."

"It's tomorrow," said Elizabeth, "because we sometimes get Tokyo on the radio shortwave band, and they always refer to Pearl Harbor as having happened December *eighth*."

("There now, I've spoken. I've answered quite as if nothing had happened.")

"I don't believe I have ever heard the Tokyo broadcasts directly," Kessler was saying. "What do they say about Pearl Harbor?"

Spratt answered, evidently relieved that the drinks had not made Elizabeth as hazy as he had feared. "They call it a glorious victory," he said, "undertaken in self-defense, since the Americans were going to attack Japan any minute."

"The rats," said Mr. Stern.

Spratt agreed and continued, "And they call General Mac-Arthur the laughing-stock of the Orient, and Roosevelt a paranoiac warmonger leading his befuddled country to destruction, and ask why we don't give in now and make peace, since we can't possibly win—most of it in a beautifully modulated feminine voice. She speaks perfect English, probably went to college in Seattle. They wind up by playing *Old Black Joe*."

"Why *Old Black Joe*?" Kessler asked.

"Don't ask me why the Japs do anything, Kessler." Spratt gave a short ironic laugh. "Why don't you all come over some evening and listen? We can usually pick up the broadcast around ten."

"Speaking of time," said Irene, "do you know it's getting very late? We really must be getting along," she suggested, turning to her husband.

To Elizabeth's inexpressible relief he agreed with her. Spratt asked for the check, and Kessler asked a waiter to get him a taxi. Elizabeth got up with the others. She heard the Sterns telling her it had been a pleasant evening, and heard herself answering. Holding her handbag tight so that the pressure of the clasp on her hand would keep her aware of her surroundings, she went with them toward the checkroom at the front, where they paused while the girl brought their coats. Spratt held her coat for her. As he slipped it around her he bent to speak to her in a low voice.

"How do you feel, Elizabeth?"

"I'm all right." She made herself smile at him reassuringly, hoping he could not hear the pounding of her heart.

"That brandy hit you for a minute, didn't it? Sure you're all right now?"

She nodded. Dear Spratt. But Arthur—somehow she had to speak to him.

A waiter approached them. "Mr. Kessler?" he said, and Kessler turned. The waiter said there was some trouble about getting the taxi. They were hard to find these days, fewer taxis in service, and so many people using them to save gas—

There would be no problem, Spratt assured Kessler. He himself had to go by the Sterns' to get a script from Mr. Stern, but he would take Kessler home with Elizabeth, and if Kessler didn't mind waiting there he'd come back and pick him up, no trouble at all.

Little as he liked making his friends play chauffeur for him, Kessler reluctantly accepted. So they would have a few minutes alone, Elizabeth thought as she got into the car with Kessler and Spratt. But could she speak to him tonight? She was not sure she could say anything coherent.

They got home. Kessler said to her, "Don't stay up to entertain me, Mrs. Herlong. I'll wait in the garden, by the pool."

Elizabeth said good night, and went upstairs while Spratt drove over to the Sterns'. In her room she looked at herself in the mirror. Her face looked back at her, strangely ordinary. She had to speak to him now. It might be more sensible to wait till tomorrow, to be alone first and do some thinking. She could go to bed, and when Spratt came in she could pretend to be asleep; he would stop by her room, glance in a moment, and tiptoe to his own without disturbing her. That might be better. But she could not wait. That man in the garden was Arthur and she had to tell him she knew it.

She went downstairs through the quiet house, out of the

back door into the garden. Kessler was there, but apparently he did not hear her footsteps on the grass.

He was sitting with his back to her, relaxed comfortably in a deck-chair by the pool, where a moon in its first quarter threw a faint rippling trail of light. The garden was cool and full of fragrance. Elizabeth halted a few feet behind him.

"Arthur!" she exclaimed sharply. "*Arthur!*"

Did he give a start? There was not light enough for her to tell; besides, the back of his chair was between them. But he heard her, and turned. His hand sought his cane and he got slowly to his feet.

It seemed to her that it took him a long time to speak, though when she remembered the scene later she thought it might have seemed so because she was too distraught to have a sense of time. He only said,

"Were you looking for someone, Mrs. Herlong?"

For an instant she could not answer. That voice of his—that she could have heard it so often and not have known!

When she did not answer, he said, "There is no one but me in the garden."

Elizabeth came toward him, and walked around to the edge of the pool so she could face his chair.

"Stop this nonsense," she exclaimed. "I'm looking for you and you know I am. Arthur—why did you lie to me? Why didn't you come back before?"

She was looking at his face, but she could not see its expression. Even the faint moonlight came from behind him. Again it seemed to her it took him a long time to answer.

"Mrs. Herlong," he said, "you are making a puzzling mistake. I don't know what you are talking about."

"You don't know!" she repeated. "Of course you know. Stop this, won't you?"

"Stop what?"

It might have been her fancy, or it might have been agitation on his part, or merely his German accent, but his words sounded so thick she could barely understand them.

"I didn't know you before," she exclaimed. "All of a sudden tonight I knew. Arthur, please, *please* stop it!"

He stood like a dark shadow against the stars, his shoulders bent as he leaned heavily on his cane. That figure as she saw it was not like Arthur, who had been erect as an Indian. A vague shadow of doubt flitted across her mind, but it was gone as quickly as it had come. No, she was right, this man was Arthur.

"And please sit down," exclaimed Elizabeth. "Stop being so exasperatingly polite, I'll sit down if you want me to." She jerked up another deck-chair and dropped into it, twisting her hands in her lap. He sat down too. Now she could hardly see him at all.

"Mrs. Herlong—" he began, but she interrupted him.

"Why don't you call me Elizabeth? You know me well enough!" She began to laugh, and checked herself. "Don't tell me I'm under a strain from Dick's going away, or that I've had too much to drink. They're both true, but they don't matter right now. Maybe it took that to stir up all the old memories that suddenly tonight showed me who you were. So stop this idiotic pretense, can't you?"

Elizabeth did not know it, but her own talking had given him time to get control of his emotions. Kessler was thinking now that all the time he had been assuring himself that she would not recognize him, he must have been unconsciously expecting this, for he was more ready for it than he knew. His fierce grip on himself made his voice very low when he replied.

"Mrs. Herlong, I repeat that I don't know what you are talking about. You think I am somebody else. My name is Erich Kessler."

"Your name is no more Erich Kessler than mine is. Please, please—I can't bear this! Tell me the truth!"

"I can't tell you more than I've told you," he answered.

Elizabeth wet her lips. "Were you shell-shocked?" she asked incredulously. "Did you lose your memory? Don't you know what I'm saying?"

"No, I was not shell-shocked, and there is nothing wrong with my memory." In the dark she could barely see him restlessly poking at the grass with his stick, as he had done before.

"Listen to me," she exclaimed. "You are Arthur Kittredge, you were born in Chicago, you came to Tulsa, Oklahoma, as a research chemist for the Lerith Oil Company, in 1916 you married a girl named Elizabeth McPherson, in 1917 you joined the army—don't tell me you have forgotten!"

Kessler's answer, when he spoke, was like the answers he had given her that other time they had sat outside in the dark talking to each other—steady, rigidly controlled, his only evidence of agitation that restless poking at the grass with his stick.

"I have not forgotten," he said.

Elizabeth sprang up. "Then you do remember me, Arthur!"

"No," he returned quickly. "Sit down, Mrs. Herlong." He spoke so forcefully that she obeyed him. "You interrupted me," he went on. "I was about to say I have not forgotten anything that happened to me before the war. My name is Erich Kessler, I was born in Berlin. I was in this country many years ago, but I was never in Tulsa, Oklahoma, in my life, and I never saw you until your husband brought me here for dinner one night last October. Now believe me." He spoke to her earnestly. Elizabeth sat listening, half convinced by his insistence. "You told me," he continued, "that I reminded you of someone you had once known, and you couldn't remember who it was. Now you have remembered; something about me—I don't know what, since I never saw him—calls your first husband to mind. Tonight, under a great strain, you suddenly realize who it is I recall to you, and your surprise is so great that you are even persuaded not only that I have some traits in common with that man, but that I am that man." He paused a moment, then resumed his argument. "Talk to me about it now, if that will be any relief to you. But there is one thing I beg of you."

"What?" she asked breathlessly.

"Don't say anything to your husband about this."

"Good heavens above, you sound as if I were a lady in a crinoline!" She heard herself beginning to laugh again, and again made herself stop. "Do you think I'm sitting here aghast at the notion that my second marriage isn't legal, that my children— I'm not such a fool as that. There's nothing wrong with my present marriage, Arthur. You're legally dead, the United States Government says you are, they even wanted to pay me a pension. That has nothing to do with it. But you're you."

"Yes, I am me," he returned with an attempt at lightness. "But I am not that other man."

"Then where did you get his eyes, his voice, his mind? I know you, Arthur. My God, man, I loved you, I was married to you—"

"You were nothing of the sort," he interrupted her harshly. "And if you don't get this illusion out of your mind you're going to be miserable the rest of your life. There is nothing I can do but deny it—no, there is something more I can do, and I'll promise you to do it."

"What else?"

"I'll go away. You'll never be troubled by me again. If I had dreamed this was going to happen no power on earth could have brought me here to destroy your peace. If you say the word, I'll go tonight."

"No!" she cried. "That won't change anything."

"Very well," said Kessler. "But you will make me a promise too."

"What is it?"

"That you will not trouble your husband with this. For it would trouble him, more than you can imagine in your present state. He'll be here in a few minutes. Your first impulse will be to blurt out words that tomorrow morning you'd give half your life to take back. Will you promise?"

She did not answer, and he added,

"If you don't promise, I'll leave Beverly Hills tonight. I will not be the means of wrecking your peace or his."

"You've wrecked mine pretty thoroughly," she said half under her breath.

"For the present. Tonight you can wreck it for good if you want to. Mrs. Herlong, you said this evening in the restaurant you would come to see me tomorrow. Will you swear to me you will not mention this idea of yours to your husband before we have talked to each other again?"

"Yes," she said faintly, "I promise that. But you haven't convinced me. Everything you've said— I know you."

They heard a car. Spratt was coming into the driveway. His voice called cheerily,

"Kessler! Ready to go?"

"Yes indeed, Mr. Herlong. I was waiting for you."

Kessler stood up and started for the car. Without paying much attention to what she was doing, Elizabeth was following him.

"Hope I wasn't too long," said Spratt. "Why Elizabeth, what are you doing here? I thought you'd be asleep by now."

They had reached the side of the car.

"Mrs. Herlong was just about to go upstairs to bed," Kessler said. "She is very tired. She'll probably be sound asleep before you come back."

"I hope she is." Spratt leaned across the door. "Then good night, Elizabeth."

He kissed her. For an instant it was as though a stranger had kissed her, and then suddenly it was not. Dear Spratt. He was her husband. This other man—but he *was* Arthur. Or wasn't he?

"These nights are really cold," Spratt was saying to Kessler as he backed the car. "The days have been bright lately, but as soon as the sun goes down—"

His voice trailed off. Elizabeth turned and went back into the house. Tonight she would say nothing to Spratt. She had promised. Later, should she or shouldn't she? Right now she could not tell. But at least, she would be asleep when he came home, or he would think she was.

Upstairs in her room, she got mechanically through the routine of undressing. In her state of turmoil it was easier to move than to sit still. That man *was* Arthur; he could deny it forever but it would still be true. "Good Lord," she said aloud, "don't I know my own husband?"

Looking around, she saw her bedroom as though she was seeing it for the first time, her fragrant, luxurious room full of beautiful objects that Spratt had given her. The room was as eloquent of his personality as of hers; Spratt was her husband, he was the father of her children, she loved him, but now it was as though she could hear herself talking as she had talked twenty years ago. "What I feel for you—it's strange to call it love, because it's so different. I can't give you what I gave Arthur, because I haven't got it to give. It's just not there any more."

Elizabeth stopped in the middle of the room. "What have I done?" she exclaimed in fright. "What would Spratt do if I told him? Shall I tell him? Can I live here the rest of my life and not tell him?"

She sat down on her bed, and suddenly she felt more tired than she had ever felt in her life. Her body ached in every muscle, her emotions were strained past the point of feeling anything more. She was utterly spent, too tired to know anything but her own exhaustion.

It cost her a great effort to make even the trivial movements of putting out the light and getting into bed. She lay there in the dark, unable to think coherently of anything except of whether or not she was too nervous to go to sleep. There were some sleeping-capsules on her bathroom shelf. The dentist had given them to her last year when she was undergoing some painful treatment. Tonight one of them would do her good, but she was too tired to get up and take it. Underneath her thoughts of the sleeping-capsules the rest of her mind was turning in rings, suggesting all sorts of vague fantastic possibilities: herself saying nothing more to Kessler, but telling Spratt that he was Arthur and leaving the rest up to them; Kessler telling her Arthur had had a twin brother from whom he had been separated in infancy, as happened in old romances; Kessler, Arthur, Spratt—she heard Spratt's footsteps in the hall outside.

Elizabeth turned over and closed her eyes and made herself breathe deeply. She could not talk to him now.

Spratt opened her door softly. "Asleep?" he whispered. She lay quite still. He tiptoed over to the bed, stood an instant looking down at her, and carefully drew up the blankets to cover her shoulder. He bent and kissed her forehead, very lightly so as not to wake her, and slipped out again, closing the door silently behind him. Elizabeth moved, covering her face with her hands as though she were going to cry, but she was too tired to cry. She said to herself, "I must get that capsule, I've got to have some rest." Then all of a sudden she was asleep, and she slept heavily, weariness closing her in like a drug.

In the room adjoining hers, Spratt was undressing quickly, opening and closing the closet doors with care so as to make no noise. He was glad Dick had not waited to join the Marines. What he was getting into was mighty tough for a kid, but when something had to be done, the longer you waited to do it the tougher it was. And having him actually in it was going to be easier on Elizabeth than these months of looking forward to it had been. Easier on himself too, for that matter. After all, no matter when your youngsters left home it seemed too soon. You knew they were going to find life a lot harder than they expected to find it, and you dreaded it for them. But you did your best to teach them to be honest, to have a sense of responsibility and to take what happened with their chins up, and beyond that there wasn't much more you could give them. Dick was a good kid. He'd be all right. Elizabeth would be all right too. She sometimes cringed before a hard job, but she always got through it and came up smiling. He was glad this fellow Kessler had turned up. Knowing Kessler had been good for all of them.

Spratt got into bed. He was tired, and was asleep in five minutes.

In his apartment, Kessler had not begun to get ready for bed. He was sitting alone on a sofa, asking himself over and over, "Good Lord, what have I done to her?"

Useless now to wish he had not come here. The damage was done. Now it was up to him to undo it. He had to convince Elizabeth that he was not Arthur, and leave her marriage as secure as he had found it. The task appalled him. It was going to require the last shred of his strength, and even with that he was not sure he was equal to it. He was giving way. The studio had been letting him work at home for the past few days. That was all right, as long as he had the story treatment ready on time. But the story treatment was quite unimportant compared with clearing up the mischief he had wrought in Elizabeth's life. Exhausted as he was he had to sit here all night if necessary, devising means of persuading her.

The strongest weapon was always the truth. Not the truth about his identity this time, but the truth about what it would mean to her if she continued to believe her recognition correct. If he could make that clear to her she would not want to believe it, Kessler told himself. Once he had done that he could rest, yielding to his weariness in the blessed thought that he need never make an effort again. He stayed where he was, thinking, until the daylight began to creep between the curtains and he fell asleep with his head against the sofa cushions.

12.

WHEN Elizabeth awoke she could tell by the sun that it was late in the morning. Her first thought was that she should have been up to see Dick off to his eight-thirty class, then she remembered Dick was gone to boot-camp in San Diego. She sat up. It was after nine, so Cherry and Brian would be gone too, as well as Spratt. Elizabeth rang her bell.

The maid came in, bringing orange juice and the morning paper. "Why didn't anybody wake me?" Elizabeth asked.

"Mr. Herlong said not to. He said you were tired."

Spratt had left her a note, scribbled in pencil across a sheet of studio stationery. "Elizabeth—Glad you're getting a long sleep. I told Cherry and Brian to go on to school without bothering you. I have to leave now, will ring you later if anything turns up, otherwise will see you tonight. All well. Chin up, the war news looks pretty good this morning, anyway nothing lasts forever. I love you, thought I'd remind you in case I hadn't mentioned it lately. Spratt."

The maid brought her toast and scrambled eggs. She had been about to ask for bacon before she remembered what a rare commodity it had become. Elizabeth laid the note on her bedside table and looked around her at the day.

She felt fresh and well, and last night's tumult seemed a long way behind her. The morning was cool, sparkling like a jewel. It had brought back her courage; today was ahead of her and she could face it. In fact, she wanted to face it, to do what needed to be done and get it over. She thought of Kessler. She had to see him and talk to him like a reasonable human being. What a fool she must have sounded like last night. It had

212

all been too much, that astounding recognition just after Dick's going. But Kessler?

Was that a fantasy or was it the truth? Last night she had been so sure, this morning it seemed more like an illusion born of nerves worn to the limit of endurance. Until those last minutes before she went to sleep she had not realized how tired she was. She had read somewhere that intense fatigue produced strange mental symptoms, like those of a narcotic that brought foolishness without unconsciousness.

But he did look like Arthur. That at least was not her imagination. It was Arthur he had suggested the first night she saw him, it was Arthur he had been bringing back all these months. Now, in the fresh light of the morning, was he Arthur or wasn't he?

If he was not, what a lunatic he must think her! But if he was, where had he been, why had he been silent, what was this going to mean? She had a picture of Arthur packed away in a closet, but it had been years since she had looked for it and it would take her a long time to find it now. Anyway, she did not need it. Her memory was vivid enough, and Kessler was there to be seen.

"I'll get this over now," said Elizabeth. "Now. Today."

She got up and went to her telephone. Apparently he had been waiting for her call, for he answered the phone himself. When she told him who she was he said, "Yes, Mrs. Herlong?" and waited expectantly.

"First," said Elizabeth, "I want to apologize for my startling behavior last night."

"Then you do know this morning," he asked eagerly, "that you were mistaken?"

"I don't know that, not yet. But at least this morning I can promise you to behave like an intelligent adult. You told me I could see you today. May I come over?"

"Certainly."

"Now?"

"Whenever you like."

"Thank you."

While she was getting dressed she remembered that last night Kessler had said he had a favor to ask of her. She must remember to tell him to go ahead, and not let what he called her mistake stand in the way. If she was wrong, he would forgive her and never mention it again, to her or anybody else—she was sure she could trust him for that. But if she was right—she shivered, and she did not know whether it was a tremor of hope or dread.

Kessler's housekeeper told her he was waiting for her in his study. Elizabeth went in and shut the door behind her. Kessler had been sitting before his typewriter, with sheets of manuscript around him. For an instant she wondered if he had been working, or if he had set the stage to make it look as if he found this so unimportant that he could go on with his work without interruption. But she thought of that only an instant. As she came in Kessler put his hand on his cane and stood up. Their eyes met, and Elizabeth said,

"I came here this morning to see if I was right or wrong in what I said to you last night. I was right."

Kessler drew in a quick breath, without answering. Elizabeth came nearer and sat down. Holding her handbag in her lap, she leaned back to look up at him.

She said, "I have not been drinking and I am not hysterical. I had nine hours' sleep, and when I woke up my impression of last night seemed like a mistake based on a chance resemblance. It was not a mistake." She smiled at him, pleadingly. "Arthur, let's face this and talk about it."

"I'll talk about it as long as you like," he answered her, and as he spoke he smiled too, as though sorry for her. "But it's not true, Mrs. Herlong."

But Elizabeth continued, "You have a scar on your arm where you were burnt by a splash of boiling chocolate one night when I was making fudge. You have another scar on your right knee, made when you and I were practicing fancy dives and you hit the edge of the pool."

Kessler sat down, and moved a pencil that was about to fall off the edge of his table. "I have so many scars," he said, "that no doubt you could find two that would fit those you are talking about." Then, supporting himself on his cane, he leaned toward her, and continued, "Mrs. Herlong, my body is such an accumulation of patches and makeshifts that to prove or disprove my likeness to any healthy man would be very difficult. I didn't grow this beard to disguise my face, but to cover some ugly lines on my chin that would make me even harder to look at than I am now. Yet you insist I resemble your first husband."

Elizabeth felt no yielding of her conviction. "It's not just that you look like him," she persisted. "It's—how shall I say it?—your mind, the way you think, the way you speak. You are interested in everything. You are full of scraps of knowledge on all sorts of subjects, picked up because of an insatiable curiosity about what goes on in the world. Your teaching Margaret to examine flowers through a microscope, your encouraging her to ask questions—it's how Arthur would have dealt with a child, and for the same reason. Your generosity, your tremendous tolerance, your encompassing love for the human race—that's not 'like' Arthur Kittredge, it *is* Arthur. Yet you—" She stopped, her eyes on him with a passionate earnestness.

"Yet I tell you I am not Arthur Kittredge. I am Erich Kessler, and you are going to believe me."

"How can I?"

"Can't more than one man be curious about the planet he lives on? Can't more than one man love the human race, as you put it?"

"You are talking in abstractions. I tell you, I *know*."

Kessler shook his head.

Elizabeth shrank back into her chair, away from him. "How

can you do this to me!" she exclaimed. "Don't you remember how I loved you?"

For a moment she covered her face with her hands. She did not know how thankful he was for that moment, when she did not see the tightening of his eyes and lips that even his grim self-control could not prevent. She got out a handkerchief and began twisting it between her fingers, then carefully untwisted it and folded it again. Her pause to regain her own calmness had given him time to regain his, and when he spoke again his voice was steady.

"Now that Dick has gone to fight for tomorrow's world," he said to her, "it would be a catastrophe to see his mother refusing to give up her dependence on yesterday."

Elizabeth started. "What on earth do you mean?"

He spoke to her in a low, intensely purposeful voice. "Mrs. Herlong, not long ago your son sat where you are sitting, defining in his own mind the question before this generation. At length he understood—I like to think I helped him understand —that he was living in one of the periods when the advance of civilization seems to halt because of forces that are trying to push it back instead of letting it go ahead as it was meant to do. He came to see that his side was the right and ultimately victorious side, because those who fight to raise up the dead past eventually destroy themselves."

Elizabeth shook her head with a puzzled frown. "I understand that, but what has it got to do with me? With us?"

"It has a great deal to do with you and me. This battle between yesterday and tomorrow is only occasionally an international affair. But it's going on all the time in our own lives. Some of us refuse to let go of what used to be. We cling to it even when it is nothing but dust and dead leaves, instead of accepting the fact that we've got to go ahead in time whether we like it or not."

Elizabeth did not answer. But she was listening to him, for he spoke so earnestly that he made her listen.

"You know men and women like this, though for the most part you've been too intelligent to be among them. You've lived past your first youth without any great regret for it, for you've acquired a richness of social experience that makes you a far more vital personality, for instance, than your daughter. You don't envy Dick and Cherry's friends. If you had to associate with them all the time you'd be bored beyond expression, for pretty and entertaining as they are, they're shallow and unfinished compared to what you have become. But you've seen men and women who have let time go by without being enriched by it, haven't you?"

He paused a moment. Elizabeth still did not understand where he was leading her, but she still listened.

"Sometimes it's so obvious that a child can see what they're doing—baldheaded grandfathers acting like fools over young girls, women in their fifties making themselves up into ridiculous caricatures of adolescence. Hasn't it ever occurred to you that they do this because they've still got adolescent minds? They've never developed to the point where they can enjoy adult pleasures in the company of adults, so they try to imitate and associate with the children whose equals they are. A ripe mentality is an achievement. It takes effort, and some people have never made the effort. So instead of growing up, they stay half-finished, and spend what ought to be their most abundant years paying their dancing partners and beauty operators to tell them how young they look. You've seen them, and laughed at them."

Elizabeth caught her breath in protest. "But you were just telling me I wasn't like that. I'm not—for heaven's sake, I'm not going to be a fat old woman who gets her face lifted and goes starry-eyed over a gigolo!" She laughed shortly at the idea. "But even if I were, what has this got to do with us now, today, with what I came here to tell you?"

"It has a great deal to do with it, Mrs. Herlong," Kessler insisted. "You're a charming woman, not because you're sixteen but because you aren't. Genuine maturity has a gracious poise that youth never has. The charm of youth is its physical freshness, but the charm of maturity is a flowering of the spirit. Those others I was recalling to you, they have no youth and no maturity either. You have maturity, you know how fine it is—don't start to be like them. Don't reach back now!"

"I don't understand you!" she exclaimed. "I want to know whether or not you are Arthur Kittredge come back from that German hospital where they told me you had died. What are you trying to tell me?"

He answered her simply. "I am trying to tell you that if you want to believe I am Arthur Kittredge, you can persuade yourself that I am. You can make yourself see me as a living reminder of a period of your life that was very happy—that perhaps has grown happier in your recollection of it."

"I didn't come here," retorted Elizabeth, "to be advised whether or not I should believe in a fantasy. I came to be told the truth."

"I am telling you the truth," he insisted. "The truth is that you can stop living in the present if you want to. You can reach back and demand that the past be returned to you. But it won't be returned to you. You won't get back what you have lost, you'll only be destroying what you have."

"But if you are—" she began, and stopped, her eyes going over him with an intense scrutiny. She had listened to him impatiently, but she had heard what he had been saying to her. He was like Arthur. But he was different too. When she had first looked at him this morning she had been sure. Now she began to ask herself again whether the differences meant another man or the changes of war and years.

"If you will let me," Kessler said, "I can tell you why you want me to be Arthur Kittredge."

"Go on," Elizabeth said faintly.

"For the past few months you have found the present very hard to take. You have been looking back into a time when you weren't aware of the demands life was going to make on you. In those days every minute was delightful for itself. You had what you wanted and you didn't know you were going to have to pay for it. You've personified that lovely thoughtlessness of youth in the figure of the man who shared it with you. You want it back—not Arthur, but the young freedom Arthur symbolizes for you."

Elizabeth started. She felt a tremor run through her, so sharply that for a moment she could not control her voice sufficiently to answer. She had never been resentful about the passage of time as some people were; actually, she had been too busy to think much about it. Or so she had believed until now. Was it possible that her looking for Arthur was only part of the universal human wish for irresponsibility? Her voice was thin with astonishment as she exclaimed,

"My God, is that what I've been doing?"

"Yes," he said, "it is."

Elizabeth was silent. She felt as if she had been accused of a sin, and found just enough echo of guilt in herself to be unable to speak in her own defense.

"You can't get it back, Mrs. Herlong," Kessler said gently. "But if you keep trying, you will lose what you have. And you have so much to lose now, so much more than you had twenty-five years ago."

Elizabeth moved forward in her chair, listening intently. The curious sense of guilt had not left her.

"As for your first husband—" Kessler began.

"Yes—what about him?"

"How old were you when you married him?"

"Eighteen." After she had spoken she realized that her answer had come as readily as though she had never had any reason for believing he knew this already.

"Eighteen!" Kessler repeated. "What did you know then about loving a man?"

"I thought I knew a great deal," she retorted.

"Naturally you thought so. How could you judge your feeling for him except by the standard you had then? But look at it now and see what it was by the standard of love you have today. A bright girlish rapture. Beautiful, no doubt, but no more than that."

"But what else is a young girl's love? What else should it be?"

"Nothing else. That's what I'm trying to tell you. But what did you lose when you lost Arthur? A lover and a playmate. You had nothing else to lose."

Elizabeth drew back and stared at him, almost angrily, resenting what he had said and fighting against having to accept it. He wanted a moment to give her time to get used to it, and then went on.

"When we get older, and are drawn into the depths of experience, it is sometimes very tempting to look back and regret the time when we were skipping over the surface without dreaming how thin it was."

Elizabeth still did not answer. All this was new to her, as relating to herself. It was as though he were accusing her of having been foolish just when she thought she was being wise.

"When we do look back," said Kessler, "it means that just then we are frightened at the challenge of being adult."

"I have been frightened," she acknowledged, still astonished at all he was showing her. "You know that."

"What we forget in those moments, of course," he went on, "is that the profoundest joys, as well as the greatest trials, are found in the depths of experience. The happiness of youth is a shallow merriment, it can't be anything else. But the happiness of maturity, I mean real mental and emotional maturity, is strong and deeply rooted because it comes of having tested this and that until we have discovered the permanent values. Cherry is heartbroken if she goes to a party and isn't dressed like the others. Some women your age are too, because they're still judging life by Cherry's standards, but you aren't, because you long ago outgrew letting yourself be heartbroken over things that didn't matter. Mrs. Herlong," he exclaimed earnestly, "you have gone so far—don't turn back now!"

"And that's what I'm doing!" she confessed. "I didn't know it. But I'm trying to go back!"

"Yes. You are looking back to the rapturous days when no war had interrupted your pleasures, when you had no son to go into danger, when there was no crisis to demand your courage. In looking for that dream of security, you have been looking for Arthur." He added, firmly and incisively, "If I were your first husband, Mrs. Herlong, I would tell you exactly what I am telling you now. You don't want him back."

Elizabeth passed her hand over her forehead, pushing back her hair. The gesture seemed to clear her eyes and her mind with them. She said, "You are not Arthur, then?"

"No. Your first husband is dead. You can't have him back, and I repeat, you don't want him back."

He paused to be sure she was listening. She nodded to assure him that she was.

"You don't want him," he repeated. "We often think we want the dead back, but actually we do not, because we have gone on without them and if they should return they would be thrusting themselves into a world that has moved past the place where they left it. If Arthur Kittredge came back to you now it would be an intolerable intrusion, not only because you have your husband and children, but because you are no longer the woman who loved him. You have changed—who does not change in twenty-five years? If he had lived, you would have changed together. But this didn't happen. You have lived with Spratt Herlong. What intimate experiences you two have had I don't know as you know them, but I know this: in the course of them you have built a citadel that only the two of you can share. That's true, isn't it?"

Elizabeth thought of the time when Cherry, as a baby, had been so ill they had feared they might lose her. She remembered when Spratt had lost his job, hit from behind by a friend he had trusted. She thought of the night when she had sobbed secretly on his shoulder at Dick's joining the Marines, and he had said, "What do you suppose I'm here for?"

"Yes!" she exclaimed. "Oh yes."

"I can be a friend of you both," said Kessler, "a dear friend perhaps, but I'm outside your essential life because I did not help you build it. Don't let me threaten it now, Mrs. Herlong! You can keep it—that depends on your self-command, not on mine. No human being can destroy the structure of a marriage except the two who made it. It is the one human edifice that is impregnable except from within. Keep it. You need it."

Elizabeth smiled, without realizing that she was doing so. "Yes," she said to him, "I need it."

"If you keep what you have, I'll be glad I came here. Because, as your friend, I believe I've been of some help to you at a trying time."

"You know you have."

"Then, can't you take what I can give you, instead of trying to make me an instrument of destruction?"

"You make it very clear, all of a sudden," she said, almost incredulously. "When I came in here, I was so sure. But—you look like him, and yet you don't look like him. You— Maybe you're right, Mr. Kessler, and I've let a chance resemblance take me back. But why was I so sure?"

"You won't like this," he answered, "but I'm going to say it anyway, because it's true."

"Go ahead. You've told me several unpleasant truths already. I shan't be angry with you."

Kessler spoke with penetrating directness. "You have never quite got rid of your first marriage. Even when you thought you had most certainly lost it, it was still casting a long shadow over your life. You have remembered Arthur, haven't you, more than you have ever confessed to your husband?"

Elizabeth sat up straight in her astonishment.

"How did you know that?"

"Haven't you?" he insisted.

"Yes. I couldn't help it. Not all the time—sometimes for years I hardly thought of him, then the recollection would come back suddenly, dreadfully. I have never before this minute confessed it to anybody."

Kessler smiled at her with a tender wisdom. "Have you remembered him at times when going ahead with your life seemed especially difficult?"

Startled, she tried to think back. She could not recall all the occasions at once, but she remembered the most recent one. It was last fall, when Spratt had said something about the imminence of Dick's going away, and she had watched him by the pool, and had resolved she was not going to think about it, and then the date on the calendar had recalled Arthur. She said frankly, "Maybe you are right. I can't be sure. But I— I believe you are right. I never thought of that till now. My grief at his death came back, when I was shrinking from the job ahead." As she spoke she felt a sense of uplift, as if suddenly released from something; she exclaimed, "Oh, thank you for making me know that!"

"Mrs. Herlong," Kessler said gently, "as you know, I have undergone some pretty horrible experiences. But they taught me something. They taught me that looking backward is the one sure gesture of self-destruction. We're involved in a worldwide calamity right now because a part of the world is looking back and trying to raise the past. If we are to save ourselves, we can't join them. We *must* look to what is before us. It's no fun, especially right now, but we've got to. The past is gone, but we're here, we're moving into the future. We can't help moving, we can only wreck ourselves trying not to."

As she heard him, she was aware of a tremendous enlightenment, not as regarded the world, but as regarded herself. "I see," she exclaimed. "You mean, I somehow let that first marriage hang over me—"

"Yes."

"—trying to recapture that first golden flush, suffering because I couldn't do it. I knew I couldn't do it, that's what I told Spratt when he asked me to marry him. But I didn't know I was still trying to find it."

He nodded emphatically. "You have still suffered now and then because of what you had lost, when what you had gained in place of it was so much more excellent—haven't you?"

"Yes—" She paused, and exclaimed, "and you are right, it is more excellent." She looked at him closely. "Mr. Kessler, you are not Arthur, are you?"

"Ah! You do want the present, then. You want today and tomorrow."

Elizabeth had a sense of freedom like nothing she had ever felt before. She drew a long breath. Her mind flashed back to that bright year with Arthur, and then lingered on her twenty years with Spratt. The two periods were as different in meaning as they were in length. She had known all along that the second had a value greater than the first. But she had never placed them side by side, as Kessler had made her do today, to see with vehement clarity how her love for Spratt overpowered anything she had ever shared with Arthur.

"Thank you, Mr. Kessler," she said in a low voice. "You don't know what you've done for me."

Kessler smiled at her gratefully, but he did not answer. It was as though, having accomplished what he had set out to do, he felt no need of saying anything more.

Elizabeth leaned back in her chair. In body and mind she felt perfectly at ease. Kessler had reached out and taken a burden from her. She thought of Arthur, of how she had loved him, of her torture at losing him, and realized that this was the first time since her marriage to Spratt that she had let her thoughts dwell on Arthur without trying to recall them, because this was the first time she had been able to think of him without pain. How foolish to have let that shadow lie over her, and in all these full, joyous years to have been unable to escape it completely. Now she was sure that Kessler had taken it away. She would never again feel herself sinking into one of those secret quagmires of anguish. He had given her freedom from Arthur simply by making her understand that she no longer had any reason to want him.

Like herself, Kessler had leaned back in his chair, and now, his whole body relaxed and his hand lightly holding his cane, he looked like a man who had accomplished a task and was now content to rest. With the point of his cane he was idly tracing the pattern of the rug.

As she looked at him, Elizabeth raised her head sharply. How often she had seen Arthur sit like that, resting in a big chair, his eyes down, when he was tired at the end of a hard day.

Her muscles tightened involuntarily. She sat up, about to begin again where she had begun this morning, and then, as her lips parted to speak she remembered what he had said. "If I were your first husband, Mrs. Herlong, I would tell you exactly what I am telling you now. You don't want him back."

He believed he had convinced her that he was not Arthur. For a few minutes he had succeeded in doing so. Now, again, she was not sure.

But as she watched him Elizabeth was convinced of something else, which was that he had meant just what he had said. He was never going to tell her any more than he had told her. If he was not Arthur, further persistence on her part would be useless. If he was Arthur, it would be equally useless. He would never tell her. She might suspect to the end of her life, but she would never know.

She understood, as in her agitation last night and this morning she had not understood, what Kessler had done for somebody, if not for her. He had resolutely moved himself into a sphere of his own, where his disaster would be only his, not interfering in any way with the normal lives of normal persons. It was all very well to say now that if she had known twenty-five years ago Arthur was making such a sacrifice, she would not have accepted it. But, if this man was Arthur—then, because she had not known, she had accepted it. And now, because she was not sure, she had to go on accepting it. If she had any magnanimity of spirit, the only return she could make him was to accept fully what he wanted to give her by letting him believe she was persuaded he was not Arthur. But as she watched him Elizabeth thought, "I never will be sure. I'll never, never know."

But today she could say that to herself without distress. Last night and earlier this morning, it had seemed of vital importance that she should be sure. Now, it was not important. No matter what happiness Arthur might have given her if he had come back from the war, the fact was that he had not given it to her, and Spratt had. Kessler had shown her that. To the end of her life she would be grateful to him. If there was anything she could do for him, it was to let him continue to believe what he so evidently wanted to believe, that he had convinced her entirely. Since that was what he wanted from her, that he should have.

But she remembered that there was something else she could do for him. He had told her so last night. She roused herself to speak.

She said, "Mr. Kessler, last night you suggested you had a favor to ask of me. I hope that's still true."

Kessler looked up, with a slight start as though her voice had recalled him from a great distance. For a moment he seemed to be getting his thoughts in order. Then he answered, "Yes, it's still true."

"I told you last night," said Elizabeth, "I'd be happy to do anything in my power for you. After what you have done for me today, I'd like to repeat that in capitals."

Kessler smiled at her. She had been right; he did believe that she was fully persuaded, and that was what he wanted. "Thank you, Mrs. Herlong. I want to put, shall we say, a part of to-morrow in your hands. Margaret."

She was astonished. "You mean you want me to take her?"

He nodded.

"But don't you want her? I thought you loved her so much."

"I do love her. But I shan't be here always."

Elizabeth sat up straight, holding the arms of her chair. "What do you mean?"

"Look at me, Mrs. Herlong," he said quietly. "Haven't you ever wondered how I have lived as long as this?"

She felt her features changing to express a surprise that, after all, should never have been there. He did look very tired. He had collected all his resources to tell her what he had told her, and now that he had finished the release of tension had let his face sag into lines of weakness and a great weariness. She answered him without trying to gloss her words.

"No, I haven't. Your life has hardly seemed to depend on physical strength—Mr. Kessler, forgive us! What a strain we have put on you! Dick, myself, all of us—we never stopped to realize you were ill."

"That doesn't matter," he answered, so quickly that it was like an interruption. "Please don't think it matters. If you let this trouble you I'll be sorry I spoke. Please!" he exclaimed in-sistently, for she had risen to her feet, ready to go before he wore himself out with any more talking.

Elizabeth sat down again. "Mr. Kessler, of course I'll take Margaret. I'll take her now if you'll let me. But don't you want to come with her? Why don't you let me take care of you, in-stead of staying here with nobody but a hired housekeeper? If you only knew how much I should like to do it!"

"No, no, that's not what I want. Thank you, but I only wanted to tell you that it's very unlikely I'll live as long as Margaret will need protection. When I can no longer be her father, will you be her mother?"

"Of course I will. No, please don't start to thank me. Spratt and I both love children; now that ours are growing up we've often said we wished we had another younger than Brian. So don't start being grateful."

"You may get a great reward for it," said Kessler. "I told you how brilliant her parents were."

"Oh, that. I hope she's all you think her, but if she isn't, it makes no difference. She's a dear child. With all my heart I hope she won't need us, but if she does, we'll be very happy to have her. Don't fear for Margaret's future." She spoke quickly and sincerely.

"I won't," he promised her smiling. "Not for hers, nor for yours."

"Thank you. Now I'm going. You are very tired."

Elizabeth had stood up again. Margaret's future seemed less important just now than Kessler's strength. The longer she stayed the more she would exhaust him. Tired as he was, he did not want her to stay; every word he had spoken had been part of his effort to keep their lives separate. She added,

"Mr. Kessler, I hope I'm forgiven for troubling you today. Thank you for making me understand that I had made a mistake."

He smiled at her again. "You are satisfied, aren't you, that you did make a mistake?"

"Oh yes." She had to make it sound true. Seeking swiftly for words, she went on, "You do look like him. There's an odd resemblance about the eyes especially, but now I see it's only a resemblance. If I hadn't been so overwrought last night when I realized who it was you'd been reminding me of all this time, I shouldn't have gone so far as to believe you actually were Arthur." That sounded convincing. Now she could thank him for what he had really done for her.

So she continued, slowly, "Mr. Kessler, I told you awhile ago that you had made me very happy. You have. I never realized before that being made happy isn't receiving something new, it's being made to understand what we have. You've done a great deal for me since I've known you. But for what you did today, I'll remember you to the end of my life."

He was listening to her intently. "I believe you mean that, Mrs. Herlong," he said in a low voice. "God bless you for saying it."

How tired he was. There was so much she would have liked to do for him. Elizabeth remembered wistfully that she had never taken care of Arthur in an illness, because in the time she had known him he had never been ill. Kessler was looking at her with eyes that seemed to her the tenderest she had ever seen. He added,

"If I have done anything for you, thank you for having let me do it."

He would not let her take care of his bodily weakness. But there was something more she wanted to give him. If he was Arthur, it would be a great acknowledgment; if he was not, he would still understand it.

She said, "Mr. Kessler, may I tell you something more about Arthur?"

Did he start faintly? She could not be sure. "Anything you would like to tell me, Mrs. Herlong," he said.

"I told you I loved him very much," said Elizabeth, "and losing him was a dreadful experience. But I've begun to understand, since I've been talking to you today, that that experience had a great deal to do with making my life since then as full and rewarding as it has been. You were right when you said that at the time of my first marriage I was a very innocent young girl. I simply had no idea of what life could do to me. I suppose it's always true of the very young, you see things happen to other people, but it doesn't enter your head that they can ever happen to you. So you don't build up any resistance, life hits you and you've got nothing to fight with.

"I had loved Arthur so much," she went on, "that when I lost him it was like the end of the world. But what kept me from going under completely wasn't my own strength, it was Arthur's. The first time I realized I had to make a new life it was because I realized that he wouldn't have wanted me to go on depending on him. If he could have seen me, he would have said, 'Depend on yourself, on your own resources.' It was because of him that I learned to do without him. Sometimes, since then, I have wished I could tell him that. Since I can't tell him, I'm telling you.

"And I'd like to tell you too, that you've made me realize today that Arthur's greatest gift to me has been my splendid marriage to Spratt Herlong. Does that sound strange? Now that I understand it, it isn't strange at all. You see, in the first place, Arthur had made me believe in marriage. I know sometimes after a first marriage has been unhappy people find happiness in a second, but they must be very much afraid to undertake it. I wasn't afraid. Besides, losing Arthur had given me a very clear sense of values. I knew what real happiness was and real suffering, I knew it so well that I couldn't waste my emotions over trifles. In all these years nothing has surprised me more than the way so many people use themselves up over things that don't matter. I'm not heroic about it, it's just that I've learned what's important and what isn't, and as long as I have my husband and children I'm simply not capable of breaking my heart over a servant problem. What happened to me when I was very young was terrible, but I've been a better wife and mother than I could have been if it hadn't happened. And I'll be better than I was, now, because you've made me see it.

"You're right, I don't want Arthur back, not now. But I'm grateful to him, and I'm grateful to you."

Kessler, who had risen when she did, had sat down as though too tired to keep standing. He had sat holding his cane rigidly, looking at it instead of at her while she talked. But he had listened, with a faint smile of gratitude, as though what she was saying brought him a great sense of peace. Now, still without looking up, he said, very low,

"Thank you, Mrs. Herlong. I hope you will never be so lonely that what anyone will say to you can mean as much as that means to me." He was silent a moment. Then, "Goodby," he said.

"Goodby," said Elizabeth. She went over to him. He was still looking down. She bent and kissed his forehead quickly. Before he could say anything else she went out.

Kessler leaned his arm on the table by him and bent his head to rest on it. She was gone and she seemed to have taken all his strength with her. He thought of Elizabeth, leaving him for years of vigorous living. He was so tired that he could hardly imagine what it was like to be vigorous.

But he had given her those years to come. She had told him so, not dreaming how much her words meant to him. He was convinced now that she did not know who he was. But he knew, and that was enough. When she told him what Arthur had done for her, it was as though she was telling him that at last he had finished what he had set out to do that day in the German hospital. He thought of what he had said to Jacoby that day. "You never loved a woman enough to die for her." It had been hard enough to die for her once. But in retrospect that seemed almost easy compared to what it had cost him today to kill his image in her soul.

But he had done that, and now that it was over he was glad he had done it. If he had not come back, the shadow of Arthur would have lain across all her life. But he had come back, and he had taken it away. He had finished. He had no reason to be troubled about Elizabeth's future or Margaret's. It would never be necessary for him to drive himself to another effort. He felt like a man who had done a good day's work and now could go to sleep.

13.

As ELIZABETH drove home she felt a vast release, as though Kessler had unlocked a store of hidden vitality within her. She looked up at the far-off mountains, glittering under the winter snow, and wished there were no gas rationing to keep her at home. But there was gas rationing, she reminded herself, there was a war, and such a surge of energy as hers was meant to be used.

She ran into the house and upstairs to her room, where she hurried to pick up the telephone.

"Dr. Myers? This is Elizabeth Herlong. May I come in one day this week to have my blood tested and see if the Red Cross can use any more of it? . . . Yes, but I haven't given one for six months, and they called me up yesterday to ask if I wasn't ready for another. . . . All right, Friday morning at ten, I'm writing it down. . . . Yes, the Marines, he's gone to boot-camp at San Diego. . . . Why, thank you, but I'm not the one to be congratulated, he is. . . . All right, I'll see you Friday."

She dialed again. "I called to tell you I'll be glad to take a shift at the aircraft observation post. . . . Whenever you need me, mornings or afternoons, it doesn't matter. . . . Really, the Boy Scouts? I didn't know that. Brian would probably love it Saturday afternoons, I'll ask him when he comes in from school. You'll call me back, then?"

She put down the phone and stayed for some minutes where she was, thinking of Kessler.

Kessler, Arthur—the names challenged each other in her mind. She thought of Arthur as she had known him, young, beautiful, so full of vigor that he seemed to defy weakness and

232

time. And Kessler, crippled and exhausted, but still powerful with his own inner strength. "I don't know," Elizabeth said to herself again. "I don't know, I'll never know."

But as she went around the house—as Cherry and Brian came in from school demanding milk and sandwiches, as she went into the kitchen to see if the cook had saved enough waste fat to warrant taking it to the butcher, as she sat down to help Brian with a knotty arithmetic problem—as she continued with all the familiar tasks, her own life closed around her with its own demands. She was glad she had said what she had to Kessler. It was all true. His was a great spirit; she and her children could be happier for having known him, without her troubling either him or herself with a problem she would never quite solve. She had her job and he had told her to stay with it. Her husband and children were her responsibilities, voluntarily undertaken. If she failed them now she was lost. Maybe one of these days she would tell Spratt about the events of last night and this morning. But not yet.

When Spratt came home that evening she only told him Kessler was ill and had asked if they would take care of Margaret. Spratt agreed without hesitation.

"Poor kid, of course we'll take her. You won't mind if she's a bit of trouble?"

"Of course not," said Elizabeth. She nearly added, "Even if she were, I'd do anything on earth for him," but checked herself. That would require explaining, and she did not yet feel ready to explain. Spratt was talking.

"Look here, Elizabeth, maybe that guy is too sick to work and is just keeping it up because he can't afford to stop. Do you suppose we could persuade him to take a rest?"

"Oh Spratt, please try! Make him let us pay for it. And please—"

"Yes, what?"

"Tell him it was your idea. I don't think he'd take it from me."

"What an intense sort of person you are," Spratt observed

with a grin. "You feel things all the way through. All right, I'll give him a ring in the morning. Rather late for it tonight."

The next morning she was up, having coffee, when Spratt came into her room.

"Thought I'd call Kessler now," he said. "If he feels like seeing me I can go by on the way to the studio." He gave her a sidelong glance. "Now that you've slept on it, do you still feel like having Margaret here?"

"Yes, if you do."

"It's all right with me."

"You're a prince, Spratt."

He chuckled. "Not me. You're the one who'll have to bother about her clothes and lessons and teeth and disposition. It won't be as easy as looking out for your own children, either."

"Who said they were ever easy?"

"Your mind's made up, then?"

She nodded.

"Okay," said Spratt. He sat down on her chaise-longue and picked up the phone.

"This is Spratt Herlong. Can I speak to Mr. Kessler? . . . *What?* . . . Yes. . . . Yes. . . . I understand. . . . I'll be right over."

He set down the phone, and turned to Elizabeth, who had been listening in alarm. "What is it, Spratt?" she asked.

Spratt wet his lips, and shook his head slowly, as though trying to get used to what it was he had just heard. He answered,

"Kessler died this morning at six o'clock."

For a moment he and Elizabeth sat staring at each other. They were speechless with the curious shocked feeling of trying to get their minds adjusted to a sudden announcement of death. Spratt spoke first, saying something about having to call the studio. For a moment he was silent again, then he stood up.

"Lord, this is strange," he said slowly. "Like being hit on

the head. He never said anything about being that sick. I'd better get over there right away."

"Yes, go right over," said Elizabeth. She felt as if there was a great deal more she should be saying. But she could not get it out now. She asked, "Why didn't he tell us, Spratt?"

"Maybe he didn't know."

"I think he did," said Elizabeth.

Spratt went over to the door and opened it. "I guess we were about his best friends, too," he said guiltily as he went out.

After he had gone Elizabeth sat where she was for several minutes, staring at the wall opposite. She noticed that as he passed Spratt had pushed a curtain with his elbow, and she studied the line of its fold, wondering why the fold was lop-sided, until her eyes followed the line upward and saw that one of the curtain-rings had become detached from the fabric. It would have to be stitched on again. Housekeeping was a thousand details a week, just like that; no matter how competently one tried to keep up with everything, there was always something to be done. Kessler was dead. Kessler, who might or might not have been Arthur, was dead. It was fortunate she had had those curtains made before the war, for it was hard to get such good material these days. She would have to be careful not to let that ring get lost, for metal rings were hard to replace now. Kessler's last effort had been made to put her life on a solid foundation. Then he had quietly let himself go. Would he have tried so hard yesterday, when he must have felt himself near the end, if he had not had more than a simple friendly interest in her? He had told her he did not expect to live long. But perhaps he did not suspect how little time he actually had, and was merely preparing for Margaret's safety in case he did not last another ten years. If he had really suspected the end was so near, why had he not told her the truth? Or had he told her the truth? She would never know.

It hardly seemed patriotic to keep good metal rings like that only to hold up a curtain. Maybe she should replace them with plastic rings and turn the metal in for salvage. But that would take a great deal of time, for each one had to be sewed on separately, and she had promised to give her free time to the aircraft observation post. You couldn't just telephone for somebody to come in and do work like that any more, as you used to. One had to have curtains for the dimout. It was very difficult to know what was the most important contribution one could make to the war, one's time for this or for that. Kessler was dead. Kessler who might have been Arthur was dead, and she did not feel anything. These last few days had taken more out of her than she had known. She was drained of emotion. There seemed to be nothing within her but a dull sterility.

But she was glad she had told him what she had at the last, just before she left him yesterday. If he was Arthur, she had told him how much he had enriched her life, and it had been so much more than she could have told him twenty-five years ago. "He said," she was thinking, "that we don't want the dead back. In one sense he was right, after a long lapse of years it's true that we have remade our lives without them. But in another sense we do want them back, to say to them all we didn't say or couldn't say while they were with us. If I was talking to Arthur yesterday, he knew by the time I left him how much fruit his life with me had borne. It was all I could do for him, but I'm glad I did that much."

There was nothing more she could do now. Nothing but sit here, staring at the curtains.

But she suddenly remembered that this was not true. There was still something she could do, something she must do at once. She must get Margaret.

Elizabeth sprang up. At the idea of Margaret, alone again in her desolate little world, she found that she was not quite as numb as she had thought. She had to get Margaret now, before the child began to feel utterly abandoned. She began to hurry into her clothes.

When she reached Kessler's apartment she found that Spratt had been there and gone, to attend to the last arrangements somebody had to attend to. The housekeeper was very busy, answering the telephone and carrying out the various instructions Spratt had given her. Margaret was curled up in a big chair in the corner where the tree had stood last Christmas. She had put on her clothes in a haphazard fashion very different from her usual neatness—yesterday's crumpled dress, one shoelace untied, the parting between her pigtails carelessly awry. When Elizabeth approached her Margaret looked up, showing a streaky little face worn out with her having cried too much.

Elizabeth did not say anything. She sat down in the big chair, for Margaret did not take up much room and there was space for her at the edge of the seat. She put her arms around Margaret and drew the untidy little head to rest against her. For a moment Margaret clung to her without speaking, then she gave another choking little sob.

"He died," she said brokenly. "Everybody that belongs to me dies."

Elizabeth felt like sobbing too. She was not used to hating anybody. But with Margaret in her arms she felt that if all the words of hate in every language could be rolled into one they could not express how much she hated fascists and what they accomplished.

"Not everybody, Margaret," she said gently. "We belong to you too."

Margaret looked up at her again. She shook her head slowly.

"No, you don't belong to me."

"Don't you want us to belong to you?"

Margaret was puzzled. "You?" she asked. "You and who else?"

"My husband, and all our family. We want you to belong to us. And we won't leave you. You'll stay with us always."

"With you?" Margaret did not understand. "You want me to stay with you?"

"Yes, we want you to come to us today. Right now. Wouldn't you like to have me be your mother?"

"You're not my mother," Margaret answered hopelessly. "My mother is dead."

"I'm not your mother, but I'd like to be. I love you, don't you know that? And I've wanted another little girl. My daughter is so big now, she's nearly grown, and I've wished so often I had a little girl to play with. Don't you want to come with me, and let me be your mother?"

Margaret considered. She scrubbed her eyes with the back of her hand. "You mean," she asked incredulously, "you want me to come live with you?"

"Yes, that's what I mean."

"For how long?"

"For always."

"And be just like yours? Like other girls and their mothers?"

"Just like that."

"What will Mr. Herlong do?"

"He'll be your father."

Margaret began to smile a little bit. "Does he like little girls?"

"Oh yes. And he likes you especially."

"And I'll live with you—in that big house with the swimming pool?"

Elizabeth nodded.

"Will Brian let me go swimming?"

"Why of course. Whenever you please."

"Would he show me his bugs and things, do you think?"

"I'm sure he would."

Margaret smiled again, shyly but more happily this time. "That would be nice. Living at your house, Mrs. Herlong."

"You needn't call me Mrs. Herlong any more, if I'm going to be your mother."

"What do I call you, then?"

"If I'm your mother, don't you want to call me that?"

But Margaret shook her head, with a frightened look. "Oh

no, do I have to? My mother died, and my father died, and I called Mr. Kessler father, and he died. If I called you mother, you—" She stopped, appalled by the enormity of it.

Elizabeth did not insist. "All right, you don't have to. My name is Elizabeth, would you like to call me that?"

"Elizabeth," Margaret repeated. "It seems funny." She paused a moment to think, and asked, "When do I go over to your house?"

"Right now. I'll drive you there, and I can come back to get your things. Unless you'd rather show me now where they are."

"I'll show you." Margaret scrambled down from the chair. She stood in the middle of the floor, still confused by this second re-orientation of her world. "It's funny," she said slowly. "It's all funny. Yesterday he was here, and now he's dead. And now I'm going to live with you. Can I bring the microscope?"

"You can bring anything you want." Elizabeth took her hand and they started for Margaret's room. "I'm going to like having you with me," Elizabeth assured her.

"I'll like it too," said Margaret. She stopped and looked up seriously. "Mrs. Herlong—Elizabeth," she said, "I'll be good."

"Of course you will, darling. Were you afraid I thought you wouldn't be good?"

But Margaret was in earnest. "I'm a refugee," she said quietly.

Elizabeth drew in her breath sharply. "So what, Margaret?"

"Some people don't like refugees," Margaret reminded her.

Damn some people, Elizabeth thought savagely. Aloud she said, "They must be very silly people."

"Some of the girls at school don't like refugees. One girl said her mother said there were too many of them in this country already and she wished all the refugees could be put on the boat and sent back where they came from."

"Her mother must be a fool. What is that girl's name?"

"Lillian Farnsworth."

Elizabeth remembered Mrs. Farnsworth babbling, "But don't

you want to do *anything* for the war?" She said, "Margaret, Lillian Farnsworth's mother is a fat stupid fool. If she ever says anything like that to you again, you can tell her that, and you can tell her I said so."

"She thinks—" Margaret stopped, and squeezed Elizabeth's hand with sudden terror. "You're not going to send me back, are you?"

"Come here with me, Margaret." Elizabeth led her back to the big chair. She sat down, and took Margaret to sit on her lap. "Darling, I told you I wanted you for my little girl. No matter what you want to call us, I'm going to be your mother and my husband is going to be your father. We're Americans, and we're going to take you into an American court and get some papers that will make you just as American as we are, and just as much our daughter as Cherry is. Then nobody can ever, ever send you back to Germany."

"You can do that?" Margaret exclaimed.

"You bet we can. Refugees can be as American as anybody else. Why Margaret, my people were refugees."

"Were they, honestly?" Margaret cried in the delight of a burden shared. "Where did they come from?"

"Oh, Scotland, France, Holland, lots of places, and one of my great-great grandmothers came from Germany, just like you. They all came here for the same reason you came here, because they weren't happy in the places where they lived and they wanted to be in a new free country where everybody could be friends. And Lillian Farnsworth's people were refugees too."

"They were! Then why does she say things like that?"

"Because she's forgotten about it, or maybe she doesn't know. All Americans are refugees, Margaret, except the Indians. They came from all over the world, some of them a long time ago, some of them just lately. Most of us are rather nice people, don't you think? We make mistakes, but we try to be nice people."

"*You're* nice people," Margaret qualified it.

"Well, everywhere, even in this country," Elizabeth continued, "there are people who are not nice. We have to learn to put up with them, even when they say insulting things. Most of the girls at school are nice to you, aren't they?"

"Oh yes. We don't eat lunch with Lillian Farnsworth," Margaret confided.

"I hope you don't. If she bothers you again, you can tell her Mr. Spratt Herlong liked you so much he made you his daughter, and only the girls you invite can come with you to go swimming in your pool."

"In *my* pool?"

"Of course, if you're our daughter won't it be your pool as much as ours?"

"Oh-h-h!" Margaret sighed rapturously. "Can I go swimming today?"

"It's still rather chilly, but we'll see. Now let's go get your clothes."

When she brought Margaret home with her, Elizabeth gave her a little room next to Cherry's, which Cherry had been accustomed to using as a sort of private refuge where she and her schoolmates could gather to eat fudge and do their lessons together. It had a single bed which, covered with an Indian blanket and some bright pillows, had served the girls as a couch. By bringing in Margaret's possessions, and adding some little-girl furnishings Cherry had given up, Elizabeth turned it into a welcoming little bedroom.

She was glad of the occupation. It kept her from thinking of Kessler too much.

At first she had very little time to think of him, and as often before she was thankful for the immediate demands which saved her from introspection. Kessler had left a brief will, giving his few possessions to Margaret, and requesting cremation. Spratt attended to the essential details.

Brian and Cherry, as well as Dick when the news reached him at San Diego, were appalled at losing their friend. They had virtually no knowledge of death. Faced by it, they were almost inarticulate. "But he was such a *good* man!" Cherry protested, as though this should be a reason for his living forever. Brian said, "It doesn't seem possible. He was—well, he was such a pal of mine, just like Peter. Gee." From boot-camp Dick wrote, "I tell you, I don't get it. A great guy like that, and Hitler and Tojo go right on flourishing. But Kessler—I guess I just don't know what to say."

In a later letter he added, "By the way, it was swell of you folks to take Kessler's youngster. Where have you put her to sleep? In my room? If you have I guess it's all right, but I may be getting off for a Sunday soon and when I do I hope she won't mind moving out for the night. I'd sort of like to be in the same old place, been there so long I wouldn't feel at home anywhere else, I guess. Just a soft-hearted sap after all."

Elizabeth hurried to write him that she felt about his room exactly as he did, and when he came home he would find nothing changed. She got back a rather embarrassed little note, thanking her.

But Brian and Cherry, since they still lived at home, found it very odd that Margaret should be established as a member of their household. She was a nice enough child, but after all, she was a stranger. She wasn't one of them. And it was their home. Did they have to have somebody else in it?

Spratt told Elizabeth not to argue with them until a good occasion presented itself. The chance came one morning when the newspaper carried an article in which an official was quoted as saying the Japanese were preparing to invade the United States. Cherry and Brian asked their father if he thought the Japs could do so. Spratt did not laugh at the possibility. But he told them what he knew about the coast defenses, and when he had persuaded them that there was no need to be overly frightened, he added,

"We're mighty lucky in this country, aren't we? We still don't have to be much worried about our house being burned and ourselves being on the charity of strangers. Pretty lucky, aren't we?"

"I'll say we are," Brian agreed.

Spratt addressed him and Cherry with a humorous candor. "You know, when I was a kid going to Sunday School, and the preacher took the Bible and read, 'It is more blessed to give than to receive,' I thought it meant everybody should put a dime into the collection plate. But I guess the Bible is a pretty profound book. You have to do a lot of thinking before you know what it's all about."

Puzzled, Cherry asked, "What's that got to do with the Japs, boss?"

"Well, sometimes I wonder," said Spratt, "what we'd be doing now if the Japs had started this war first, instead of the Germans. We weren't very well prepared back in '39 when it all began. If the Japs had attacked then I guess they could have invaded California, and if they had we'd be refugees now in the Middle West or maybe some foreign country, that is, if we'd been able to get there. Scary notion, isn't it?"

Brian whistled. Cherry exclaimed, "For pity's sake, boss!"

"We would have, wouldn't we?" said Spratt. "But instead, because it started on the other side, we've still got everything we ever had, and we can take care of Margaret instead of having to ask foreigners to take care of us."

They looked uncomfortable. Spratt grinned at them and continued,

"You know, I'm finally beginning to get what that fellow in Sunday School was talking about. 'It is more blessed to give than to receive.' You're mighty right it is—it's a sight more blessed *to be able* to give than it is *to have* to receive."

Their eyes opened wide. Cherry began to laugh. Her father chuckled as he asked her,

"Get it, Cherry?"

She hesitated, then nodded slowly. "I guess—I do," she assented with some reluctance.

Half under his breath Brian was repeating, "It's more blessed to be able to give than it is to have to receive. Gee, boss, you're funny."

"Okay, maybe I am," said Spratt. "But it's not funny to be on the receiving end. I hope you never have to try it."

Brian scowled at the newspaper, which still lay half open before him. "Gee," he said, "everybody's in so much trouble."

As that statement was incontrovertible, Spratt let him reflect without interruption. After awhile Brian concluded,

"I guess it's all right for Margaret to live with us. I guess it just seems funny for her to be living here instead of with Kessler. It sure is bad about him. I miss him."

"You and me both," said Cherry.

They made no more audible objection to Margaret's being with them. But both of them, especially Brian, found it hard to get used to the fact of Kessler's death.

With Margaret it was different. She had been uprooted once, and was not incredulous at having it happen again. She had loved Kessler more than the Herlong children and had needed him more, she sorrowed for him more than they did, but she did not share their surprise. Margaret knew about death. She was not astonished at it, but she was afraid of it.

Margaret was afraid. Fear went through her whole personality and gave her foster-parents a problem for which their experience had not prepared them. Elizabeth and Spratt knew how to cope with childish faults, but their children had not known the meaning of insecurity. Margaret knew that better than she knew anything else.

Living in their home, she made very little trouble for anybody, for she was a good-tempered child and a very bright one. She picked up her playthings, studied her lessons and asked permission to do what she wanted—she was a good little girl, but she had not lived with them two weeks before Spratt and Elizabeth were saying to each other that her goodness, rather than any lack of it, gave them concern. A child who tried so hard to please everybody was not natural. But Margaret had spoken a simple truth when she said to Elizabeth that everybody who had belonged to her had died. In spite of all the reassurance Elizabeth was trying to give her, both in words and in a general attitude of affection, Margaret was still not at ease. She was happy with them, but happiness threatened her with its own loss. It was as though she felt herself in paradise on probation, and thought that by being very good she could make a pact with destiny.

Before long such excellence of behavior had won unqualified approval from Brian and Cherry. She was much easier to have around than they had expected, they said. Brian showed her his collections and Cherry let Margaret come in and look at all her clothes, for it was fun to display their treasures for a spectator who was so delighted at receiving attention and who never touched anything out of turn. But their parents found Margaret's attitude ominous.

"I don't know how to deal with it!" Elizabeth said to Spratt. "Impertinence or bad manners I could handle. But this is new to me. Our children were perfectly unacquainted with fear."

Spratt spoke through his teeth in a low angry voice. "My God, Elizabeth, those brutes! This is what 'mental cruelty' means, not a convenient phrase to get divorced with. Margaret got out of there with a whole body, but what they did to her mind!"

"And there are millions like her," Elizabeth said savagely. "I go cold and sick thinking of them."

"Thinking of millions won't help Margaret," said Spratt, who customarily moved from the general to the particular with all possible speed. "Let her see you love her and like having her around. Don't pet her, just make her feel wanted. Don't ask her about Germany, or Kessler either. If she ever talks just let her do it, as you said Kessler did when you were prettying up her Christmas tree. She'll get it out of her eventually—it may take years, but she'll talk if she knows you want to listen."

"Make her feel wanted," Elizabeth repeated. "Yes, I believe I can do that."

The next day she said, "I have a problem, Margaret, and I need you to help me."

"Me? Help you?" Margaret came and sat down by her. "Have you got some trouble, Elizabeth?"

She was still afraid to use a title that would have suggested to fate that Elizabeth was her mother. By this time she called Spratt "boss" as the other children did, for that title had no threatening connotation for her, as "father" had, but she continued to address Elizabeth by her first name. Knowing how Margaret felt about it, Elizabeth did not suggest a change.

"Oh no, not trouble," she answered, "it's just this. I knitted Dick a pair of socks and he's crazy about them, he says they are ten times as comfortable as the ready-made socks they get in the Marines and he wants a lot more. But with taking care of the house and watching for planes at the observation post, I really haven't time to make so many. Would you make some socks for Dick if I taught you how?"

"Oh yes!" cried Margaret. Then, uncertainly, "Do you think I could learn? Could I make socks good enough for a Marine to wear?"

"Of course you can. The first one seems complicated, but after that they're easy, so easy you can learn to knit without even looking at it."

"Ah," Margaret sighed eagerly. "Would he wear them, do you think?"

"Why Margaret, if you knew how much he wanted them! Will you really make them? I'd be so grateful, and so would Dick."

"Oh yes, yes! When can I learn?"

"Right now. I have some needles and yarn in my room."

The idea of doing something important was a stimulant for Margaret's wounded soul. Elizabeth could have knitted a dozen socks with the effort it took to teach Margaret to turn a heel, but Margaret needed a place in the universe more than Dick needed socks. In her next letter to Dick, Elizabeth asked him to send a word of encouragement. Dick had no literary gifts, but he had an understanding spirit, so he scribbled back,

"Dear Margaret, I hear you are making me some socks. That's swell of you. I sure do need them. Yours as ever, Dick."

Margaret was not used to receiving letters addressed to herself. She was thrilled, and thought it enormously polite of him to have scrawled in tiny letters on the corner where civilians would have had to put a stamp, "Free. Thank you, Congress."

She spent some time studying her name as he had written it on the envelope. That night when Elizabeth came to tuck her in bed, Margaret detained her. "I've got something to ask you," she said bashfully.

"Go ahead." Elizabeth sat on the edge of the bed.

"You won't be mad with me?"

"Not a bit."

"Well, I was thinking—it would be nice—you said I was going to be American—" She hesitated.

"Indeed you are," Elizabeth encouraged her.

"—and your little girl just like I was born to you—" Margaret paused again for confirmation.

"You are my little girl."

"Well—my father—Mr. Kessler, he is dead and I belong to you now, and I thought it would seem more like I really belonged to you if—if—" She stopped again.

Elizabeth spoke gently. "If you had the same name as the rest of us?"

Margaret nodded vehemently. "How did you know? Do you mind? Can I?"

"I know because I was going to ask you what you wanted your name to be. You remember I told you we would get you some papers making you our little girl and an American. We are getting them, so you can be Margaret Herlong from this minute if you want to be."

"Can I? Oh, thank you, Elizabeth!" Margaret put her arms around Elizabeth's neck and hugged her. "Will you tell them at school I've changed my name?"

"Suppose I go to school with you in the morning, and see your teacher."

"All right. All right. Then—Elizabeth."

"Yes?"

"Then nobody can *ever* make me go back to Germany, can they?"

"Never, never, never. Why Margaret, we couldn't let you go back now! We'd miss you so."

Margaret sighed with drowsy happiness. Elizabeth drew the covers over her and gave her a final good night kiss. She went out to find Spratt.

"We haven't finished yet," she told him. "She's still afraid. But we've started."

"If she knows we want her, that's enough for now," said Spratt.

14.

THE spring that year was late and chilly. Every night a fog rolled in from the sea, and for half the day it made a thick gray cloud over the sky. In the cool weather the winter flowers continued to open, but even the calla lilies were smaller than they had been, as though they knew their time should be over and they were as tired of blooming as everybody was of looking at them.

Then, all of a sudden, one morning the sun began to shine on time, and almost simultaneously the country burst into flower. There was still snow on the mountains, but in the valleys the magnolias and the purple jacaranda trees began to bloom, roses tumbled over the fences, poppies and lupin blew on the slopes, and along the canyon roads were hundreds of acacia trees shaking their golden curls. The birds made an enchanting racket all day, and at night there was always a little wind and a thousand small rustlings, while in the dark the scent of jasmine swept out in an invisible cloud to enfold the whole town of Beverly Hills. To Elizabeth, who had always been deeply aware of the beauty of the earth, the sudden flowering brought a heightened sensitiveness, in which, no longer occupied with the immediate duties of adjustment, she thought a great deal about Kessler.

She wondered if they had hastened the end by asking so much of him. That he had been eager to give it did not ease her feeling that they should not have asked it. At last, one evening, she said this to Spratt.

"Did we demand too much, Spratt?" she asked. "If we did—" She stopped, looking at him guiltily.

Spratt sat down by her and put his hand over hers. "Suppose we did, Elizabeth?"

"Not you. Except maybe in expecting him to work at his job when you didn't know he wasn't equal to it. But Brian and Dick, and especially myself."

Spratt answered, "I don't know. But if we did, it was what he wanted. Kessler wasn't the sort of man who could endure to feel useless."

Elizabeth heard him gratefully. "Do you really believe that? You aren't just trying to make me feel better?"

"No, I'm not just trying to make you feel better. I think more of you than that. If you took your problems to him, and Dick took his, if Brian used up a lot of his energy with bats and bugs, none of you did anything he wasn't asking you to do." He smiled at her, understandingly. "You'd be like that yourself, Elizabeth."

"Would I? I don't believe I've ever thought about it."

"Well, think about it a minute—what's worse than being thrown away in a corner like a wornout coat? If I had five more years of activity or ten more of uselessness, I'd choose the five. What do you say?"

She did not hesitate. "I'd choose the five, too. Anything would be better than feeling nobody wanted me."

"Then don't be troubled about Kessler. He did what he wanted to do, he had what he wanted and he knew he had done a good job. When is there a better time to call it quits?"

Elizabeth did not answer. Her chin on her hand, she was silent for several minutes—for so long, in fact, that at last Spratt gave her a broad comprehending grin, saying,

"Go ahead and say it, whatever it is."

Elizabeth raised her head slowly. "I've not known whether or not I should say it. Maybe I shouldn't. But I'm going to, because I can't bear to have anything between us that isn't open for us both to look at. Spratt, do you remember I told you Kessler reminded me of somebody?"

"Why yes. Did you finally remember who it was?"

She nodded. Looking straight at Spratt, she said, "He reminded me of Arthur."

"Oh," said Spratt. After a moment he added, "That's curious. A crippled German—I thought you said Arthur was strong as an ox and all that."

"He was. I suppose that's why I couldn't place the recollection for so long."

"Well, I'm glad you got it figured out if it was any relief to you. Funny how those chance resemblances tease us sometimes. But why should you be scared to tell me that?" Spratt asked with some amusement. "After all these years you don't think I'm working up a case of jealousy against Arthur!"

"No, not that," said Elizabeth. She was tempted to leave it there, but after a moment's hesitation she continued. "Spratt, you remember the night after Dick went to boot-camp, when we had dinner at Chasen's? I'd had too many cocktails, and with that brandy afterward—maybe it was that, I don't know, but all of a sudden I realized who it was he had been reminding me of, and I got a downright conviction, not that he looked liked Arthur, but that he *was* Arthur."

"My God," said Spratt. "You must have really been tight!"

"Maybe I was. But anyway, that's what I thought."

Spratt was staring at her in amazement. "I hope you didn't spill any of this to Kessler."

"Yes I did. That same night. When you left him here while you drove over to the Sterns' to get that script. Of course he told me he wasn't."

"He must have thought you were a lunatic. Elizabeth, stay away from Manhattans. They're insidious."

"That's not all I want to tell you. I went to see him the next day."

"To apologize?"

"To see whether or not I was right. He did look like Arthur —maybe 'look like' is the wrong phrase. I mean, in the way he thought and spoke and acted, he *was* like him. He told me again that he wasn't Arthur. But he told me something else too, and this is what I want to tell you now." She spoke earnestly. "Spratt, he reminded me of what a ghastly tragedy it would be if Arthur, or any man long dead, should by some miracle return to interfere with the lives of people still living. He reminded me of all that you and I have together, all the things I should have known and thought I knew, but never until then knew so completely—of what it means to be married for twenty years, to have built a citadel of refuge for each other—" she was looking directly at him as she spoke—"he made me see this, all new and fresh as if it had just been given to me, what we have, and how much I love you."

Spratt took both her hands in his. "My dear girl," he said gently, "did it take that to make you know?"

"Do *you* know how much I love you, Spratt?"

"Of course I know," said Spratt.

He paused, but she waited, for she saw that he was about to say more. Spratt was not a romantic lover. His devotion to Elizabeth was far more evident in what he did than in what he said, and he accepted her affection for him in the same way. Now he told her so, still holding her hands and smiling at her tenderly as he spoke.

"Don't you prove it with every step you take and every word you say?" he asked her. "Why Elizabeth, I get it every time you answer the phone. It comes across. You say, 'Yes, Spratt, this is Elizabeth,' and you might as well be saying, 'Spratt, here's the one human being in the whole world who's always on your side, who believes in you no matter what kind of fool you make of yourself, who knows you better than anybody else on earth knows you and in spite of it somehow still thinks you're a swell guy.' I get it every time. Do I have to tell you that?"

"No, you don't have to tell me. Only sometimes it's good to be told."

"I love you too, Elizabeth," said Spratt. "Don't you know it?"

"Yes, oh yes." She smiled at him happily, pressing the hands that were holding hers, and her spirit felt warm and at ease. She went on, "Mr. Kessler didn't need to make me understand how much we loved each other, I knew that. But what he did make clear to me was how much more we loved each other now than we did when we got married, how much we had built up between us, a few big things and ten thousand little things that we share with each other and not with anybody else. Like tonight when we were having cole-slaw for dinner and you said to me, 'Remember that wonderful cole-slaw we had at that funny little restaurant in San Francisco?' It's such a trifle, but all those trifles— You get it, don't you?"

"Sure, I get it," he returned. "I guess that's marriage, isn't it?"

"That's right." She went on, with a shade of diffidence. "Spratt, do you remember, when you and I first talked about getting married, I told you about that—that golden rapture of being in love with Arthur, and how I never could have it again?"

"I remember," he answered simply, in a low voice.

"What I want to tell you now," she said slowly, "is that somehow, while I was talking to Mr. Kessler, I understood for the first time how really unimportant that has become. It just doesn't matter, because it doesn't matter. I love you now more than I ever loved Arthur, and I want you to know it. Do you understand?"

To her astonishment, Spratt gave a low matter-of-fact sort of chuckle. "Yes, my dear, I understand it, and it's about time you understood it too. If I remember right, I told you then I didn't want any rapturous adoration from anybody. I wanted just what we've got. You and me and the youngsters, counting on each other as we do. That's what I want, and if I know you after all these years, it's what you want too."

"It is!" she exclaimed fervently. "You've made me a very

happy woman, Spratt—that's what I'm trying to say, and I love you more than I've ever loved anybody else in my life. That's all."

"I suppose every girl has a romantic hero when she's very young," Spratt said coolly. "But if she turns into a sensible woman," he added, with a warning rebuke in his voice, "she doesn't go about trying to find him again."

"I deserved that," Elizabeth acknowledged. "But it's over. You don't know how completely over it is."

"I think I do. If it weren't, you wouldn't be telling me all this, would you?" Spratt smiled at her wisely. "You didn't tell me when you thought you saw Arthur's face on poor Kessler. Elizabeth, that still isn't troubling you, is it?—I mean Kessler's looking like Arthur."

"Oh no! You're right—if I were still troubled about it I'd never have dared to mention it. It's all gone—it just doesn't matter."

Spratt stood up. He examined a tiny spot on the window-curtain. "You could have found out, you know," he said dryly.

"What do you mean? How?"

Still without looking up from the curtain, he said, "Soldiers in the last war were fingerprinted. I believe the prints are still on file in Washington."

"Oh!" Elizabeth started. She sprang up too, and went to him, taking his arm so he had to turn around and face her. "But it doesn't matter, Spratt! That's what I've been telling you. I was mistaken, and even if I wasn't—it's not important. Arthur isn't there. Don't you understand?"

Spratt took hold of her elbows and pulled her close to him. "You dear goose, of course I understand. I haven't been married to you for twenty years without knowing you have more imagination than is good for you. If you didn't have a tough practical magnet like me to pull you down from your flights of fancy, heaven knows where you'd have got yourself by now. You've been terrified at Dick's joining the Marines because once before in your life you saw a man go off to war and not come back."

"Did you know that?" she gasped.

"Of course I knew it. It's about time I said so. Dick knows it too, if I'm not mistaken. You've been going around not mentioning what was on your mind because you were so afraid of it. Why didn't you mention it?—or why didn't I, for that matter, since I'm supposed to be the tough member of this partnership? Well, I'm mentioning it now. Nobody can promise you anything, but there are a few plain facts you might look at. Men aren't dying in this war the way they did in the last one, they have blood-plasma and the sulfa drugs and plenty else they didn't have in those days. When people like you say they want to face facts, why do they always mean they want to face unhappy ones? Why the hell don't they pick out a few pleasant facts to face while they're doing it?"

Elizabeth drew a long breath. She lifted her chin and smiled at him suddenly. "Spratt, you're wonderful. Of course I knew that, but I've been so scared I didn't think of it. Why didn't you remind me before?"

"Heaven knows. I'm not the only goose in this family. I suppose I kept hoping that if I didn't say I knew what you were thinking about you'd stop thinking about it, and I didn't want to think about it either. But my dear, what with remembering and being afraid, you've had Arthur on your mind for about six months. No wonder as soon as you got a drink too many you went about seeing him. Now listen, Elizabeth. You and I are both up against too much, right now, concretely, to be worried by any past abstractions. Get it?"

Elizabeth remembered what Kessler had told her. She nodded. "I do get it. Maybe you still don't know how well."

"All right, maybe I don't. But we've got a job to do. We've got to make a decent life for ourselves and our children, and we've got to take that poor scared kid of Kessler's and undo Hitler's work on her. We can't start breaking our hearts, for instance, by remembering that she's just one of millions and we can't do anything about the others. You're the sort who's in danger of that sort of worrying, you know—it's a temptation, but it's no use."

"I know it's no use. I can't save the world, though I'd like to. If you catch me forgetting to stick to my own corner of it, remind me."

"Never fear, I will. I've seen too many people wasting their energies on cobwebs when they might be doing a job of work." He kissed her hard. "I love you, my dear, and I know you love me better than anybody else. Now go say good night to the children, and tell Cherry if she wants to finish reading *The White Rose of Flanders* she'll have to get it from the library. The copy she took out of my room belongs to the studio story department."

Elizabeth kissed him back and went out to do her motherly missions. She was thinking how clear things became when you finally summoned courage to take them out and look at them.

She took back the novel, over Cherry's protests, and made Brian bring in a book on water-culture of plants he had left outside to catch the dew. "Nobody will ever explain these things to us the way Mr. Kessler did," Brian said regretfully. "He was just about to help us build a tank. Gosh, it's a shame about him."

She agreed, and went to Margaret's room. Ready for bed, Margaret was waiting for Elizabeth to come tuck her in. "Will you keep something for me?" she asked.

Elizabeth said she would. Opening a box she had brought from her earlier home, Margaret gave her a silver fountain pen.

"It belonged to my father—Mr. Kessler, I mean," she explained. "The boss gave it to him for Christmas. It's such a pretty pen, and he used it a lot. But we mostly write with pencils at school. Will you take care of it?"

Elizabeth picked up the pen. Its polished surface gave back a bright reflection of the bedside light.

"Why yes, Margaret, I'll keep it for you," she promised. "Then when you're older and want a pen for your writing, I'll give it back to you."

Margaret got into bed, and Elizabeth opened the window.

"It's getting colder," Margaret observed.

"There's still snow on the mountains. The boss says he can see it when he drives home through the canyon."

She kissed Margaret good night, and took up the pen again. It occurred to her that if there was still any ink in it, the barrel should be emptied before it was put away. She unscrewed the cap.

The reflection of the light made a bright clear line along the side of the pen. As she removed the cap and exposed the lower end, Elizabeth saw that just above the point, the line of light halted in a blur.

Laying the cap on the table, she took out her handkerchief. The smudge on the silver surface appeared to be a light one, and she held the pen nearer her eyes to see if it could be rubbed off with the corner of the handkerchief or if the silver would require polishing before it was put away. Holding the pen at the upper end, she turned it to catch the light at the edges of the dull spot, and saw that what had appeared at first to be a formless blur was actually the strong clear print of a thumb.

Something caught sharply in Elizabeth's chest. She was sure it was a thumb, because the print lay diagonally on the holder, just above the inner edge of the pen-point; whoever had last used this pen had been a writer accustomed to hold it as low down as possible, his fingers sharply bent. As clearly as if it were a recollection from yesterday she could remember herself saying, "Arthur, doesn't it give you a cramp in your hand, holding a pen as close to the point as that?"

Her heart was pounding so hard that she had difficulty in keeping her voice level as she asked,

"Margaret, has anybody used this pen since—since you came to live here?"

There seemed a breathless space between her question and Margaret's answer, though actually Margaret answered without hesitation. "No, why? Is there something the matter with it."

"Oh no," said Elizabeth. "I was just wondering."

"Father carried it in his pocket," Margaret added. "He liked it very much. Nobody ever used it but him."

"I see," said Elizabeth.

Her hands, holding the pen in the right and her handkerchief in the left, were trembling, and so numb that she could hardly feel what she was holding. She tried to pick up the cap from the table, dropped it, and stooped to recover it.

"Good night, dear," she said, still bent so Margaret could not see her face. "I'll put this away for you."

"All right. Good night, Elizabeth."

Still holding the pen carefully by the upper tip, Elizabeth put out the light with her free hand and went out, closing the door behind her. Standing in the hall outside, she waited, taking deep slow breaths to make her heart be quiet. When her hands were steadying she lifted the pen again, and watched the reflection of the hall light on the lines and ridges of the print. Suddenly, almost to her own surprise, she brushed it with her lips, a swift light kiss like the one she had given Kessler the last time she had seen him. Then, quickly, before she could be tempted any more, she began to polish the pen with her handkerchief, rubbing hard. After a moment she held up the pen to the light and turned it around. The reflection along the polished silver was unbroken.

The pounding in her chest was gone too. Her hands were no longer trembling, and no longer numb. She felt a vast inexpressible sense of triumph.

Taking the pen into her bathroom, she let out the ink and filled the barrel with water two or three times to clean it. When it was dry she replaced the cap and put the pen away in a drawer of her desk to wait until Margaret should have need of it. As she closed the drawer she laughed, softly and proudly.

"Now I have conquered," she said in a low voice.

From his own room next door, Spratt called to her. "What are you doing, Elizabeth?"

"Putting away a fountain pen that belonged to Mr. Kessler, the one you gave him last Christmas. Margaret asked me to keep it till she was old enough to use it at school."

"Oh, I see. I'm glad she still has it."

Elizabeth smiled, a happy little secret smile. You never did tell everything. Not everything. She never would tell Spratt she had rubbed out that thumb-print because she had believed it would assure her that Kessler and Arthur were the same, and she did not want to be sure. It was enough for her to know that in rubbing it out she had rubbed Arthur out of her life, and left herself and Spratt free to go forward into the future together with no shadow of yesterday between them.

Spratt called, "Do you want to come in here and listen to the news? It goes on in five minutes."

"Why yes," Elizabeth answered. "I'll be right in." From outside she heard the wind, blowing down from the mountains where there were still ridges of winter snow. "I'll be there in a minute, Spratt," she called. "But first I'd better get you an extra blanket. It's going to be a chilly night."

She brought the blanket from the hall closet. "Thanks," Spratt said when she entered. He grinned at her appreciatively. "You think of everything, don't you?"

"I like taking care of my family," said Elizabeth. She came to sit on the arm of his chair. As Spratt leaned back to look up at her she bent over impulsively and kissed him. He slipped his arm around her waist, and she rested against him while they listened to the voice of the radio announcer and the sound of the wind as it rushed down from the snow on the mountains.